A JOURNEY FOR HOPE

BRIAR CREEK LOVE BOOK TWO

STACY T. SIMMONS

ISBN: 978-1-951839-82-6

Celebrate Lit Publishing

304 S. Jones Blvd #754

Las Vegas, NV, 89107

http://www.celebratelitpublishing.com/

In loving memory of Stacy T. Simmons.
May her words continue to bless readers for many years to come.

To Midge,
you have been so
supportive of my
precious Stacy. Thanks!

Love,
Betty Isakonas

"For I know the plans I have for you," declares the Lord, "plans to prosper you and not to harm you, plans to give you hope and a future."
-Jeremiah 29:11 NIV

"Hope is the thing with feathers
That perches in the soul
And sings the tune without the words
And never stops at all."
-Emily Dickinson, The Poems of Emily Dickinson

CHAPTER ONE

"Vroom. Vroom!" Giggles followed as a whirr of blond hair and extended arms, circled the makeshift desk in the living room, followed by a fifty-pound, stocky yellow Lab. A bark accompanied by more aeronautical sounds slipped into the earpieces of one very frustrated aunt, Hope Fuller.

"Jack, I'm in a class." As her six-year-old nephew continued his spiral-dance around the desk, she tried to maintain focus on an online tutoring student. The lemonade glass on the desk caught her eye as the liquid listed in the container. She shifted it away from his "propeller" arms. "You're doing great, Bryce, please read the sentence again." Hope put a hand over the microphone. "Jack, can you and Ranger find someplace else to play?"

"Okay, one more." Jack whirred past the side of the desk tilting back and forth. His hand brushed the glass, knocking the lemonade over.

Hope held back a screech hovering in her throat. "Bryce. I'm so sorry, I need to go, we'll do double lessons Thursday." Hope pushed from the seat while she picked up her laptop. "Jack, we need a towel, quick. There's lemonade on the keyboard." She prayed her laptop would be okay. It was her first big purchase since graduating with her Master's in Art Education last month.

Jack sprinted away, seemingly unaware of the disaster. Ranger, the dog, followed his young owner and yipped at his heels. Jack brought back a small cloth effective as a sponge soaking up a substantial pool in their backyard.

"Here." Faith and her very pregnant belly waddled on scene with a large towel and began blotting the sticky drink puddled on the table. "Jack, said he'd spilled your lemonade."

"Sorry." His lower lip quivered, and the boy's small shoulders drooped.

"It was an accident." Hope touched her nephew's shoulder, no one could stay upset at this precious little boy. His face brightened. After a few sprays of cleaner and swipes, it was back to normal. "Go on, Ranger wants to play with you." She heard excited quick pants and yowls from the lab.

Jack ran to his dog, crisis seemingly forgotten.

"Is your computer, okay?" Faith ran a hand under the laptop. "It feels dry."

Hope pressed the On button and it flashed to life. "It's working. Thankfully the keys only got a few drops on them. You know what this spill reminds me of?"

"What?"

Hope took the damp towel from her sister and continued to sop up the mess. "First date?"

Her sister slid into a chair a smile crested across her face. "Mine and Caleb's blind date where he spilled cola on my expensive white dress."

"Exactly, though it all worked out, didn't it?"

"We've been married three years. I'd say, yes, it did." Faith touched her eight-months- rounded-belly in all its pregnant glory and grinned. "Thanks again for coming to help."

"You've already thanked me three times, and I got here from

Florida the day before yesterday." Hope held a hand under the dripping towel and carried it to the laundry room down the hall. Upon returning, she asked. "Still have that dress?"

"No, I gave it away a couple years ago."

"But that was a nice dress, you should've saved it." Faith's husband Caleb walked into the room with a grin. "You could wear it on a date night now."

Hope's eyes went to Faith's midsection.

Caleb hugged his wife. "Um, not right now. Soon."

Hope sidled next to her brother-in-law and whispered. "Great rescue." Caleb's reply was a dimpled smile.

Her brother-in-law pointed to the light beige rug near the computer table. "Having trouble drinking, Hope?"

"No, Jack was playing and knocked over my lemonade."

"Oh, no. Yesterday, Faith told me he was loud during your classes."

"Somewhat."

"I love my son, but nothing is quiet with him. He'll start twice a week summer church camp soon." Caleb sat down beside his wife and took her hand. "Which we know doesn't solve the noise problem completely. Last night, we came up with a solution. Did Faith tell you?"

She glanced at her sister. "What kind of solution?"

"We know someone who opened a coworking office space. They have a small one that's not rented. Do you want to use it for the next month?"

"That sounds perfect. I'd rent it, but I don't have a car."

Faith flicked a hand toward the driveway. "You can use mine. Caleb can drive me where I need to go, or if he's working, Taylor's a few blocks away. She has helped me out more times than I can count." She leaned over to her husband. "This guy is willing? You did ask him, didn't you?"

Caleb lifted his shoulders up a notch. "I'm sure I said something to him."

"As long as they're okay with it. I'll work from there tomorrow if there's a table and chair. Would 9am be too early?"

Caleb nodded. "They're there by then."

"Do I know them? I've met a lot of your friends from the area."

"You might." Faith's impish smile widened. "I'm not telling."

Hope swallowed a groan. What exactly was Faith up to this time?

Coffee in one hand, computer bag in the other, Hope said a quick goodbye to the family, and got into her sister's big, red, minivan, eager to begin the day of teaching. Giggles threatened to arise, as she glanced around the vast interior. Hope figured she could hold at least eight friends with room to spare in the metal monstrosity. She shifted into reverse and pulled S.S. Behemoth from the driveway. Soon, tree lined streets turned into rows of stores with brightly colored canopies shielding the windows from the North Carolina sun. She glanced at the address on her phone and located a parking spot close to the office.

Hope gathered her laptop bag, and snack Faith packed her. Climbing the two concrete steps to the door entrance, she paused, unsure of whether to knock, or open the door. Prickles of anxiety chicken pecked within, knowing she'd soon meet this person who let an absolute stranger into their office.

"Go on in." From the doorway of the adjacent shop, a lady motioned toward the door. In the mid-morning sun, the rays cast a glow on the woman's halo of auburn hair, her face partially concealed by science lab goggle-sized eyeglasses. "He's in there."

Hope managed to collect a semblance of manners and thanked the woman. She pushed the office door open, sunlight from the hallway brightened the dark entry way. She saw a light down the hall. "Hello?"

"Who's here?" A very masculine voice rejoined from the glowing room.

Didn't Faith or Caleb tell him I was coming? She swallowed past the dryness in her throat and croaked. "I'm here to work in the empty office. What I mean to say is my name's Hope Fuller." She heard some squeaks and groans from the office, then footsteps.

A tall man appeared at the end of the hall. As he drew nearer, her eyes grew wider in recognition of the familiar face. She stood staring for a moment longer than considered polite. "Dylan?"

A smile lit up his face. "What're you doing here?"

Strands of nerves fired, as confusion overtook her. "Caleb and Faith said this was all worked out with the office owner. They didn't say it was you." The strap from the heavy bag slid from her shoulder, following gravity's pull. She grabbed for the handle. And missed.

"I've got it." Dylan caught her laptop before it crashed to the hard tile floor. He saved it and held it out to her. "Neither my brother nor sister-in-law said anything to me."

"Thanks." Hope clutched the bag to her body as if it were Wonder Woman's shield that she could use to draw superhero strength.

"I'm surprised. In a good way. You look great." Dylan's mouth turned up. "What are you doing here?"

She mentally inventoried her outfit, the green knee-length dress with a ruffle on the shoulders she'd purchased on a day trip to Paris, dark flats, and compact gold earrings. *Not bad.* Hope fought against the urge to check her hair. "Thanks, so do you. It's been a while. The reason I'm here is our . . . I mean my impending niece or nephew. I finished my master's degree and have some time on my hands before I find a teaching job, so I can help with the baby for a while when he or she arrives." Her nervous chuckle bobbed below the surface as she clutched the bag tighter.

"Last time I saw you was Christmas at Caleb's and Faith's?"

"Yes. Seven months." She took two steps back and smiled. "This was a ridiculous idea. I'll go back to their house. It should be quieter today."

"Let me guess. You need the quiet because of Jack." Dylan's lips curved upward. "He's an energetic little guy."

"Between his and Ranger's noises, I'm not sure how I'll be able to do my work with all the distraction." Hope shrugged.

"How long do you need the space? I've got someone interested in it by the end of summer."

"A month at most."

"It should work. You always have had a big heart." Dylan motioned with a hand for her to follow. "Anyway, it slipped my mind you were visiting. I've been busy passing the bar exam, starting this business, and my law practice. Let me show you the office." He ran a hand across his neck and exhaled as he entered the small space. "There's not much here, an old desk from college, and a chair. I'm planning on donating it soon. I can get it out of here if you'd like."

"It's works well, my laptop will fit perfectly on it." After settling her things on the time scarred wooden desk, she glanced at Dylan, his blond hair seemed shorter than when she'd last seen him. But those blue eyes, they were still the same. "Thanks for agreeing to rent the space." Hope quickly assessed the serviceable chair. She frowned at the dust covering it. "Do you have any furniture wipes?"

"In my office, do you have time to catch up?"

Hope glanced at her phone. "About an hour."

"Good. I'll get those and my chair, hang on." He walked out of the office, rattling accompanied his footsteps back, and he pushed a large mahogany colored leather chair into the small space and gave her the canister of wipes. "What kind of job are you doing?"

She took three of them and scrubbed on the chair. Once satisfied, she dropped the used cloths into the trash. Hope touched a finger to the chair's damp surface. Where to sit? Glancing around the office held no quick answers to the situation.

She chose to perch on the desk's edge trying to look a mixture of both professional and casual ease. "I'm tutoring elementary school kids online, until I get a teaching job."

"That's not a bad idea, online tutoring. Anything else in the works?"

"I have several interviews via video lined up in Tampa for an art teacher." The room seemed smaller with Dylan an arm's length away. She fiddled with her pink-polished fingernails and tried not to glance into his captivating eyes. *Stop it, Hope.* She shook her head.

"I hope you get one of those positions. You're not hiding a paralegal or law doctorate in your list of accomplishments, with the Art Education Master's degree, are you?"

"No, I'm not hiding anything." Hope wasn't sure how to take this teasing side of Dylan. She decided to join in. "How long have we known each other?"

"Are you referring to the time we were friends, dated for a couple of months, and switched back to friends?"

"Your gift for words hasn't changed," Hope grumbled. "This is why you're the lawyer and own this office. Big shot." She twisted her lips in a smirk.

"Not me. I'm a far cry from a big city attorney." He shifted in the seat and shrugged. "This isn't all my office. My uncle and I went in together. It's mostly his. I'll manage the tenant for him. I couldn't afford this. Not with my waist-deep pile of law school loans."

"Completely get it. I've got some loans on my master's

degree." Hope pulled out her wallet and looked for a credit card that had some "wiggle room" on it. "Let me take care of my bill. How much do I owe you?"

Dylan quoted a reasonable rate. "You can get it to me later today, I'll work up a bill."

"Thanks." Her computer beeped. "Class is starting in a few."

"I'll write down the internet access code." He pulled a business card from his back pocket and wrote down the needed numbers. Dylan gave it to her, "Have a good class." He pushed his chair out into the hallway and closed the door behind him.

All through tutoring, Hope found herself mentally wandering to the occupant of the other office. Three years before, after igniting the simmering fires they had for one another, they decided to end it after dating for a few short weeks. Hope made a resolution in that dreary little box of an office, to not journey down a path redirected by a faulty GPS—toward Dylan.

CHAPTER TWO

The minivan lurched into the driveway, and Hope moved the cumbersome gearshift to park, mulling over how she'd respond to Faith's questions about the day.

Jack ran to the car a wide smile on his face. "Aunt Hope, hi, come inside. Mom said dinner's soon."

She opened the door and took her things from the van "Something's missing, let me see your teeth." Her nephew opened his mouth as wide as he could, and Hope inspected every tooth. "One's missing. Who took it?"

"The tooth fairy."

"She takes teeth?"

His blond head nodded in affirmation as his tooth-gap showed. "Yes."

"I think I'll call you Jack-o-lantern then."

"Aunt Hope!"

"Kidding." She brushed a kiss on his forehead. He wasn't family by blood, but of the heart. Jack's mom had passed when he was not more than a toddler. "Let's get in, I'm hungry, aren't you?"

Jack shook his head.

No sooner had they stepped inside then her sister walked into the foyer.

"Come peel cucumbers for the salad. Tell me about work."

"I'll be there in a moment." She raised her laptop bag higher. "Let me put my things away."

"Hurry, I want to hear how happy you were with your surprise." Faith hugged her and walked from the room.

Oh, I was happy. Let me tell you. Hope's phone vibrated. She dug it from her purse. A text from her longtime best friend, Amelia.

What's new? How's Briar Creek and the family?

Hope's thumbs flew across the keyboard as she sat on the corner of the bed. *S.O.S. Ame. I saw Dylan today.*

He's there in Briar Creek? Where?

She shifted further back into the bed. *Surprise, he is. I'll be doing my tutoring in his spare office.*

So, he'll be your work husband. LOL!

Her mouth tingled with laughter as the phone shook in Hope's hands. *Ha. Ha. We're friends. Nothing more.*

If you had to be pretend married to someone, that hunk would do.

Her lips turned downward. She replied. *Not funny, Ame.*

Hugs. Keep me posted. Tell your family "Hi."

I will. Thanks. Later.

Hope plugged her phone into the charger and went downstairs.

Faith handed her a paring knife. "What took you so long?"

"Ame texted me to see how I was doing. She said to tell all of you hello." The thin streamer of cucumber peel curled around her finger. She shook it off and finished the salad.

During dinner Faith asked about Caleb's day, Hope's brother-in-law provided the largest portion of the conversation. Followed closely behind by his son.

After dinner, Hope noticed Faith rubbing her lower back. "Go shower. I'll clean up."

"Thanks." Faith slowly walked through the doorway.

"Aunt Hope, can you throw the ball with me?" Jack's big brown eyes looked at her.

"I'd love to. After I clean up dinner."

"You two go, I'll do it." Caleb began to rinse the dishes by the sink. "If y'all could go to the park down the street to play. I need to turn on the sprinklers, this summer heat is scorching the grass."

"Sure, can I take the van?"

Caleb nodded. "Mmhmm."

"Get your stuff, Jack, and I'll meet you at the van."

"Okay." Jack's feet pounded the wooden floor as he ran from the room.

"We'll be back soon."

"Have fun. Appreciate you taking him."

"We will. See you." Hope made her way upstairs and sorted through her things to find some bottoms to change into. She found a pair of purple yoga pants and a tie-dye tank and put them on. Looking in the dresser mirror, her hair sprung like a Slinky around her face. With a few flicks of a wide-bristle brush and a large hair-tie, she was ready.

Jack waited by the front door carrying a sports bag that was bigger than him.

"Let's take your glove and ball." Hope plucked through the contents of his bag and found the items. "Let's go."

Her nephew jerked open the door and sprinted to the van. Hope grabbed the keys off the hall bench and soon was pulling from the driveway.

As she stepped from the van, birds were singing a night lullaby to their little ones tucked in the crook of a tree. Soft intermittent peeps chorused in tandem to the crickets' chirps. She found an open spot away from other park-goers, and they readied for practice.

"Square your shoulders, Jack." Hope instructed as she stood

to her full five-foot nine-inch height. "I'll help you aim your pitch."

"You've got it wrong." A male voice from behind her, pushed his way into the conversation. "He needs to plant his lead foot. Keep it straight and turn his body as he throws."

Hope spun, teeth gritted. Who was this wannabe baseball coach? She tossed the ball to Jack and turned. She surveyed the gray workout shirt that left no doubt that the baseball expert was physically fit, and her eyes went to his face. She'd know that cleft chin anywhere. "Dylan, do you mind?"

"I do, if you're going to incorrectly teach our nephew." A scowl slashed Dylan across his face.

Lava shot through her veins and steam blew from her lips ready to erupt. "Didn't I mention to you that I was the softball captain at my school, and I played on the winning intermural league team at Florida State?"

In two steps, Dylan was next to her. She saw the beaded perspiration on his muscled arms he stood so close. "Are you giving me your resume?"

"No." Hope pivoted away from Dylan. "Stating my skills."

"In high school, and college I played baseball. We were the intermural state of North Carolina champions, two years in a row," taunted Dylan. "Let me show him."

"Come on, Uncle Dylan." Jack coaxed.

Jack threw the ball past Hope. She turned in time to see him catch it. And smile. *Aggravating man.*

"Watch the master." Dylan stepped a few feet in front of Jack and gave him a series of complicated instructions.

"Ok, I'll throw it to you." Jack threw the ball straight to his target, Hope.

Dylan protested. "Hey, I thought it was for me."

Jack shook his sweat-darkened head. "Nope. You're next."

Hope sauntered past Dylan and pretended to nudge him with an elbow. "Guess I'm his favorite."

Her nephew laughed loudly. "You are one of my favorites. Uncle Dylan's the other."

"Thanks, Jack." Dylan held a limp towel to his side and dropped it.

As Dylan tossed the ball to her nephew, she had to admit, the man had a skill with teaching. Jack's pitching was stronger.

"One more toss, slugger, then the second string will help you." Dylan chuckled.

"More like the star player." Hope threw a ball that rolled on the ground. She clamped down on her teeth in frustration.

Jack scooped it up with his glove and rolled it back to her. "Let's do it again, Aunt Hope."

She glanced at Dylan who was sitting on the top of the wooden bench. "Don't you have somewhere to be? Like the next country over?"

"No, I've already finished my five-mile run, I'm resting and observing." He bowed his head as his shoulders shook.

Hope stood tall and wiggled her arms out. "Square your shoulders more."

Dylan instructed. "Plant your lead foot."

She half turned to face him and wagged a finger in his direction. "No comments from the grandstand."

"You're too serious, Hope." Dylan laughed. "Baseball's meant to be fun."

Hope's ears burned. She knew how to have fun, and she'd show him her skills too. "Jack, can I toss the ball to your uncle?"

"I'll watch." Jack ran past her, and she handed him a water bottle from the bag by her legs. "Thanks."

Dylan stood across from Hope. He swung his arms around, as if he needed to stretch. He cracked a big grin and spoke. "Go easy on me."

"I'll throw it when you tell me." She tensed her arms in preparation.

"Ready."

As the sun slipped lower in the sky, the rays cut into Hope's vision, and she shielded her eyes with a hand and threw as hard as she could.

"Ow!" Dylan clutched at his eye.

Worry brewed with the moans coming from Dylan. Hope ran over to him.

"Did you throw it blindly? I'm going to have a black eye tomorrow."

"I'm sorry, the sun was blocking my vision, I thought I could do it."

Dylan pointed to his face, stop sign redness ringed his left eye. "You didn't."

"Jack, get me the water bottle from the bag." Hope shouted.

Her nephew ran next to her, his brown eyes rounded. "Wow, Uncle Dylan."

Hope put the sweating water bottle to his eye as he winced and stepped back.

"I need an icepack. I've got to get home."

"We'll drive you, I brought Faith's van." She took the bag and gestured to Jack for him to get his gear.

"I guess, it'd be faster."

All fifteen minutes of the drive, Jack filled the uncomfortable spaces between her and Dylan with talk. Pulling into the circular driveway of a cabin at the foothills of the mountains, Hope noticed the large porch out front and the cheery brown-red planks covering the modest home. Dylan alighted.

"See you tomorrow?"

With a wave, Dylan walked up his pebbled sidewalk.

"Wait until I tell Mom and Dad what you did to Uncle Dylan."

Hope prayed a sinkhole would open and swallow her before she saw the expressions on their faces. Shame washed over her, as she recalled the baseball-sized ring around Dylan's eye. Tomorrow was going to be tedious day.

~

Dylan turned on all the lights in his office and went to the washroom at the end of the hall to survey his eye. Red lines bisected it, and the ripe dark plum color shadowing his eye only accented the inflammation. *And I have a client meeting today.*

The front door chime rang as it opened. Dylan shut off the light, and headed to his office, not caring to see the cause of his throbbing eye. He closed the door behind him.

A knock sounded.

"Come in." Dylan busied himself by turning on his laptop and glancing over the client notes for his meeting.

"Good morning." Hope put a coffee cup on his desk. "I went by Hawk's Creek Coffee."

"Mmhmm." He looked up from the screen. The yellow dress she wore made her red hair more fiery and her gray-green eyes brighter. Dylan's gaze averted back to the screen, and his heart picked up speed as if he'd done a gym cardio workout. "Thanks."

"I brought this too." She handed him a clear bottle with transparent liquid. "Witch Hazel. Soak these cotton pads several times a day and put it on your eye."

Dylan opened the cotton pad package. "Does this work?"

"Caleb said it did. How are you feeling?"

Hope hovered between the door and chair in front of his desk. He was raised better than to let a woman stand awkwardly in his office. "Sit. I mean. Please sit. It's better. I iced it most of the night."

She complied with his invitation and took her place in the chair. "How's your eyesight?"

"While it looks awful, I can see well."

"Thank goodness."

He noticed the pink on her cheeks. Dylan enjoyed the show of slender arms in her sleeveless top and long legs peeking from her skirt. *She's changed, still beautiful, but more polished. And we're friends. Strictly friends.*

"I asked what time your meeting is. You didn't respond, everything okay?"

Dylan shook his head, straightened, and adjusted the collar of his pressed shirt. "Too little sleep last night. I forgot to get your number in case I'm running late."

"I'll write it down." Hope took a pen from his desk, jotted down her number, and pointed to the cup with the pen. "Drink up, the coffee's strong. It was funny to be back there, the last time was when Faith and Caleb were on their honeymoon. And we were dat—"

A door creak interrupted Hope, Dylan stood and glanced at the hall. "My clients."

She rose and went in search of her own workspace.

A familiar floral scent remained in his office. He sniffed the air before going to meet the couple. What was the perfume called? Summer Days. With the memory, he smiled. It was the one he'd bought for her before their relationship had drifted into friendship.

Dylan's voice carried down the hall as she closed her laptop, after the last tutoring session for the day. She packed her things and walked to the receptionist area. All it contained was a grey chenille sofa she'd seen in his apartment some years before and several generic waiting room chairs. She scanned the wooden wall behind the receptionist area. It was the only interesting feature.

"I know." Dylan lifted his shoulders. "It needs something."

Color. Style. New furniture. "I think with a few changes, it could be great. The pattern of wood on the wall is really nice."

"It was a last-minute addition to the remodel."

A chord struck in his tone, resonating with Hope. "Do you need to borrow my artistic eye?" *Poor choice of words.*

"Way to bring up my present situation."

Faith stepped closer to the doorway. "Not intentional."

Dylan touched his eye. "It'll be my souvenir for a while."

Hope put her hands on her hips. The present good mood flickering toward annoyance. "I felt awful about it and have apologized. I don't know what else to do."

"Maybe it's because I'm exhausted. Maybe it's not." He frowned. "All of this reminds me of what happened between us. Why we ended. Why we are better as long-distance friends."

"Agreed." Hope threw the door open and stepped toward the minivan. Dylan's wasp-stinger words hurt her heart. All the disappointment, and sadness at their faded relationship came showering down. With this many holes in their relationship, could the tatters be mended, and they become better friends?

CHAPTER THREE

"No classes today?" Faith's kind voice came through the cracked open doorway.

"I do." Hope turned in the bed and swiped her eyes. "I have some around eleven."

"You've got an hour then." Faith slipped into the room.

"I wish I could cancel them." Hope pulled the soft yellow sheets toward her neck and shook her head.

"You love teaching, what's got you down?"

"Dylan rehashed why we broke up."

"Ouch." Faith sighed softly. "You two. You began as friends but stopped that part of your relationship when you dated. It never developed both sides of being friends and boyfriend and girlfriend. Did it?"

"Here's what happened. We fizzled out as quickly as a roman candle once we were together. Even though we haven't talked in a long while, I still . . . aagh," She pushed a curl from her face. "I don't know."

Faith poked her shoulder. "Every time I mentioned you at a family dinner, he asked about you."

She pushed up against the fluffy pillows and glanced at her sister. "Probably a kind gesture."

"I can't speak for him. I think you two can turn this boat around and not let it crash."

Hope threw the covers back, then tidied them. "You've been married to your river outfitter for too long. A boat analogy. From you."

"I know. Fear kept me from boating for a long time. I missed out on a lot of fun times." Faith grabbed her arm. "Don't be me. Dylan was a friend once. He'll be one again."

Hope stood and hugged her sister. "This is going to sound sophomoric. I'm not sure we can be friends."

Faith smiled softly and spoke. "Miracles do happen."

"They do." Hope pushed from the bed, a mischievousness firing inside her. "You're a fairly good big sister, have I ever told you?"

"Fairly good?" Faith pointed to herself. "I'm the best."

She hugged her sibling's neck. "You are."

Faith grinned wryly and moved toward the hallway. "Jack's calling me." Faith started to close the door behind her. "Love you. You're a pretty good sister, too."

"Love you too. Thanks for the compliment."

Once changed into work clothes, Hope dashed from the front door, toast in one hand, bag in the other. Her red flats mimicked the determination in her steps. The Fuller family didn't back down from anything. Dylan Gaines was one large, albeit well-formed, challenge.

Big Red, her newly given nickname for the Mom Mobile, swooped into the parking spot a short time later. Hope glanced down at her denim shirt and cherry red pants, smiling she alighted from the van.

She got as far as the steps up to the sidewalk when a voice greeted her.

"Good morning. You need this leopard scarf. It'd look marvelous with your outfit." The friendly lady who helped her the other day waved the scarf in her hands. "You could wear it as a belt."

"Good morning, I didn't get your name the other day. I'm Hope Fuller." She ran a hand over the soft fabric.

"It's Minne, Minnie Pickering. Pleased to get to know you. Are you and Dylan a couple?" Her crimson lips pursed and unfolded like a Chinese fortune teller Hope had played with in middle school. "He's what I'd call a catch."

She waved a hand in front of her and shook her head. "No, nothing like that. I'm borrowing his extra office space."

Minnie snapped her fingers. "Too bad. Do you have time before work to come into my store?"

The eye-catching window display intrigued her. "I'd love to."

The shop owner clapped her hands together and chortled. "Wonderful!"

Minnie hooked Hope's arm with hers and reeled her into the store. The scent of lavender and tea rose permeated the area, reminiscent of a garden she toured, Queen Mary's Garden, in London.

"Welcome to Minnie's Treasured Things. If you don't see it here. You don't need it." Mrs. Pickering dipped her impossibly crayon red head down and shot it back up as if it were tied to marionette strings. "I'm a purveyor of yesterday's treasures."

"I can see." Hope noted the tower of hats on a wooden hat rack by the oval mirror, some feathered, some plain, and a few leopard models scattered in the array. Along the walls were racks of clothing in all hues, reminding her of Joseph's coat of many colors. She walked over to the antique perfume bottles and picked up a light blue one. "I love this one."

"You've got good taste. That's one I picked up during a trip to Paris last year with my husband. I almost kept it for my collection. But beauty needs to be shared." Minnie waved the scarf in her hands. "How about this? Interested?"

"Oh, yes, thank you. How much do I owe you?" Hope went over to the gold and mirrored checkout desk. A large green parrot squawked from his wooden perch behind the counter. "I didn't realize you had a pet. He's beautiful."

"Pedro. He's my assistant. The cheapest employee on the books." Minnie pushed her large black glasses back to the bridge of her nose. "Zero, for the scarf. It's my gift."

"Thank you so much." Hope wove it under her beltloops. It ended with just enough left to make into a knot. Perfect.

"Come back and visit. That perfume bottle will be waiting."

"I will, thank you, Mrs. Pickering."

"Call me Minerva or Minnie. Tell my friend, Dylan, over there 'hello.'"

"Sure. Bye." Hope departed the store. Sunlight reached the middle of the sidewalk, to Hope, and seemed like a Heavenly hug. She'd look forward to visiting Mrs. Pickering. Minnie.

Hope pulled on the office building's door, locked. She knocked. No response.

"Coming." Dylan called, jogging up to her, "Court case ran late." He unlocked the door.

She held it open for him. "Your hands are full, go first."

As Dylan passed, his arm brushed hers. He looked at her, then entered. Her cuff came undone, and she groaned. It had taken her a while to button it one-handed.

"Someone's in a bad mood." Dylan pivoted halfway, his lips flashed an almost unnoticeable smile and kept on course down the hallway.

"No, that's you." Attempting to put the tiny pearl-sized fastener through the sleeve's buttonhole, she called out. "It took me a hot minute to get this closed."

"Let me see."

She walked to his office.

"Which sleeve?"

Hope held out the unclasped one.

Dylan easily slid the button through the hole and glanced up at her. "I was a jerk yesterday. Sorry, I said those things."

He's trying to be nice, Hope. "Appreciate it."

He tapped the frame of his office doorway and bent his head toward the desk. "I have a nine thirty phone call."

"And I was just leaving." She walked back to her office. The squeak of the chair down the hall and his voice in conversation with someone alerted her to the fact the call was taking place.

At least they had a start toward rekindling their friendship.

Hope's brain power was diminished after lunch. Back-to-back math classes tested her art educator brain. She stretched her neck before packing her laptop back in its bag.

Someone rapped on the door.

"Come in."

Dylan entered and stood in front of her desk. He pointed to the computer. "Wanna leave it here, I've got an alarm if you're worried."

"That'd be nice to not lug it back and forth until tomorrow. I'll take it back to their house this weekend."

"I like mine at home on the weekends too. It keeps me company when I'm watching games." Dylan looked away. "I multi-task, that's all I meant. I'm not a hermit. I date."

"I didn't say you didn't." Hope alighted from the seat and took her handbag's strap. "See you tomorrow."

"Hold on." Dylan walked with her to the hall. "Do you want to go with me Saturday to some furniture places in Asheville? I'd really like your opinion. We could also talk about why we've not spoken in over a half a year."

Longer than that. They stood face to face, her heartbeat picking up pace. She'd exhaled, not realizing it'd been captured in her lungs. "I'm supposed to watch Jack so Faith and Caleb can go on their date night."

Dylan held the office door open for her. "We'd be back in plenty of time."

Darn! Hope stepped into the hallway. "I'll let you know. Bye." She pushed the main door open and walked through it. Mind marking off a "do-go" or "don't-go" checklist. It'd require some prayer time. Lots and lots of it.

CHAPTER FOUR

Dylan wouldn't stop talking. He filled in all the quiet spaces of the car with chatter. Hope now knew where Jack got his talkative tendencies. "Nice weather, isn't it?"

"I guess, I was talking too much?"

Hope held two fingers close together. "A little. I couldn't even hear the radio, and it's pretty loud."

"Sorry." Dylan turned the volume down. "You were so quiet, I wanted to keep up the conversation. Tell me about London."

"I studied in King's College and was able to volunteer at the National Gallery." Hope played with a strand of her hair, winding it round and round her pointer finger as she glanced out of the window. "I worked with some great people in the children's area. To see those kids, enjoy art, it was a thrill."

"I loved my time in Oxford during my junior year. I'm going back someday." Dylan turned on the signal. "I'd like to find out why didn't we talk. I tried texting you about eight months ago."

"I lost my old phone. So I bought a new one, with a different number." She tore her gaze from the whirring scenery and onto his face. "My email never changed."

"Mine didn't either." Dylan's glance flicked to hers. "All

throughout law school it never changed. Yet, I didn't hear from you."

"It sounds like a pitiful excuse, but I was busy, either studying or volunteering." Hope ran a finger over the leather armrest, not meeting his eyes. "And I went out with museum friends on the weekends to Paris, exploring markets, and museums. It was wonderful."

"It does sound great. I could've reached out to you, too. But law school is no joke. I either was in class or preparing for an exam or mock trial."

"Neither one of us were at fault. The timing wasn't there." Hope glanced at Dylan's profile. His clean-shaven face was drawn in concentration. "Maybe we can—"

Dylan interrupted. "We're here." He pulled the car into the parking lot and turned it off. "What were you going to say?"

"It's not important." Her shoulders tensed in frustration. "Let's go shop."

Dylan's face turned serious. "Browse."

She threw up her hands in acquiescence and grinned. "Fine. Browse."

Hope meandered in and out of furniture displays while Dylan wore an expression much like one of the dispassionate, marble statues she'd observed in London's National Gallery. She kept her attention on the decorations and not on the sullen man trailing her around.

Hope ran a hand over the arm of a light beige sofa. "Do you like this?" When she received no response, she turned to look at him. Dylan sat on a swamp water brown sofa. Her stomach did cartwheels. "You like that?" Her voice rose on the last syllable.

"It's big and comfortable."

It was the size of a Greyhound bus. "You want something smaller, the room isn't large."

"Maybe I'll put this in my house, someday."

She went over to the price tag and flipped it over. There

were several extra zeroes on the end of the number. “Um, did you look at the price?”

He leaned over and absorbed the high dollar amount. “For this? Let’s go look at the one you chose.” Dylan put his six-foot one body in one corner of the sofa she’d selected. “Not bad, it’d appeal to women too. I won’t only have male clients. Good call.”

“That’s why you wanted me with you, to save you from making a bad future purchase.” Hope breezed ahead of him. “Did you take a photo of it?”

“No. I’ll catch up to you.” Dylan wove through several clusters of people and snapped a shot.

Having watched him retreat, she glanced the other way grabbing something from the display in front of her, feigning interest.

“That’s uglier than the man sofa.” Dylan laughed. “It’s probably just as expensive.”

Hope caught the low price on the tag. Shifting her eyes to what she held in her hands, the grip she had on it wavered. It was a puce-colored vase which had a person’s face carved into it on a clock. “I thought the color was, vibrant.”

“Sure, you did.” Dylan took the ‘humanoid’ vase and set it back on the display rack. “You can buy it later. When I get my brown man-sofa.”

“Do I have to? I really don’t want to see it again.”

Dylan let loose an easy chuckle. He picked up the vase and pointed to the clock face. “The hour hand is near his right cheek and the other is near the left eye. Four o’clock. We need to get you back to babysit.”

A quick peek at the hideous object confirmed his announcement. Her thumbs flew over the keyboard in a text to Faith. “Let’s go.”

Conversation drifted to different subjects in the car. He spoke of sports and history. She regaled him with talk of design and family. It made her realize how vastly different they were from one another, which made conversation interesting.

"Thanks for going." Dylan stopped to let her out. "Don't forget to buy that clock vase online."

"And you can get the caveman sofa set." She opened the car door. "Night."

Dylan gave a quick wave and pulled away. She hurried inside ready to have a night of fun with her nephew.

Later, after Jack was put to bed, Hope showered and threw on her pj's. She tiptoed downstairs to not wake him up and sat on the family room sofa. Her cell phone was blinking. She picked it up and read the message.

I thought you might want a photo to remember your art piece by.

As the photo of the vase materialized, she had to laugh.

Thanks, I'd forgotten how cute it was.

When's your birthday? It looks like it'd make a great present.

Sorry, can't tell you, I'm allergic to ugly presents.

See you later. You can remind me of your birthday then.

Not a chance. Night.

When she scrolled through the channels, an ad for the furniture store was on. She was almost positive the spokesperson stood near the ugly vase, but half of the lady's body covered it up. No doubt it was done on purpose. Hope giggled and continued to channel surf. Once Faith and Caleb arrived home, she caught up on their date night and headed to bed. As she plugged in her phone, the photo blipped on the screen for a second. It made her giggle again. Dylan did have a funny side. She appreciated his odd sense of humor.

Faith peered over her coffee cup in the kitchen. "Can you watch Jack? Mrs. Settles was going to come sit today but is sick."

"Sure. It's a light day anyway. I only have two tutoring

sessions. Poor thing, I hope she's better soon. She's been Jack's sitter for a long time." Hope leaned into her sister. "Do you have something pressing, maybe a mani-pedi."

"I wish. I can't see my toes beyond 'the bump.' Caleb polishes them for me. It's Briar Creek Bakery. Willow and Ryan are taking their engagement photos today."

Hope leaned back into the chair. "Two matches from the Briar Creek Bakery so far. You and Caleb, now Willow and Ryan." She gave a sly smile. "I wonder if there's more?"

"Maybe, someday. We've got some high schoolers working, give them a few years. I'd better go. I hope my coffee making skills aren't lost. It's been a few months since I worked."

"I'll go." She gestured for Faith to sit down. "You stay home. You've only got four more weeks until the baby comes."

"It's more restful there. My son's one bundle of energy. At the bakery, Mondays are slower." Faith pushed from the table to stand and flexed her back. "I need to tell Jack bye. Text me if you have anything come up."

"I will."

"Thanks." She waddled from the kitchen.

Hope viewed the sweet scene of her sister and nephew hugging and Faith brushing a kiss on his forehead.

"See you two."

Both Jack and Hope waved, and Ranger smiled in his own canine way as a spool of drool marked the tile floor.

"Eww, Ranger." Jack ran and grabbed a paper towel.

"I'll help." Hope found the antibacterial cleaner under the kitchen sink and sprayed after Jack wiped it up. "Paper towel, please?"

"Here." Jack thrust the mile of paper into her hand. "Can we go swim?"

"Of course. I don't have to tutor until this afternoon. "

"Yay!"

Her nephew ran down the hall to his room. She cleaned the

rest of the breakfast mess and went to put on her own suit as well. Before one toe reached the patio, Hope had sprayed and rubbed sunscreen on Jack and then, herself. The smell of tropical beaches scented the air in the kitchen. It lifted her already great mood.

Jack pointed to her. "Aunt Hope, you look like a ghost!"

She surveyed Jack's skin. What wasn't covered by red and blue dinosaurs on his swim trunks was a nice shade of never-seen-the-sun. He favored one of her beloved British actors who played Doctor Strange, Benedict Cumberbatch. With a thatch of hair over his forehead, and his strong chin, he could almost be a younger version of the actor. "Missed a spot." Hope sprayed the small patch. "Let me rub it in." Hope smoothed his arms with a palm. His skin appeared underneath the sunscreen goo like a Polaroid photo developing. "Back to yourself. I'll grab the towels, need anything else?"

"Maybe my squirt cannons. I don't know where Mom put them."

"I saw them in the garage the other day. Let's go get them."

"Okay."

The duo grabbed the squirt toys and then headed outside.

Rainbows reflected the jets of water from Jack's cannon, Hope screeched as the tepid water hit her face, which delighted her nephew. She waved her hands in the air in surrender. "Have you ever played Marco Polo?"

"Yup." Jack's brown eyes twinkled in the sun. "Mom says she's the champ of her family."

"She did?"

"Mmhmm, you and Aunt Grace never won. That's what she told me."

Competitiveness rose within her. "Let's play. I'll show you a few tricks to beat your mom and dad." Hope eyed the stone grotto and waterfall in the pool, the perfect place to hide and lie in wait. "Stay on the shallow side, please."

Jack kicked to the other side of the pool across from Hope. He squeezed his eyes closed. "I'll find you. Ready?"

"I am." She used small shallow strokes to cut through the water. Her years of swimming at the beach and her family's pool came in handy.

"Marco."

"Polo."

Her nephew's legs beat against the water, he was zeroing in on her. She stayed still.

"Marco." He was a foot away from her.

She turned her head to the side and shouted. "Polo!" Jack's hand touched her shoulder. "Aah, you tagged me!"

Together, Hope and Jack laughed.

"Your turn. I need a head start." Jack started to swim away.

"I'll count to twenty before we begin." She bent her head side-to-side to clear the water from her ears, closed her eyes and counted. "Marco."

"Polo!"

She was stymied. The lower voice didn't belong to her young nephew. "Caleb, are you home?"

"No."

Hope opened her eyes. On the other side of the pool, Dylan crouched next to their nephew.

"Hi." Her smile wavered like the lapping pool water in front of her.

"Hello. Faith told me where you were. I went to the coffee shop a while ago."

"Oh, gosh. I forgot to let you know I'd not be in the office today." She shielded her eyes from the sun as she looked at him. "Was she doing, okay? I told her I'd go in for her."

"Fine. She was sitting with some friends from church and chatting. Ryan and the rest of the crew won't let her work." Dylan ran a hand in the water. "Can I join you two? My last meeting ended early and Jack's always asking me to swim." He held navy trunks in his hand. "I came prepared."

"Of course. You were a Weeblo when you were a boy. What is the Boy Scout motto? Oh, Always at the ready."

"It's Webelos. Be back in a moment." Dylan disappeared into the back door of the house.

While he was gone, Hope threw her arms to each side and spun in the water, creating a whirlpool. All the activity had shifted the back of her suit higher, so she scooted to a place where she could adjust before Dylan returned.

He stepped from the house, with a red towel around his neck, reminding Hope of Jack's reading cape. Her eyes stopped at his uncovered upper body. Muscles hugged his ribcage in a pleasing fashion. Hope busied herself and scooped some leaves out of the water.

"Aunt Hope made a big wave, Uncle Dylan." Jack announced.

"She did?" He slid into the water beside him. "The whirlpool. I've seen her do that before, it's cool. Do you have the basketball?"

"Nope. It's over there." Jack pointed to the landscaping next to the grotto.

"I'll get it." Hope pushed off the side of the pool, the stamped concrete warm under the summer sun. She dunked her hands into the pool.

Dylan's eyes went to her hands. "You, okay?"

She glanced at her light red hands and nodded, as her hair trickled salt water onto her shoulders cooling her tanning skin.

"I'll get it." Dylan alighted from the pool, and she noticed his strong legs and back as he dug around the green plants. *He's a gym rat. Always has been.* A cold hand touched her arm. She turned and smiled at her water-speckled nephew who jumped up and down.

"I gotta go."

"Go. We'll start the game when you get back."

Jack left small, wet footprints on the concrete decking as he ducked into the house, Ranger yipping at his heels.

Without any preamble, Dylan jumped off the side of the pool, cannonballing into the water.

An Old Faithful-esque plume of water shot from the depths of the deep end, and gravity pulled it, right on top of Hope.

She sputtered and wiped her face, praying her contacts would stay in place. Hope cupped her hands and pushed against the water.

"Hey!" Dylan's hair flopped in his face as he moved through the water toward her.

Sparkles of awareness to his proximity electrified Hope. She searched for a way to escape. Dylan cut through the water like a homing signal tracking its target. When his head was in the water, she swam to the bench under the waterfall, and remained still.

"Aunt Hope. Where are you? I see Uncle Dylan, but not you."

She laughed, the echoes bounced off the roof of the stone structure. At once, Dylan dove under the water and popped to the surface beside the bench. Her heartbeat picked up pace. He came closer to her. She shrank back against the rough bench, shoulders hunched in false terror. "Don't you even try it."

As he began to wrap his hands around her legs, someone laughed. Hope switched her gaze to the new entrant into the grotto.

Jack splashed closer to them. "I see you two."

A triumphant smile in place, she had a reprieve in the form of her forty-pound nephew.

"Later." Dylan swam toward the little boy. "Basketball time?"

"Yeah. Are you playing, Aunt Hope?"

Her waterproof watch dinged, signaling she had an hour before tutorials. "Sorry, I can't, tutorials are in an hour. We'll need to get out of the pool, Jack."

"Aw."

"Let me take over, I've got a match against this hulk of a ballplayer."

"You sure?"

"I don't have anything pressing today, go teach."

"Thanks." She climbed up onto the tanning ledge and reluctantly headed inside. Hope glanced out the window at the "boys" at play. Her heart warmed.

As she finished the last tutorial, a plate slid across the desk. It contained a small apple and a crustless turkey sandwich, her favorite. She bit into the sandwich as the garden freshness from the tomato popped onto her taste buds. She looked up at Dylan. "Yum. Thanks."

"Can I show you a few things I bookmarked for the office?"

"Okay. Scoot next to me." Hope pushed lunch and her laptop to the side to leave room for Dylan's beside it, and Jack sat on the ground nearby rolling the ball to Ranger.

As he clicked through several of the pieces, she was surprised to see a level of sophistication he'd not had in college nor displayed in the furniture store. Band posters covered his dorm walls the few times she'd been able to visit him at University of North Carolina. "Go back to the last page." She pointed to some chairs featured in the display. "These look like the chairs and side tables you had on the list."

"I don't know anything about design." He shrugged. "I trust your taste. What for the walls?"

"Can you add wood on the opposite wall?"

"It'd be too pricey."

Hope gestured with a finger to the screen. "Wall art would be more affordable, or, maybe a mountain photo, one of Blue Ridge. "

"Great idea. Would you do the photo?"

Hope paused to reflect on his question. Serious photography was in her past. She'd moved onto the education of people about art. "Can I let you know?"

He touched her hand as he closed his laptop. "There's something you're not sharing. You were a talented photographer. Maybe someday you'll tell me?"

With nothing to add to the conversation, she bit into her sandwich.

"See you tomorrow."

She waved as he left the room. A motor turned over a brief time later, and Hope looked out of the window and saw Dylan pull away. As she took her plate to the kitchen, the colors from the remaining vegetables out on the counter gave her an idea for a photograph. Courage comes to those who trust in themselves. She wasn't sure she was brave enough to follow through.

CHAPTER FIVE

Undulating Blue Ridge Mountains covered in a shroud of gray-purple mist caught Hope's attention on the drive to work. She pulled to the side of the road and clicked a photo. In the phone screen, Hope scrutinized the light, and wished for her Canon EOS, instead of the no-frills cell phone she held in her palm. The colors in the majestic peaks reminded her of the new office furniture and décor in Dylan's waiting room. Reborn wisps of the need to create uncurled inside her. She tamped down the rhapsodic rush of excitement and aimed the car toward work. There were classes to teach.

She reached the office and had clicked on her laptop before Dylan greeted her. "Morning."

"So, did you think about what I'd said the other day? Doing a photo?"

Hope detoured around the question. "I saw the most beautiful thing on the drive here." She began to pull out her phone but stowed it away in the desk drawer. "Never mind."

"Show me." He moved to the side of her desk. "You've got me curious. What was it?"

Hope pushed aside the reticence to reveal the beauty she'd

seen. It wasn't show-and-tell day at work or anything. She retrieved her phone and thumbed through the photos, turning the screen in Dylan's direction. "This."

"Gorgeous." Dylan grinned. "That'd make a nice piece of wall art, blown up, of course."

Hope fiddled with her laptop, not meeting his eyes, her shoulder muscles tensing.

"I'm so accustomed to the scenery here, I've forgotten to appreciate it. Silly, huh?"

"No." She shook her head and her shoulders relaxed that he hadn't pressed the photograph idea. "It's the same with me living in Florida. People are enamored with the beach. I've got one a few miles away from where I live, which I love to visit. It's not the same excitement though for me as it is for tourists."

"Have you been to the mountains?"

She put her phone in her desk and answered. "No."

"How about I take you hiking?"

"Sure, I'll go. I packed tennis shoes."

"The trails are rocky and steep, hiking boots would be safer."

Hope stared at Dylan. "They work for hikes back home."

"Let me guess." Dylan ran a hand in a straight line. "Smooth trails."

"Yes."

"On the way out, Saturday, we'll go to Pickering's General Store. They've got a great selection of hiking boots."

She shook her head. "I don't think I need them."

"I read in the Briar Creek Gazette someone injured their ankle on a trail last weekend."

She eyed her ankles and winced. "I don't know."

Dylan leaned on her desk. Too close to Hope for her comfort. "I don't want you to get hurt. Besides, won't you hike again?"

"No." She leaned back in the hard chair. "I mean, yes, I will. We'll go to Pickering's."

"I'll pick you up at nine." He pushed from the desk, arms crossed.

"That early on a weekend?" Hope smirked. "We'll need coffee."

"My brother and sister-in-law own a coffee shop and bakery. I go to their house for coffee." Dylan grinned.

"Fair enough."

Wearing her broken-in faded jeans and her second favorite top, Hope walked into the kitchen while her sister and brother-in-law were having breakfast with Jack.

"You're dressed, and up early. Saturday tutoring?"

"No."

Caleb stirred his coffee. "Honey, Dylan told me he's taking Hope on a hike."

Faith's brows arched. "Your idea of a hike is from the pool to the boat dock in our parent's backyard. Are you sure you're up for it?"

Her sister's glib remark caused Hope to reply more sharply than intended. "And you didn't go boating until Caleb got you to try it. I'm getting hiking boots, so I'll be going more than once."

"I think it's great to be active." Caleb rummaged around in a cabinet. "Faith, honey, do you know where the wheat germ might be?"

"I know, Dad." Jack popped from his seat and headed to the cabinets.

"Never mind, son." Caleb shook the pouch of wheat germ on the table beside him. "Who says dads can't get pregnancy brain?"

Hope caught Faith's surprised look and joined in with one of her own.

"Okay." He sat down at the end of the table and began to

munch on his cereal. Jack slurped the last bit from the bowl and glanced at Hope. "Can I go with you?"

His parents simultaneously said. "No."

"Why not?" Jack's bottom lip hung down.

Hope raised an eyebrow in surprise, "Are you going someplace?"

"Yes, and Jack's going with us." Faith took a quick sip of her juice.

Jack leaped from his chair and pulled on his dad's arm. "Where are we going, Mom and Dad?" His big brown eyes smiled. "Is it fun?"

Caleb cleared his throat and spoke. "Well, your mom and I are taking you to the zoo."

"I love the zoo! I'll go put on my shorts." Jack ran to the doorway.

Hope pointed to her sister's significant belly and shook her head.

Caleb grimaced. "Hold on son. No, not the zoo. The grocery store?"

Jack paused his steps. "That's not fun. I'd rather go with Aunt Hope and Uncle Dylan."

Hope's heart went out to her nephew, she would love to have him join—another time."

Faith whispered to her husband. "B-O-O-K."

"The library. I bet they have the new Pirate Joe adventure. Go change. We'll take you in a few minutes." Caleb instructed.

Jack ran from the kitchen. "Whoopie!"

"If they don't have the Pirate Joe book, someone is in a bad situation." Faith quipped.

"I bought it online the other day. It arrives today." Caleb's smile was as large as his win. "I was pretty sure you'd like some time alone with my brother."

Her smile fell. "I'm always up for a hike." The doorbell rang. Hope pushed from the table and stood. *Thank goodness, no more time to question me.* "I'll get it, you two keep making eyes at each other. It's too sweet in here for me."

She departed to laughter from her family. Hope pulled the door open and waved Dylan inside with her free hand. "Morning, come on in." It was hard not to notice his muscular legs showing beneath his khaki shorts and a broad set of shoulders wrapped in a blue Henley. *Nice.*

"Thanks, what's so funny?"

She winced. *Maybe he didn't see my observation of him.* What do I say? "Apparently, I am. Shoot, I forgot our coffee."

"Oh." His mouth was set in a smirk, Dylan's voice lowered. "You are funny. I appreciate your humor."

"Thanks." Hope wasn't sure what else to say, when Ranger brushed up against her leg, she reached down to pet him. *You are a great dog, Ranger. Perfect timing too.*

Awkward silence surrounded them. Of the three sisters, Hope was known to be the least funny.

"I'll go say hi." Dylan walked into the kitchen as Hope followed. "We can get some to drink before we leave too."

The family chatted for a bit, and Hope and Dylan excused themselves after getting their to-go cups of coffee. Once outside, she climbed into his dark silver, two-door coupe. "Nice car. You traded up from your green Gremlin."

Dylan turned the soft Christian rock higher before stating, "It died my last day of law school. Lots of memories in that car. It was a draw for the ladies."

She bit the inside of her lip to keep from laughing. "The last time I saw that car, it had more tape on it than paint."

Dylan's eyebrows headed toward his hairline. "No, it didn't."

Hope narrowed her eyes at him.

"Well, okay, it was held together with prayers and tape."

They neared the large sign for Pickering's General Store on the right of the highway.

"We'll get your boots, then head to the trails. They aren't but ten minutes up the road."

As they stepped inside the store, the wide wooden planks creaked, and her eyes trailed to the old signs hanging on the walls, some for cold drinks, others for gas stations. "This place is really cool."

"I like it. Jack and I have spent some time here. He likes the candy section in the back. Don't tell his parents." Dylan winked.

She made a zipping motion with her fingers on her mouth. "I won't say anything. As long as you buy waters."

"Deal." Dylan stuck out a hand, and Hope shook it.

"The boots are back here." He pointed his thumb away from them. "I bought mine here a few years ago."

She followed where he led. Passed the tall cabinets lined with jams, jellies, and toys from yesteryear, stood racks of clothes and the display of ladies' boots.

After trying on four pairs, she settled for a comfortable pair in bright red. "These are it." She rose from the wooden bench, "Sorry it took a while."

"You have to get ones you like, the trails will still be there." Dylan smiled.

At the main checkout counter, Hope added a few jams and jellies alongside the boots. "For Faith's buttermilk biscuits."

Dylan's eyes lighted. "Text me when she makes them, I'll be right over."

The older gentleman motioned to the rest of the array. "I've got more if you want them."

"These are good, thank you."

The man picked up on of the glass jars and grinned. "You chose one of my wife Minnie's favorites." Pick smiled. "That's My Jam. She loves red raspberries."

"I've met your wife. She owns Minnie's Treasured Things. Right?"

"She does. My Minnie is a special woman, there's not

another gal like her in the world." He brushed out his white moustache with a finger. "She makes the jams, let her know if you like them."

"I will."

Hope and Dylan alighted from the store a short while later. She balanced her large boot box with her bottle of water, sack of jams, and candy for Jack, herself, and Dylan.

"Need a hand?"

She gave him the boot box, "Appreciate it."

"How about letting me hold the candy bag too?" Dylan reached for the bag in between them.

"You want this?" Hope waved a blueberry stick candy in front of him.

"Yes." Like a bird after his prey, he shot out a hand, took the candy, and popped it halfway into his mouth.

As the sweet scent from the candies beckoned to her, she found a strawberry one and did the same. When she looked at him, she grinned. It took a lot of self-restraint to not point out his lips were stained blue. Something about his kid-like enjoyment pleased her.

A short jaunt down the road, and they were on the trail's lot. Walking along a meandering path, Dylan narrated what they saw. "That green fringe is a fern," he teased, "and that brushy tailed thing is a squirrel. Grandfather Mountain has many unusual things."

Hope rolled her eyes and swatted his shoulder. "We have those in Florida."

"So, you do." His voice held a note of humor.

Hope giggled.

They stopped at a roaring waterfall. The force of the water shot droplets onto her face. Before she could get it off her, Dylan swiped it away with a finger. Heat didn't ebb in the place that he'd touched. Shyness overtook her, and she looked away.

After an hour's worth of hiking, Dylan spoke up. "We're at the end of the trail, I know something unusual."

"More trails? I'm ready." She swung a foot in front of her. "So far, my feet aren't hurting."

"Told you the boots would work." Dylan squinted at Hope. "They do have a lot more trails. We could do those another time. I was thinking of something else, the Mile High Bridge."

"The view must be amazing."

"It is. And when the wind blows, which it usually does, it swings."

Her stomach danced at his words. "A high swinging bridge?"

"Mmhmm. We don't have to go."

"No, I'd like to see it." *From afar.*

Walking the short distance to the bridge, Hope drew clean pine-scented air into her lungs. The bridge before them swayed in the light breeze.

"Ready to cross?"

She wasn't sure if she wanted to admit to being scared or not. Hope pinched her lips together. The bridge wouldn't best her. "Ready." Her footsteps clanged on the metal slats. Increasing wind gusts caused the bridge to shift and sway. Hope halted her steps. Dylan took her elbow. She smiled up at him. His warm hand was comforting. In his closeness, he smelled wonderful. Beyond the clean air, his cologne was fresh and vibrant, with hints of ginger. She breathed in the manly scent.

"We're close to the best part." Dylan squeezed her elbow lightly. "We can turn back if you want to?"

"Let's keep going."

Hope managed a smile as her pulse ka-thunked when they reached the middle. When she noted the gorgeous, green-treed mountains and the craggy, jutting rocks below formed a deep crevasse, her strong resolve began to flounder like the bridge underneath her feet.

"Let's stop for a sec. We'll take a photo." Dylan retrieved his phone, his arm slipped around her shoulders. "Looking great."

As they stood side to side, Hope was confused by the swarm of emotions hitting her. His familiarity was both confusing and exhilarating. The wind decided to make its presence apparent, and blew harder, lifting Hope's ponytail ends and whirled in her face. With the creaks of the bridge as it pitched like a porch rocker, her formerly steady legs jelled. Dylan's grip became a bit firmer as the wood structure swayed.

"Let's head back quickly." Dylan pointed to the swirling mass of heavy clouds a short distance away. He took her hand. "Looks like the weather's changing. Storms coming."

They doubled back to the gentle walkway which led to the parking lot, right as the clouds let go of their stores of surplus water. She dropped his hand, ran ahead of Dylan, and held her arms overhead to deflect the showers.

Dylan unlocked the doors and motioned to her back. "Backpack."

She wiggled out of the soggy nylon straps and gave it to him before getting into the car. From the rearview mirror, she saw him sprint to his trunk and throw their bags inside then jump into the automobile.

A rumble of the motor, and arctic air blew through the vents. Hope rubbed at her cold arms.

"Sorry." Dylan cut off the air. "I'll set it to heat. Press the button on the door, it'll turn on the seat warmers."

"Th-anks." Hope's teeth chattered. "It reminds me of London this past spring, cool and rainy."

"Let's get you home, you're bouncing on the seat like Jack when he watches his favorite show." Dylan pressed the button, and warm air charged through the vents. "I remember that you get cold easily."

Surprise made her teeth halt their chattering. "You do?"

"Who could forget that time at the movies, when it was so

cold, I had to run next door and buy a sweatshirt for you from Old Navy?"

He remembered. Hope hugged herself with the thoughts of his recollection of their dating days. "I still have it, it's one of my favorites."

Dylan remained quiet. She glanced at him and noted the small smile on his face.

As Dylan pulled away after they'd said goodbye, the sun broke through the clouds, adding perspiration to her skin. She fumbled with the keys in her wet hands at the front door. The door slowly opened.

"I see you got caught in the rain." Caleb smiled. "It canceled the rest of my river trips for the day."

"Sorry for both of us." Hope stepped inside as bumps rose on her arms from the blasting air. She rubbed her hands together.

"Taylor and Jarod are here with the kids. Looks like you need to change."

"That I do. I can't wait to see them." She looked at her soggy, baggy clothes. "Be back soon." Hope squished and squashed upstairs. A hot shower was never so welcoming. After dressing in comfortable clothes and putting her hair up in a damp bun, she headed to see her friends.

Downstairs, Jack chased after three-year-old Joshua who was cackling and running after Ranger in the kitchen.

"Slow down son," Joshua's 'dad, Jarod, followed behind the young runners. "Hey Hope, I owe you a hug later."

"Hi Jarod. Go get 'em."

Entering the family room, she saw Olivia's strawberry blonde hair that matched her mom Taylor's. "Hey, Taylor. Good to see you."

With her little girl on her hip, Faith's best friend broke into a huge grin. "Hope, I can't believe it's been so long. Congratulations on your masters."

Hope hugged Taylor.

Hope said pointedly. "Thank you. I saw y'all on your last trip, when you were visiting your family in Florida."

"True." Taylor touched her daughter's nose. "Everyone wanted to see the twins. Who could blame them though?"

Little Olivia's petite nose turned up, and she exclaimed. "Hi!"

"Hey, Olivia, you are a beautiful girl." Hope touched one of her legs above her frilly sock.

Olivia tucked her face into her mom's embrace.

"She's quiet compared to her brother's loudness."

Joshua ran into the room and wrapped his arms around his mom's legs, his sandy blond hair plastered to his forehead.

"Go sit, Josh, I'll get water for you."

"I can get it." Hope looked at Taylor, "Sippy cups?"

"In the plaid bag."

As she pushed back, snacks, toys, some other unidentifiable kid things, Hope located two cups. "Found them."

"Thanks."

"Jack, I'll get some for you too. You look warm."

Both Jack and Joshua were sitting in the corner where his toys were located, playing with cars and trucks. Apparently, Jack had heard his aunt because he gave her a nod.

Once all the children were hydrated, Hope found a spot in a chair near the sliding glass door. Conversation moved from raising kids, church, and the upcoming baby. A shard of longing poked at her heart. *I'd love to have a family of my own. Babies. Handsome husband. Like Faith and Taylor have.*

"I am sure glad you're here Hope, Faithful needs to rest as much as she can." Taylor patted her friend's tummy. "Faith tells me your masters is in education."

She pulled away from her self-reflection and answered, "It is, in art."

"You'll be teaching in Tampa, I guess?"

"There are several schools that I'm interviewing with next week online."

"We've got an opening in my elementary school."

Hope noticed the shift in her sister's posture. She leaned forward. "In art?"

"I'd have to check with the principal. I think so and it was open a few weeks ago. Are you interested?"

Shock rendered her tongue unmoving.

"If you're not, that's okay."

"No." Hope wet her lips. "I never thought about being able to live here. Please ask."

"We'd love that, Hope." Faith's eyes glistened. "They'd have an aunt nearby."

The doorbell rang and Jack whirred past the grownups to answer it. A deep voice blended with Jack's higher tone as the pair walked into the room. Dylan's hair still bore the comb-marks from his shower.

Something within Hope shifted. *He's a friend.*

Caleb announced, "We might have a new resident here in Briar Creek."

"Taylor and Jarod, are you expecting?"

"No, guy." Jarod waved his hands. "We're blessed with our two. It's Hope."

"Hope?"

She looked at him. His face didn't give away any emotion.

"She might be teaching here next year." Faith volunteered.

"Here." Dylan repeated.

"Brother, did the rain clog your ears?" Caleb hit one of his ears and further stated. "Faith said here."

"I think that's—"

Faith stood wringing her hands. "Oh my gosh! My water broke." The carpet darkened underneath her feet. "I'm so embarrassed."

"Don't be. I'll go get the towels." Hope gave her sister a quick hug and ran from the room.

Caleb ran across the room and grabbed his wife's hands. "I'll grab the bag." Furrows showed between his eyebrows as he turned to exit.

Hurriedly, Hope grabbed a bunch of towels from the linen closet and returned to the family room placing them over the spot.

Caleb came into the family room with the big bag. "We'll call y'all. I can't believe the baby is three weeks early."

"It's starting to really hurt." Faith clutched her midsection.

"I'm texting the doctor now." Caleb darted a glance at Hope. "Hope, will you stay with Jack?"

Tears stung the back of her throat. "Of course, and don't worry about telling the family, I'll call." She grinned. "I'm so excited for you, it's going to be all right."

Hope gave her brother-in-law a quick squeeze. Her gaze lingered on her sister's face and then gave her a hug too. "You'll be great. Love you, I'm praying."

Faith's lips quivered. "I don't know. I'm scared." She kissed Hope's cheek. "Love you. I'd better go."

"Don't be. Jesus is with y'all." Hope blew her family one more kiss.

"Hang in there you two." Dylan and his brother hugged. Then he turned to his sister-in-law. "Faith, you are amazing, you've got this. I'll be praying, too."

"Thanks. Ouch." Faith held onto her midsection and bent at the waist. "We need to go. Now."

Both parents kissed Jack before leaving.

Taylor and Jarod gathered up their kids and departed behind them.

Dylan turned to Hope. "I'm going to stick around if that's okay."

"You can keep me calm. I'm sorry you're not going to the

hospital." Hope swiped a tear from the corner of her eyes. "Faith and Caleb and the baby will all be good. I wish I could be there."

"I'm hopeless with kids." Dylan touched Hope's arm. "I'll need your help when that baby gets home."

"You don't, you were amazing that day in the pool. You're a great uncle."

"I appreciate that."

He came closer to her, and her heart missed a beat. Heat from his body touched hers.

"I'd better get this cleaned up." Hope blotted at the floor. "Can you get the cleaner, it's probably under the kitchen sink."

Dylan nodded and headed to the kitchen. He returned soon after, "Here it is."

"Thanks." Hope glanced up at Dylan. "It's getting toward dinnertime. We'd better figure out what to feed this nephew of ours."

"Chicken!" Jack said.

"Uncle Dylan will cook, and I'll help."

He shook his head and his mouth turned down. "I'm not the best cook."

"Remember my char-broiled brownies?" Hope rose and pushed him into the kitchen. "Besides, I still need to get these towels washed."

"I warned you, as for your brownies I can still smell it and see the smoke from your dorm kitchen." Dylan thumbed through his phone. "We'll look up a recipe. Or get delivery."

Hope put her hands on her hips. "Our siblings don't do delivery. Remember?"

"Neither one of us are professional chefs, like Faith. We'll order, or risk food poisoning." He studied his phone screen. "Dinner Delivery it is."

Hope tossed a glance back at Dylan as she passed by him with the armful of towels. "Please make it healthy." *Although I'd secretly love a juicy burger right now. Cheese. Pickles. Mayo.* She started the wash and returned to the kitchen. "You know what I'd really like?"

"A burger?" A grin split his face.

"How'd you know?" She turned to face him. "I wanted a burger."

Dylan laughed and pointed to his phone screen. "I ordered one for you, you can eat it later."

"You are a smart man."

"I know."

Hope smirked and headed toward Jack's bedroom to start his shower. "Conceited, too."

"I heard that."

She smiled. *He's still the same. I missed our friendship.* A dip in her midsection caused her to push pause on any other musings. They were most likely too dangerous.

After a delivered chicken dinner was enjoyed. Jack's lids began to close as he sat on the sofa. She patted his leg. "Time to go to bed, you've showered and had a little snack."

"Uncle Dylan? More?"

"You had two pieces of chicken and a snack. Kitchen's closed." From across the room, she saw Dylan's smile in the low-lit room. "Story time?"

Jack covered his right eye with a hand. "Pirate Joe."

"Lead on." Hope scooted from the sofa, and she and Dylan followed Jack to his room.

The adults sat near on the bedroom rug, as Jack dove into his bed and Ranger followed.

Jack pulled on his blanket. "Will my mom be, okay? You know my other mom died." Jack's mouth wobbled. "Is Mom going to love me after the baby is born?"

Her hand flew to Jack's arm with the barrage of unexpected

questions. Hope gathered her thoughts, then spoke. “Sweetie, she’s going to be fine. People have babies every day. As for loving you, you are her son. She got to choose you. Your mom loves you so very much.” She looked at Dylan who had his head bowed. She whispered, “Say something.”

“Your mom in heaven loves you very much. She asked Faith to be your new mom since she couldn’t stay. Your mom here, loves you, too.” Dylan cleared his throat. “She’s going to be fine and so will the baby. And you get to be a big brother.”

Hope reached over and squeezed Dylan’s hand.

Jack settled into his pillow. “Good.” He took the book off his nightstand. “I’ll start reading and Uncle Dylan will finish wearing the reading cape.” The little boy opened the book and began to read.

She flicked a smile at Dylan and whispered. “You’re it.”

Dylan got up from the floor and unhooked the cape from the back of the door. He whipped it around his shoulders and tied it in a loose bow.

“Red’s your favorite color, isn’t it?” She held the cape’s edge in her hands. “You look like a Book Nerd.”

Throwing the small cape over one shoulder, he winked. “A handsome one.”

“So, you claim.” Hope surveyed him head to toe and shrugged. “You’re not bad.”

“I was irresistible if I remember not so long ago.”

Aargh. Leave it to the lawyer to throw her own words back at her. “Maybe I had sunstroke. It was at Clearwater Beach on a hot August day.”

“I rest my case. Defendant is guilty as charged.”

Jack’s book fell in his lap and his sleepy eyes pointed in their direction. “Uncle Dylan.”

“You’d better read attorney. The jury is getting angry.” She slid a glance to her nephew. “Correction, sleepy.”

Dylan's warm reading voice lulled Jack to sleep after Pirate Joe found the first clue to the invisible treasure chest.

"He's snoring." She pointed to Jack's door and mouthed. "Let's go."

They tiptoed from the room, and Hope flicked on the hallway nightlight and shut the door partway. In the foyer, Dylan stretched and yawned. Hope kept her yawn behind closed lips.

"You did well in there, Uncle Dylan."

"Thanks. You were great too." Dylan yawned again. "I need to go. Tomorrow's going to be busy. My folks drove from Asheville and are at the hospital. How about your family?"

"My mom texted they're at the airport now. They'll land at eleven and go to the hospital."

"If you want to go, I can stay with Jack."

"I appreciate it. I'll stay here. The baby probably won't come until tomorrow."

Dylan waved as he stepped through the door. "Night."

"See you later." Hope shut the door behind him, went into the quiet family room and cleaned up their glasses. Tucked into bed a short bit later, she was grateful for its comfort. Hope began to pray for her sister and her own future. She wasn't sure what outcome would be best, whether it was a career to begin here as a teacher, or in Florida. As a prayer was said for a quick answer, guilt twisted inside at her selfishness.

CHAPTER SIX

Morning glowed through the blinds waking Hope from a fitful sleep. She scooped up her cell phone and read the "still waiting" message from Caleb sent at 5 am. She eased down the hallway to Jack's room and opened the door. The mess of linens and a furry head let her know both boy and dog were still sleeping. As she rounded the doorway to the kitchen, she sniffed rich vanilla coffee. Hope picked up the pace and flew into her dad's outstretched arms.

"Dad, I'm so glad you're here."

Her dad kissed her forehead. "Me too. We had to get some sleep. Your mom and Grace were sleeping in waiting room chairs." Smiling he handed her a mug of coffee. "It appears our little grandbaby wants to delay the arrival."

"Not for long, dear." Her mother stated as she entered the kitchen, already perfectly dressed with all her jewelry and makeup on. "Good to see you, honey."

Hope wrapped her arms around her mom's slender body. "I'm happy to see you. Is Grace here too or is she still at the hospital?"

"Yes, she's asleep upstairs." Her mom held her at arm's length and put her hands on each side of her face, smiling. "We've missed you. Only with Grace at home, it's quieter. I can't wait to have you living nearby again."

Hope couldn't meet her gaze. *I don't want to disappoint them. They were strict with us growing up, but now they're grandparents, they've grown softer.*

"Is Jack up yet?"

"I checked on him, but he was still asleep."

"Not anymore." Grace came into the kitchen followed by a still sleepy boy.

While Jack received hugs from his grandparents, Hope and Grace chatted about the baby.

Grace motioned to the rear of the house with a finger. "I saw some hiking boots in the mudroom when we came in. Was Faith hiking?"

"I was."

"Those are your boots?" Grace shook her head. "Not you Hope. Your idea of a hike is to the shopping center or beach." Her sister lifted a dark eyebrow at her. "You didn't hike with Faith, I trust."

She leaned into her sister and said with a whisper. "I was with Dylan."

Her sister folded her arms. "This is news. Last time you mentioned him, you two were barely friends any longer. How'd it go?"

"I've got to catch you up on a few things." Hope's lips lifted. "It was fun. We saw a waterfall and walked over a swinging bridge, until the rain came."

Grace held a hand to her chest and crooned. "Sounds pretty romantic. Date worthy."

"It wasn't." *Was it?* "Two friends out for an afternoon hike. Don't make more out of it than it was, my romance novel reading little sister."

"I'm not majoring in writing at University of Florida because of my lack of imagination."

Hope said, "True. I can't wait to read your first novel."

"You'll be waiting for a while. I'll start writing after I graduate." Grace took the cup of coffee their dad offered. "Thank you. Maybe if I do a children's book someday, you can do the photographs for it. What do you say, Hope?"

A lump stuck in her throat. She'd not told anyone about halting her art.

Her dad walked to the breakfast room table with a serious set to his face and suggested, "Girls, and young man, let's finish up and get ready. We need to get back to the hospital."

Hope's mom said softly, "Honey, Jack can't be there that long. It might be a while still."

The doorbell rang, and Jack ran to get it with Hope trailing behind him. They returned with his sitter, Mrs. Settles.

"Good morning, everyone, Caleb called and told me the wee one's arriving soon. I'll watch Jack and bring him to the hospital when his sibling's here."

Hope hugged the kind older woman. "Thank you."

"Jack and I'll be fine. Let's make you breakfast and then you can show me your latest library book." Mrs. Settles winked at Hope and her family as Jack pulled on her hand. "Please congratulate that beautiful couple for me. I can't wait to see the little baby."

"We will," her mom said. "Dear, remember we brought Hope's camera. Can you get it for her?"

"My camera." Joy lit in her heart momentarily, until displeasure snuffed it. "Where was it?"

"The back of your closet at home. I wasn't sure why it was there. It was like you were trying to hide it." Her dad handed her the camera. "We thought you'd like to take some photos of today and as a family."

An arrow of dread hit home. "Sure, wait. It's not been

charged in, um, a long time." She took the case from her dad and brought the camera out, the weight of it familiar in her hand. After pressing the on button, no light appeared. "I'll have to charge it later. I can take pictures with my phone." Hope put the camera on the foyer bench. "I'm ready to go."

As the group went to the driveway, two cars were front to back.

Dylan alighted from the car in the rear and walked to where her family stood. "Good to see y'all. I wanted to check if you needed a ride to the hospital. Caleb texted me you were here."

Hope wanted to catch up with her family, but the pull to be alone with her friend played tug-of-war with her thoughts.

"We can't all fit in the rental car. Hope, ride with Dylan, and keep him company." Her mom's pointed instructions were like she was in her courtroom arena, direct and not to be questioned.

"Okay, see y'all there." Hope sped to the passenger door and sat in his car

"This worked out well." Dylan beamed. "Too bad you don't have your camera."

"My parents found it in my closet and brought it. No battery though."

"Good. You can take that photo for my office later on."

What's with him and the photo? Hope merely smiled. After buckling in, Dylan's motor revved to a roar as they pulled from the driveway. "You aren't going to speed, are you? My parents need to follow us."

"Your dad already has the address plugged into his GPS. We need to get to the hospital. The baby's coming soon."

"Our niece." Hope crossed her arms and shot him a smug look. "Girls are fun."

"I don't know the first thing about girls, neither does Caleb. We're a family of males."

"Your mom? Does she count?"

Dylan tapped the steering wheel with his fingers. "Of course, but she's the only one in the immediate family."

Hope crossed her arms over her chest. "I'll teach the baby when she's bigger how to play softball."

Dylan turned toward Hope, eyes still focused on the road. "Does that mean you're going to live here?"

"No. I have the interview in a week. Who knows if the principal here is hiring?"

Dylan muttered something under his breath.

"What did you say?"

"I'd like it if you were closer. We have fun together."

It caught her unaware. She thought their time together was a chance to get her opinion about his office decorating. Nothing more. "That'd be cool."

Dylan reached over and covered her hand with his own at the traffic light. Once they pulled from the intersection, his palm still lingered, and the warmth grew on the back of her hand. Puzzled by his "very friendly" gesture, she moved her hand away.

His cheeks reddened. "I was thinking about work, didn't mean to leave it there."

"I do that sometimes too." *What? Hold hands with some guy I used to date? Think about work and do something odd?*

"We are here, let's find a place close to the main entrance." Dylan swerved into a spot between two larger cars. He got out and waited at the front of the car.

Hope jetted from the car, and both made their way to the hospital's entrance.

The two entered the lobby to wait for her family. Sounds of soft music and squeaky wheelchairs filled her ears from the atrium.

"I'll text my parents to see what's happening." Dylan walked away.

She spied her father's brown and grey head above the crowd.

Her family panned the area for them. Hope waved them over.

"Hey, Dylan's finding out the latest from his parents. Where's the elevators?"

Grace pointed to the left as she pulled her bigger sister's arm. "How was the car ride? Did you both talk about anything?"

"All right, Ms. Nosey, we talked about whether I'd be getting a job and staying in Briar Creek."

Grace's brown eyes enlarged. "What are you talking about? What happened to the other job?"

"Shh." Hope put a finger to her lips. "There might be an art teacher position in Briar Creek Elementary. Taylor's checking for me. I haven't interviewed for the Florida job yet, it's next week."

Their mom came up beside Grace, her courtroom interrogation gaze in place. "What are you two arguing about? Your dad and I could hear it."

Hope glanced to her sister through slitted eyes.

"Nothing, mom." Grace shook her coal black hair and grinned. "You know we always dig at each other."

Dylan swept beside Hope and stated, "Girls have all these emotions."

Mr. Fuller laughed as they walked into the elevator. "Dylan, being surrounded by women has made me a happy man for many years. I hope my new grandbaby is a girl."

Hope's mother brushed a kiss on Dad's cheek. "I married a smart man."

"You're outnumbered, Dylan." Grace bobbed her head and smirked.

Hope reached across their parents and high-fived her sister.

Dylan sighed.

Beeps and a voice coming over the loudspeaker greeted them once they exited the elevator. The frigid air chilled Hope's arms only in short sleeves.

Steps away, Hope's dad knocked on the door softly. "Can we

come in?"

A pink uniformed nurse ducked from the door. "Family?"

"Yes," Hope's mom stated. "Can we see our daughter and son-in-law?"

"Mom and sisters?" The nurse questioned.

The ladies nodded

"She been asking for you three." The nurse pointed down the hall. "You can wait down the hall, it'll be a while, gentlemen."

Once the door widened, she heard panting and grunting. Hope's midsection squeezed tight as they walked into the room. She noticed Dylan and Caleb's mom, Georgia, sitting in a chair by Faith's head. Hope averted her eyes from the blue blanketed area on her sister and went over and gave Mrs. Gaines a hug. "Hi, it's good to see you." Another groan from her sister made her a little dizzy.

"Good to see you too. Looks like the little one's coming soon." Mrs. Gaines gestured to the bed. "Your sister's doing a great job of keeping calm. My Caleb looks as pale as an under-baked pie. Same as when Jack was born."

A quick glance to her brother-in-law left no doubt he was as white as his mother stated. Hope patted his arm and went to the other side of the bed beside her mom and sister.

"Need anything?" Hope rubbed Faith's shoulder. "Doing, okay?"

"Glad for the medicine. I'm so-so. Thanks." Faith attempted a smile.

Grace grinned. "You're doing really good. Better even than the time you won the award for best brownies in Girl Scouts."

Faith wrapped a hand around her middle and laughed. "They were burnt."

"Exactly, see you're awesome."

A swooshing sound caught their attention and another medical staff person whisked into the room. The nametag on her coat showed her to be the doctor. She immediately examined Faith. With a smile, the doctor patted her sister's bent legs. "Faith now's the time to really push. Do you want everyone in here?"

"I do. They are a comfort."

As she and her mom stood to the side along with Mrs. Gaines, Hope prayed as Faith followed each step the doctor instructed. Rising above the beeps of the monitoring device behind her sister came the lusty cries of a baby.

The doctor held the red and white infant above the blanket. "Dad, come cut the cord."

Caleb moved closer to the little one and snipped the umbilical cord.

"Tell us what the baby is, son." Georgia Gaines decreed.

"She's a girl." Caleb's eyes shone.

Hope grabbed Grace and hugged her. Happy wetness covered both of their faces. She looked at her mom, who was crying and laughing as well. In reflex, she began to snap photos with her cellphone.

Faith sputtered from the bed. "Can I see her?"

With several gentle swipes of a cloth, the cherub was placed on her mom's tummy. She squeaked and squalled as she threw her arms and legs into the air. Her light red hair haloed her tiny head.

Hope took several photos, and checked on the screen. Her niece's dewy skin made her smile. "She's gorgeous, congratulations. What's her name?"

The proud new parents looked at one another and winked.

Faith covered the baby with a bit of blanket. "It's Isabella Catherine Georgia Gaines."

Right then, all three men, grandfathers and uncle, came in the room. They gave each other pats on the backs.

"What a beautiful name." Mrs. Gaines said softly. "She's got both grandmothers' names. I can't believe it." She fastened an arm around her husband. "Steve, we've got a girl."

Mr. Gaines kissed his wife's forehead. "Let's get to spoiling her, Grandma Georgia."

Dylan's mom must have noticed him hanging back from the group because she waved a hand for him to come over. "Come see your little niece."

The proud uncle's eyes were bright with moisture as he cleared his throat. "Congrats, you two, Isabella's beautiful."

After the nurses took the newborn for her measurements, Hope started to stow her phone away. She, Grace, and Dylan excused themselves to let the grandparents talk with the Faith and Caleb.

"I'm going to text Amelia." She glanced at her screen. "Hmm, I've got a voicemail from a number I don't recognize."

"Don't fall for the auto expiration scam call." Dylan retorted.

"I won't." After the second time listening to the message, Hope took in the information and went back to the two.

"Amelia doing okay? Did you fall for the scam?" Dylan shook his head.

"No, I didn't text her yet. I've got an interview in three days with Briar Creek Elementary." Her smile widened. "We'll see what happens."

"It's going to happen. They'll hire you." Dylan grinned.

"Awesome." Grace walked toward the window down the hall, cell phone in hand. "I'm going to text my friends that I'm an aunt again."

An air-conditioned breeze blew on Hope, and she shivered. Dylan wrapped his arms around her. She stepped back.

"I'm warming you." His arms tightened in comfort. "Not making a move on you." Dylan whispered into her ear.

In his arms, it was like a homecoming, warm and familiar. She smiled into his shoulder, as waves of remembrance in times past crashed over her. Hope only prayed she'd be able to safely make it back to "shore."

CHAPTER SEVEN

As Hope folded the third pile of laundry for the day, she glanced over to Grace, and held up a tiny pink frilled onesie. "Isn't this the most precious thing?"

"Ah-dorable." Her younger sister, reached into the basket and pulled out a ladybug patterned hat. "Our niece is going to be the best dressed little baby in Briar Creek."

"Thanks for doing the laundry girls." Her mom sat near the basket and dove a hand into the pile retrieving a yellow checked blanket. "Grandmother duty at 3 am this morning wore me out. Isabella was so sweet though."

"You know they appreciate it, Cat." Their father's dimples showed. "Isn't she the most gorgeous grandbaby."

"You know she is." Cat placed the folded linen onto the pile. "I can't wait to show the beautiful photos you've taken, Hope, when your dad and I get back to the law firm."

"Thank you. I'm happy you like them. Thank goodness my cellphone takes pretty good photos."

"It's more you than the cellphone sweetie." Her dad softly stated. "You have skills, you need to be more confident in them."

Not sure how to reply, she smiled at him. *It's hard to be confi-*

dent when your supposed college friends think you have absolutely no talent compared to their flashy photographs.

Caleb entered the room, a burp cloth over his shoulder, and a hand on Isabella's pink pj'ed back. Proud big brother, Jack, tagged along, stopping to tickle his sleeping sister's feet. She wiggled and grunted.

"She ate a few minutes ago, I'd better go change her."

"I'll help, dad." Jack grabbed a diaper from the end table. "Let's go, Isabellie."

Both disappeared from the room.

A few minutes later, loud footsteps pounded on the wooden floor. Jack ran into the room, his cheeks puffed out like a blowfish before he exhaled. "Nasty!"

"You did that too when you were a baby, son." Caleb followed him, gently placing the baby in her grandmother's outstretched arms. "Being a dad is a great arm workout. Jack was about two pounds lighter. My daughter loves to eat. She's only been home a few days, and my biceps are ripped."

Hope's dad grinned and flexed an arm. "Wait until she gets bigger, it's even more of a workout."

Grace glanced at Hope, and they giggled.

"You were little once." Their dad admonished. "Cat, how about some time for Isabella's Grandpa?"

"Not now. Lunch should be arriving soon. Can you go check please?" Cat gently rocked her granddaughter and kissed her red curls. "Hope, would you mind helping him?"

After Hope put the folded clothes back into the basket, she laid it down on the hall bench. "Sure, glad to. Is it here, Dad?"

Alex opened the door and swung his head to the outside. "It's coming right now. Good afternoon, come on in."

Georgia and Steve Gaines came through the door bearing a deli tray and fruit.

"Thanks, Mr. and Mrs. Gaines," Hope took one of the trays from Mr. Gaines' hands. "Is Dylan coming too?"

"He'll be along shortly, that busy man had a meeting today." Georgia informed. "Plus, he's getting dessert."

"That's the best part." Steve smiled and placed the containers on the counter. "Our youngest is driven by the law and food, he won't want to miss this. Alex, is our granddaughter up?"

"She sure is, if you can wrestle her from my wife's arms." Hope's dad chuckled as they went into the family room.

Grabbing the basket from the hall bench, she heard the creak of the door. She whipped a glance toward it as Dylan strode through, wearing a navy pair of pants and a pink plaid shirt. "I like the pink."

"I bought it online as soon as I knew Isabella was, well, Isabella and not Isaiah."

"Looks good, I've got this pile of laundry to put away." Hope wiggled the basket.

"Let me put this pie in the fridge, I'll help."

Her mouth fell open at his offer, but she snapped it shut like one of the clutches sold at Minnie's shop. Shifting the cumbersome basket, she climbed the stairs.

Putting the things away were a matter for someone more organized than her. She put the laundry container on the pale blush recliner and opened every one of the weathered white dresser drawers to see what each one held.

"See the roses in the picture?" Dylan came into the room and rocked back on his heels. "I got at least five burns from the glue gun when Caleb and I made it."

She scanned the light and dark pink faux rose wall above the crib, it covered a quarter of the good-sized room. "That's really pretty, did you make one in case the baby was a boy?"

"No. Caleb and Faith knew she was a girl from the sonogram four months ago."

"Those stinkers, Faith told me weeks ago that they'd locked the door to the room so no one would know." She waved the onesie she held in the air. "I'm jealous you knew."

He took the little outfit and put it away. "I only knew because of this wall of roses." Dylan picked up a soft miniature castle laying on the changing table and smiled. "This is new."

"I got it for the baby in London." Hope hugged it. "I hoped she'd be a girl even then. Every princess needs her own castle."

"They do." He nodded. "We've got one in Asheville."

"A castle?"

"As close as we'll get in America, The Biltmore Estate."

Hope put the stuffed toy back on the changing table. "I went there as a kid, it was huge. I'd like to see it again."

"I'll take you."

Before Hope could reply, Faith popped her head in the door, and stepped inside. She put her sleeping daughter in the crib. Hope took note of the rings under her sister's eyes that spoke of late nights, but joy shined in Faith's smile. "Thanks, you two. Are you coming down for lunch?"

"I'll be there in a bit. I want to stare at Isabella."

"She is gorgeous. I can't believe she's mine and Caleb's. Please shut the door behind you when you leave. See you." Faith grabbed the video monitor and left the room.

Isabella's soft noises drew Hope closer to the crib. Her round cheeks puffed in sleep. "Come see, Dylan."

"She's a beautiful baby." Dylan said softly. "Isabella looks a lot like the Gaines side of the family."

Holding a strand of her red hair away from a shoulder, Hope harrumphed. "This little doll gets her rose red hair from my side."

"She does, but she has a cleft chin, like mine." Dylan pointed to the dent his own.

"I suppose." Hope ran a gentle finger down her niece's hand, the skin smooth and soft. "She makes me want to have children someday."

"You do?" Dylan's eyes rounded.

Hope shrugged and a smile edged her mouth. "Of course, two kids would be perfect."

Dylan opened the door for Hope. "I'd like three or four, maybe more."

Hope lost the ability to breathe. *Three or four?* She quietly exhaled before speaking. "That's a big family. What'll you do if your wife works?"

"We'll hire a nanny, or she can stay home as long as she'd like. It's up to her."

"That's reasonable." Hope stepped into the hallway. "A woman has more choices in how the kids are raised these days." She straightened her back, ready for a quick response in case he turned "caveman."

"Exactly."

He's changed, more open to things. Hope grabbed onto the handrail and accidentally touched his hand. She pulled it away and hurried downstairs, doing her best to ignore her ramped up heartbeat.

Dylan looked at Hope's back as she sped down the stairs. *She's in a hurry, must be hungry. I know I am.* As he entered the kitchen, he staked out a spot at the breakfast table. All were taken.

"We can go outside." Hope balanced a plate of food and her iced tea as she opened the door. "Under the pergola, there's some shade." She waited for him to fill his plate.

He bobbed his head in understanding and followed her to the rectangular wood and glass table and set his food down. "Good call, it's crowded in there."

"It's fun to see our families together. They get along so well."

"It is. Your parents and mine meet for lunch in Asheville when they visit."

He bit into the veggie sandwich, which tasted like mowed grass. *Yuck, it must have been meant for Caleb. He's the health freak.*

Suddenly, Hope laughed, and her eyes shined in the sun he noticed. His insides jolted. *This sandwich is horrible, I'll probably need something to settle my system. But I'd stay here forever to see the light in her beautiful eyes again.*

"I like a salad sandwich." She moved a wedge of ham sandwich onto his plate and took the other half of his.

He'd never been more thankful. As he brought the piece to his mouth, he smelled the meat and muffled a sigh. Hope was one generous friend. "I could've eaten the other half."

"But you wouldn't."

He noted the smirk Hope directed toward him. "True. Did you want to see something else in the area?"

"Like what?"

Dylan took a sip of his drink before he spoke to wash the grassy taste away. "One of Caleb's kayak customers is manager of Tweetsie Railroad. He gave Caleb passes."

"That's the one in Blowing Rock. I've passed by it. It looks like a fun amusement park."

"It's a nice place. Caleb's asked me to take Jack. We can do it together. They've already been as a family, several times, and I haven't been there since I was a kid. Plus, it will give them some time with Isabella and get some rest."

"Could we wait until my family goes back home?"

"Definitely. How much longer are you staying?"

"Three more weeks, it'll help Faith get into a routine with both kids."

"We'll go next weekend then. Did you hear anything about the job here?" His sandwich hung between the plate and his mouth as he awaited the answer.

"The phone interview went well, I'll know late next week on both. Taylor hasn't said yet."

"Oh." Dylan wasn't sure whether he should be relieved or worried. She didn't seem excited about the job here.

"If I did get the job. I wouldn't want to live here and impose. They don't need me hanging around."

"There's plenty of places to rent." Dylan drank his water and eyed Hope. Her red hair flamed in the bright light. Her grey eyes reminded him of still pools near a trail he frequented.

"Did you bring your suit, Uncle Dylan." Jack pulled on his shirtsleeve.

"Oh, I didn't hear you come outside."

He saw the odd look Hope gave him, like he was a science experiment.

"I yelled when I came out because Mom and Dad said I could swim. Can you hear?" His nephew shouted into his perfectly working ear.

He snapped his head to the side away from Jack's trumpeting and nodded. "Yes. I was thinking."

Jack changed course in his questions and turned to Hope. "Will you swim with me?"

"What about me? I can get my trunks and be back in less time than it takes for you to change."

Jack ran back inside.

"You'll lose. Your home is at least fifteen minutes away."

"Twenty." Dylan gathered their empty plates and got up from the chair. "I always keep one in the car, just in case." He put an elbow to hold the door open and she stepped inside. A light scent of berries followed her. He followed Hope and disposed of their trash. Since the pie was already cut, he performed a "taste test," then went to his car.

He came back inside and headed for the half bath down the hallway, passing Hope on the way there. Her long hair covered her shoulders, reminding him of a work of art. She was delicate and angel-like. *Darn sandwich!* He turned back and glanced at her shapely legs beginning to tan for the summer. The door slammed before he got to the bathroom. Dylan knocked on the door. "Jack, I was going to use it."

"I beat you, Uncle Dylan," Jack belly laughed.

"Use my room." Hope offered on her way to the pool. "Don't peek at any of my stuff though."

"I won't. Is your camera charged?"

She paused. "Maybe. I didn't check."

"Is it in the room?"

She nodded.

"I'll bring it down." Dylan traveled upstairs and into the third bedroom, careful to not wake his niece sleeping next door. Once he changed, he took the camera, threw his clothes back into his car, and grabbed the towel.

"Have a good swim son." His mom smiled and gestured outside. "Someone's waiting on you. And I don't mean my grandson." She patted his arm, her voice lowered. "Don't tell me there's not something going on, I can see it and so can your dad."

"We're friends, Mom." He glanced to his dad who was watching a golf game with Mr. Fuller and Caleb in the other part of the family room. "How's the North Carolina guy looking?"

"He's fourth right now." His dad squinted at the screen. "Make that fifth."

"Maybe he'll come around." He stepped outside, the June sun beating on his head. "Hope, do you have some sunscreen?"

"Look on the table. Jack and I put ours on already."

He grabbed the bottle and sprayed himself down, head to toe and got into the pool.

"You didn't rub it in." Her fingers went to his face as he squinted in the light.

"Uncle Dylan, you're a ghost."

"I'm coming to get you then." He held out his hands and growled as Jack swam in the other direction.

~

She tried not to look as Dylan chased Jack in the pool, his back had streaks of white on it. *I'll tell him later.*

"I'm swimming too." Grace dove like a dolphin into the deep side and surfaced beside her. "Your old friend's looking pretty good right now."

"I was watching our nephew play."

Grace slung her hair back, flinging water in Hope's face. "I don't believe Jack was the object of interest. No. It's the six-foot one lawyer with the bluest eyes and great hair."

Hope splashed her sister and looked heavenward. "I admit nothing."

"But your smile says everything. You used to do that when you saw him. Kinda soft. Very goofy."

Sisters, the world's worst critics and world's best friends.

Her sister put her arms up on the side of the pool and languidly kicked in the water. "What are you going to do if you get a job in Florida and the one here, which one would you take?"

"I'm not sure. I'd have to really pray hard about it." *I hope that's not the case. It'd be too hard to come up with the right choice.*

She climbed from the pool to sit in a lounge chair and toweled off.

"Want your camera?" Dylan yelled from the pool. "It's on the table."

"Maybe later."

He turned to play with Jack, which relieved Hope. Grace laughed and splashed their nephew who squealed.

Jack declared. "Marco Polo time."

Dylan waved a hand in the air and grinned. "I'll referee."

"I'll show you who the winners going to be." Grace had a smirk on her face.

"Oh, yeah?" Hope threw down the towel and jumped into the

pool surfacing next to her very soggy nephew. "We'll team up. Aunt Grace is pretty good at this."

"Jack can play with me." She crooked a finger at their nephew. "Come on over. We'll win."

Their nephew swung his eyes between Hope then Grace. "I can't decide."

"Look what you did Grace." Hope's lips formed a line before she sputtered. "You've confused our sweet nephew."

"He'll want to be on the winning team, with me." Grace said. "I always won when we played Marco Polo, or he can take his chances with you."

Hope stood beside her nephew. "You and I are a team."

"Aunt Grace, next time we'll be a team."

Grace gave his hand a shake. "You've got it. Who's ready to lose?"

"Not me." Jack dove underwater and began to swim to a corner.

"Go easy on him Grace. Count to ten before you start searching."

"I will. Don't worry." Grace turned away from them and began to count down.

Hope pointed to the deep side of the pool. "You go that way, Jack and I'll go to the grotto."

"Okay." Her nephew splashed in the water away from her.

"Good luck teams." Dylan swam away.

She found her nephew in the shallow side, and they tip-toed to the grotto as Jack held onto the ledge.

The two teams played until the sun lowered. Jack barely hung onto his paddling skills as the last "Marco" was shouted, tiredness playing around his eyes.

"Our winners are Team Hope and Jack!" Dylan pointed in their direction. "Congrats!"

"We won buddy." Hope followed her seal-like nephew as he jumped onto the sun deck. "Good going."

"We did it. Can I have some of Uncle Dylan's dessert?"

"Go check with your parents." Hope instructed. "I don't want to say the wrong thing."

He threw the door open, dripping small lakes onto the floor.

Grace waved the towel like a matador. "Your towel!"

"Too late." Dylan pointed to the camera. "I didn't see him get it out."

"No, I was too busy having fun." Hope's eyes skimmed past his to the bag. "Another time. I need to get prepped for the interview tomorrow."

"Come by the office afterward, please, I want to see know how it goes."

"It'll be after one, is that still, okay?"

"I'll be waiting."

She ducked into the house and went upstairs to shower. No one was in the family room when she went inside. Dylan's family must have gone back to his house. Muffled voices confirmed her sister and brother-in-law were taking care of their children.

Hope didn't bother with makeup after she finished her shower. Ranger sniffed her feet as she entered the hallway, presumedly detecting the peach scented body wash. His cold nose made her giggle. She headed toward her bedroom.

"I brought your camera bag back to my room." Grace met her in the doorway and gestured toward the other room across the hall. "I believe Dylan thinks you have a phobia about that thing. Is there a memory card in it?"

Probably. Glancing around for a quick change of subject, Grace's purple shirt looked very familiar. "Hey, isn't that my t-shirt?"

Grace pulled it away from her body and seemed to inspect it. "Darn laundry, things get mixed up when we do a big load." She started for her room.

"Sure, they do. Next laundry day, I'll grab it. Not you."

Grace sighed.

Later that night, Hope knocked on Grace's door. "Can I have my camera?"

"Let's see if it still has the card." Grace pulled it from the bag and began to scratch at the hard plastic body of her sister's expensive camera. "How do you do it?"

"Come in my room, you're being too loud, almost everyone's asleep." She flicked on the light and sat on the bed. Once Grace sat down next to her, she opened the small door and pressed on the minute card. It sprang out of the holder like a Jack-in-the-box, landing on the floor. Hope picked it up. "It's there." She waved it in her sister's face.

"Don't try to put me off. I know all your delay tactics."

She grumbled and popped the card back in place, turning on the camera. With a whirr, it lit up. Hurt seized her throat. She swallowed around the ache as hard as a peach pit. The first one saved on the card was of Faith's surprise party when she moved to Briar Creek. She paused to remember the fun event on the deck of Caleb's river outfitter's business.

"Keep going, that party was fun. I can't believe it was four years ago." Grace's nose crinkled up. "Look how little our boy was. Jack was teeny tiny."

"He was." She exhaled again and flicked to the next photos. Her fingers flicked through the memories. Moving day for Faith. Caleb's proposal on the water. As the next photo slid into place, she bit the inside of her mouth as her teeth clamped together. She and Dylan had their arms around one another in the easy fashion of an established couple. His smile kissed her heart through the lens.

"Good picture of y'all, was this at FSU?"

Hope bobbed her head. "During a Noles game." She lowered the camera. "I don't want to see anymore right now. I can see all the mistakes I made. . .with the photos." Hope clicked the camera off.

"Do you have a fresh card?"

"I don't know. I'll check." She brought the cumbersome bag from the floor to her bed. It depressed in the spot from the weight of the extra lenses. A glimmer of plastic caught her eye. She pinched the square and brought it out, still cocooned in the factory wrap. "I do."

"Replace the old one with the new one."

She stared at her sister. "Why, I'm not going to use it. I mean anytime soon."

"Hope Abigail Fuller, you're not one to back away from whatever it is you're trying to avoid. We've got two beautiful children in this house." Grace put a finger on the bed. "I need Auntie bragging photos."

Grace is right. Why am I letting a bunch of college kids dictate the enjoyment I'll get seeing the precious children in photos later. If I take the other job, I don't have to snap art, just my family.

She fumbled trying to remove the full card from the camera. On her second try, she succeeded and tucked the memories away. *Fresh starts.* Hope put the new card in place.

"A new chapter is opening for you." Grace grinned at her. "There's one thing you have to do."

"What? I'm drained from swimming." Her shoulders drooped.

"First take a photo of me. Then, you need to tell Mom and Dad about the interview. You haven't yet, have you?" Grace jumped off the bed and posed by the moonlit window. "Get my good side."

"You don't have one."

Grace stuck out her tongue, and Hope snapped a quick photo. She eyed it on the screen, it looked pretty good.

"Hey! I have two equally wonderful sides." Grace proclaimed with a toss of her dark hair. "Another photo, please."

The camera whirred as Hope shot several more candid

pictures. Showing them to Grace, she earned a big hug. "You're really talented. You know that."

"I guess."

"Don't listen to the doubts, we all get them. You are good. Now, our parents need to hear something from you."

Hope stowed the camera away and put it in the corner of the room, not looking at her too wise sister. "I will. There's not been a chance to tell them."

"They're probably reading. Go tell 'em. I'll be in my room if you need to talk."

Hope squeezed her sister's bony knee. "You're all right."

"I'll take that compliment, now go." Grace pointed to the door and opened it. She waved a hand. "Quickly. Before they're asleep."

She was torn between wishing there were no light underneath the door or divulging her plans to them. A whispered prayer later, she knocked on the door.

"Come in." Her dad's ever patient voice instructed. "We're still awake."

Her heart beating a new pattern as her slick hand opened the door.

She didn't want to hurt anyone, whether she stayed in Briar Creek or went back home. Whatever way she chose, it was something she had to risk to find a new beginning for herself.

CHAPTER EIGHT

"I'm glad you talked to us last night, sweetie." Hope's mom smiled at her as she entered the kitchen. "Pour a cup of coffee, you've got an hour before you leave."

"I wasn't sure how you'd take it, Grace talked me into saying something before today to y'all."

Her dad flipped a pancake with sous chef Jack beside him. Her father glanced at Hope. "Me too. We're proud of you. We'll visit two of our daughters here if you get the job. You'll be a wonderful teacher, look at all you've done in your internships and the online tutoring."

She moved beside her dad and gave him a side hug as Jack patted her hand. "Thanks. Chef Jack do you have a pancake for me? They look great."

Jack struggled to lift the blue-striped bowl off the counter to check.

Hope jumped around to Jack's side to rescue the quivering bowl. "Got it, there's enough for all of us."

"You'll be next after we finish Gigi's she wants another tiny one."

"I can't wait, I've not had pancakes since being in England."

She poured the coffee and sat across from her mom. "How was the baby last night?"

"She woke up three times, Faith said. You just missed them, she fed Isabella and they went back upstairs to try to rest."

"I'll have some time with my little darling later."

"I'm getting in all the grandchild love since we leave soon. If I didn't have several cases coming up in court, we'd stay longer." Her dad put several coin-sized pancakes on a plate. "Gigi's pancakes are ready, sport."

Jack, the young chef, grabbed the plate and delivered it to his grandmother.

"Looks perfect." She brushed a kiss on his forehead. "Thank you."

"Welcome, Gigi," Jack ran back to his G'Pa, "Can I flip this one?"

"Of course," Hope's dad put his hand over his grandsons, and they flipped the pancake onto the pan.

"Nice job, Jack!" Hope cheered.

"Thanks." Jack's smile was Hope's reward for the well wishes.

Breakfast finished, Hope readied for the interview. Coming downstairs, she saw Dylan standing there with an apple.

"Morning. Who's that for?"

"A teacher needs this." He handed it to her. "I wanted to give you something before your interview. Minnie tried to give me a handbag to bring to you before I got into my car."

"I'd take both."

Dylan's single dimple showed. "It was orange with tiger stripes."

"Good call. Thanks." She wasn't sure if she should hug him or not, so she patted his arm and opened the door. Her dad's car blocked Big Red. "Sugar cubes! I'm trapped. Faith said I could use her van."

"I'll take you, It's on my way."

"Sure. Bye, everyone."

"Best wishes honey. Thanks, Dylan." Her dad gave her a quick hug.

"You're welcome, sir."

Both walked into the humid June day, she lifted her hair from her neck.

Dylan must have noticed as he said, "I'll blast the A/C. You look pretty in that dress."

She got into the car and smoothed the black and white patterned knee-length dress. "Thanks, I hope it's not too wild for the interview."

"You're an art teacher. You need to look, vibrant."

"Good point."

He pulled to the brick and stone elementary school's drop off and turned to face her. "I know you're nervous, interviews are well. . .stressful." Dylan patted her hand. "Act like Merida, you look like her. She was fierce."

"From Brave?"

"The one."

"My hair matches hers, thanks for the ride and the pep talk. I'll text you when the interview's over."

"Keep the car." He dangled the keys between them. "I can walk to work. It's only three-blocks. See you soon." Dylan alighted from the car and began to walk down the sidewalk.

After checking her makeup in the oval mirror on the sun visor, she said a prayer for peace and the right words to say before grabbing her oversized black bag and locking the door. Despite the heat, a cool breeze ruffled the air, calm settled within. *Thank you, Lord.* She pushed open the door and was greeted by a woman sitting at the receptionist desk.

"Good morning, Ms. Fuller. You're Principal McTier's ten o'clock?"

"Yes."

"I'm Beatrice Skomp, it's nice to meet you. Call me Bea."

"Thank you, Bea. It's great to meet you as well. Please call me Hope."

She sat down and adjusted her dress to cover more of her knees and noticed a string on the hem. Hope glanced to see if Bea was looking, and pulled it from her skirt, throwing it into her bag.

A voice stated nearby. "Hope Fuller."

She pulled her gaze from the bag and looked into a set of hazel eyes and a heart-shaped face which was surrounded by dark brown hair. "Yes."

The smiling woman held out a hand. "Betty McTier."

Hope shook her hand. "It's nice to meet you."

"You as well." Principal McTier motioned with a hand as a grin set jauntily on her lips. "Come on back, thanks for coming in."

"You're welcome, I appreciate you taking the time to interview me."

"Taylor sang your praises. She's one of our best Kindergarten teachers." The principal closed the door behind them and went to sit behind her desk.

Hope found a chair across the desk, and the interview commenced. She wiped a damp hand on the side of her dress hoping Principal McTier wouldn't observe her nervous action.

Principal McTier wound down the hour-long interview and promised to have Bea schedule a second interview with the two assistant principals.

"Thank you, Principal McTier. I'll look forward to it."

"It's Cathy, and I enjoyed getting to know you Hope. We'll be in touch."

All the tenseness drifted away as she stepped to the parking lot. Hope started the car and pulled from the parking spot. A tire squealed as she went to the main street. *At least I left an impression.*

She overshot the parking spot and had to back out. The tires squealed with the large turn into the spot.

Dylan popped his head from the door like he was waiting for her to arrive. "How'd it go?"

She gathered her things and pulled herself out of the car. "It went well, thanks. I'm getting to the next round of interviews." Hope ran a hand along her hair, unsnarling a tangle caused by the light wind. "The program sounds amazing."

"Come in." He held open the door. "Better than the Florida jobs?"

"Different, the hours, school environment, it all sounds small town. Which is nice."

"Briar Creek's twenty-thousand residents thank you for saying that."

Hope sat in one of the comfortable chairs in the reception area. "You know what I meant."

Dylan sat across from her. "Would you take it?"

"Probably. I can't believe I've only got two weeks more here. If I don't get the job." She picked at another string on her skirt and snapped it off. "I can't tell you how much I appreciate you letting me take over an office."

"It's been nice, we've had a lot of laughs."

"We have." Hope motioned toward the receptionist's desk. "You know you need a receptionist for your practice? This pretty desk is going to waste, plus, your phone is ringing more and more."

"I'm a procrastinator, I can do this for a while longer."

She gave him a firm glance. "Not so sure, I sign for your deliveries and have shuttled a client a time or two back to your conference room. I'll be gone soon."

"You wouldn't consider being the receptionist?"

"Oh no." Hope flicked a grin. "My major's education. Not organization."

"Will you help me interview some people?"

She let the idea marinate for a moment before speaking. "I've never done that, but since I just went through two of them myself, I'll help."

"I'll go on Joblist and put the notice online." Dylan tapped the desk before he left. "Tweetise with Jack this weekend?"

"After church, Sunday works."

"I'll get you home."

Both climbed into the car, and for the abbreviated ride to the house, they chatted about inconsequential things.

When Dylan turned into the driveway, she noticed the rental car still in its spot. "Thanks again."

"Glad to do it, tell your parents goodbye for me, and Grace too."

She shot a smile to Dylan, closed the car door, and hurried to knock on the front door. It was pulled open by her dad.

"Tell me about the interview." Hope's dad's eyes crinkled at the corners. "Did you nail it?"

"I've got a second one scheduled for next week."

Hope's dad enclosed her in his arms. "I was sure of it. Cat, come hear about the interview, while I get our bags."

Isabella cooed in her grandmother's arms. She rocked her back and forth while Hope told her mom and Grace the good news. "I never doubted it sweetie, what are you going to do about Florida?"

"The interview will still take place, unless they offer me this job." Hope brushed a soft hand over her niece's precious curls. "I don't want to leave my precious nephew and niece."

"It's someone besides them you don't want to leave." Grace shot underneath her breath. "Begins with a D—"

Their mom interjected. "Grace, go help your dad, and Caleb."

"Yes, Ma'am." Grace walked out the door with a sad expression.

"Thanks."

"You're welcome. Do you have any feelings for that handsome young man?"

"I'm not sure, mom, maybe."

"I won't tell your dad, but I hope you do. He's pretty amazing."

Hope giggled. "You never stop surprising me."

"I think your niece surprised me herself." Cat pulled the baby away from her body. "Darling girl, you need a diaper change."

"I'll take her so you can get ready to leave."

"No, she's all Gigi's." Cat tickled her granddaughter's stomach as they went upstairs.

She found her big sister in the family room sorting laundry. Faith glanced up from the stack she was making. "Did it go well?"

She held up a thumb in the air. "Next interview's coming."

"Thank the Lord! I need more family here." Faith swiped a finger over her lashes. "Darn, post-pregnancy hormones."

Hope took the rest of the basket to the other sofa and poured it out on the cushions. "I've got this. You go sit, didn't someone want four feedings last night?"

"She did, it has to be a growth spurt. That's what the Cuddles and Love app said it could be." Faith waved her phone in the air. "I always keep that tab open, in case."

"You are one awesome mom."

"I try, thanks."

Faith's lips turned up. "Jack's excited about Saturday."

"Didn't we go as kids when Mom and Dad took us to Beech Mountain?" Hope folded a soft blanket and put it in the basket. "And the Land of Oz as well?"

"We did, I remember sitting on that big plastic brown horse. You and Grace fought over the smaller grey one."

Hope shook her head, her curls tickling her neck. "Figures, we always have something to say or do to one another."

"Girls, we're getting ready to leave." Hope's mom placed

Isabella in her mom's arms. "I'm going to miss my grandkids." She ran a finger under her eyes. "Send me photos every day, and we'll video chat a lot."

"We will, Mom." Faith rose from the chair, and Hope halted the folding.

Jack ran in between them and to his Gigi. His little arms surrounded her neck. "I'm gonna miss you and G'Pa and Gigi."

"We will miss you too, we're coming soon though." Her mom kissed his cheek.

Hope pulled her phone from her pocket and took a quick photo. After everyone hugged, her parents and sister climbed into the vehicle. Caleb closed the trunk and walked over to his wife and kids.

Grace hung from the window of the car. "Tell Logan I'm not wearing that hat."

Hope glanced at Faith who rolled her eyes. "If he asks." Grace harrumphed and closed the window, a grimace across her face.

Hope's mom declared. "Hope, bring him to Florida for Thanksgiving."

"I might not get the job. As for *him*, we'll see."

"It will, sweetie. Love all of you." Cat waved along with her husband and closed the door. Grace was head down facing her phone.

"Honey, we've already planned to go to Florida." Caleb asked his wife. "Who's your mom talking about?"

Faith grinned as she shielded the sun from their daughter's face. "Another Gaines."

"Got it. I'm on team Dylope, too."

Faith groaned. "Couldn't you think of another name?"

He lifted his shoulders. "Hopdyl?"

"No way." Faith pulled on her husband's arm. "It sounds like something in the produce aisle. Let's get back inside." Jack walked next to his parents to the door.

Dylope. Hopdyl. Why ruin a perfectly great friendship with those bad names? She rewound the invitation for Dylan at Thanksgiving. A gentle light glowed in her thoughts. *Thanksgiving might look different this year.*

Jack tugged on Dylan's hand. "Let's go, Uncle Dylan."

At that point, she was glad she'd changed from her church sandals and into tennis shoes. Hope walked next to her excited nephew and rejoined. "Come on Mr. Pokey. We're almost to Tweetsie Railroad's entrance."

"I'll show you I'm not Mr. Pokey." Dylan ran beside his nephew and nodded to Hope to lift Jack up and swing him between them.

"Cool! Can we go on the railroad first?"

They breezed through the entrance with the passes and took the winding path to the train station. The shrill of the steam whistle made Jack hold his hands over his ears, yet the grin on his face remained. Hope boarded the bright red and forest green car first, followed by Jack, then Dylan. As the train pulled away, the force of the steam engine's thrust pushed Hope back into the bench, and her hair began to flutter like streamers. She took the hair tie from her wrist and made a ponytail.

"Your hair looks like a horse's mane, Aunt Hope." Jack played with the ends covering her arm. "It's soft."

"And pretty." Dylan exclaimed.

She looked out of the open-air train car and smiled. "Thanks."

Over the wooden trestle bridge the train clicked and clacked. Jack grabbed both of their hands and held onto them tight. "Here comes the show!"

"Don't give it away, honey. Someone might never have come

here before." She shifted his hair out of one of his eyes. "Like me. Is it gonna be scary?"

"No. It's fun, these cowboy guys hold us up."

"Sounds fun?" Hope playfully shrank in the seat. "Who'd going to protect me from the bad guys?"

Jack pointed a thumb at his chest and then poked it into Dylan. "Me and Uncle."

"I feel safe now." She unkinked her spine and giggled.

All of a sudden, two men leapt onto the train as it came to a halt. On the other side of the train was a wood and paint "town." The bad guys came from behind the town hall, and began "shooting" at the good guys, who pretended to go get their posse. When the bad guy came inside, he scowled at Jack. Hope checked to make sure he was okay, as the brushy moustache and scowl was off-putting.

"I'm protecting my Aunt Hope." Jack crowed at the man. "You don't scare me."

The actor's lips twitched under the brushy moustache, and he sidled down the aisle, spurs jangling.

"You saved me." Hope kissed Jack's head.

Dylan tapped his cheek. "I did too, do I get one?"

Unexpectedly her heart lurched in time to the train starting back on the tracks. "Friends don't K-I-S-S."

"There's a rule to break, Missy." Dylan's accent was part cowpoke, part European sounding. "You owe me."

Hope kept quiet, while waves of emotion pounded her inside.

Grinding wheels on the track as they slowed told the passengers the ride was finished. The conductor in his blue striped coveralls that strained at his body's equator, walked beside the train. "All right folks, we've reached Dusty Gulch, go saddle up on one of those rides in the Kiddy Corral." With a wave, he sidled away.

As they alighted, Jack ran ahead toward the sky ride. "Let's go pan for gold."

"Who's paying for the bucket of gems?" Dylan lifted an eyebrow. "The other can pay for our snacks."

"Maybe I'll find a diamond with Jack, I'll get it."

"More like quartz, not worth the bucket you purchased."

"Don't be a grey cloud." Hope eyed her race-walking nephew. "We'd better hurry, Jack's almost there."

They walked side by side to catch up him.

As she and Jack's lift climbed into the bright sunny sky, Hope held a firm grip on his body. "I want to make sure you're going to be okay." Her stomach turned. "Do we ride this thing down too?"

"It goes even faster."

She couldn't wait.

After they rode the cute kids train ride through Mouse Mine, Jack escorted them to the gold panning area. The long water sluice ran with the force of a small car's engine.

Jack scooped his pan into the small bucket of rocks and shook it in the water. The mud shot like 4th of July fireworks with his frenetic shaking.

"Please slow down, your shirt's getting dirty." Hope pointed to the lines of mud on his light blue t-shirt.

"Okay." He lifted the pan from the raging water, and there was one flake gleaming on the screen. "Surprise, I'm rich!"

Dylan chuckled and proclaimed. "You're buying the snacks then."

Her nephew looked down at the pan then back up at them. "I don't think this will pay for it."

"Probably not." Hope scooped out the flake and put it in the baggie they'd been given. "Try again."

Goldminer Jack panned for half an hour and had eight little flakes. With each success, both Hope and Dylan praised his skills. Jack wiped a wet hand on his blue and yellow plaid shorts. "Can we get a snack now? I'm hungry."

All gobbled some popcorn, and an elephant ear. She didn't feel the least bit of guilt at eating the junk food. She deserved the extra carbs because she had to ride the kiddy airplane with Jack, the Whirl-a-Whirl and spinning barrel, while Dylan watched. He'd claimed motion sickness.

"Gift shop!"

Hope smiled at Dylan, who shook his head. "You want to be the fun Uncle, don't you?"

"Of course."

"Let's go."

Exiting, Jack held a stuffed horse that he'd claimed was for "Isabellie" and a cowboy hat. Big kid Hope wore an inexpensive "silver" bracelet with her name on it.

"Thanks for this." Hope put a finger under the bracelet. "It's cute."

"You rode all the rides with Jack, I wanted to thank you. Since I couldn't K-I-S-S you." Dylan's smile caused his strong cheekbones to be more pronounced. "I'm kidding, you know that. Or maybe I'm being serious." He moved a curl that was flying in the wind back in place.

Always a flirt. "I do." Hope's mouth rounded and her throat dried. Before she could speak, Dylan had gone ahead with Jack. Kids aren't the only ones surprised at this day. She certainly was.

For King and Country's music surrounded them as the motor turned over. Hope checked to make sure Jack was secure in his seat.

"I double checked it twice."

"You're awesome."

Dylan smirked. "I know."

She shoved his muscled shoulder, and did it once more, for herself.

"Why twice?"

Because you have great muscles. No, I can't say it. "I wanted to."

"How about me?" A high-pitched voice questioned. "Am I awesome?"

She peeked in the back at the precious young boy, his black felt cowboy hat covered one eye. "You are much more awesome."

"I'm so wrecked." Dylan shook his head and moaned.

"It's okay, Uncle, I think you're Superman."

"Can I call you Clarke, then?" She stifled a burst of joy. "Need a phone booth?"

"No thanks, Lois."

"Good one."

"You're my Kryptonite."

Silence filled the car as she pondered his words. Does he still have feelings for me? Her phone buzzed before she could say anything. She read the message.

"The Tampa school has invited me to a second-round interview." She grabbed his hand.

"I didn't know you'd had the other one. It went well I see."

"You didn't ask about it, so I didn't tell."

"Maybe I was hoping it wouldn't be as good as Briar Creek Elementary, shoot, this isn't good. Tampa."

"Why?"

"For me."

"Oh." She shuddered as the sun rays of warmth covered her. *He still cares for me.* Now she was more confused than ever. Could they become more than friends? Was there even a chance?

CHAPTER NINE

Dylan pulled on his light gray dress shirt and buttoned it, slid into his pressed black pants, and pulled on his ebony shoes. He sped through the kitchen, paused to feed his pet Beta fish, Spartacus, grabbed a protein shake from the fridge, and exited. Interviews for his receptionist were today, and he didn't want to be late.

As his car thrummed to life, he experienced a small bit of a thrill at the power of his V-8 engine. The tires clung to the winding mountain road as he turned onto the main highway headed for town. Before arriving, he stopped at Caleb and Faith's bakery to grab coffees for himself and Hope.

Pushing the door open, Ryan the manager and baker spied him through the crowd. "Morning Dylan, I'll get your and Hope's drinks ready."

"How'd you know?"

"She's working in the same office as you, thought you'd bring one to her too." Ryan prepared the to-go beverages and gave them to him. "No charge, you're the boss' family."

"Thanks. Are the pre-wedding nerves setting in?"

"I'd marry Willow tomorrow if I could." Ryan grinned. "It'll happen to you, buddy. You'll meet someone you can't stop thinking about. Then it turns into more." Willow walked by Ryan, and he gave her a quick kiss on the cheek. "You want to elope?"

"And miss the party my mom and I have planned for almost a year. No way." She rolled her eyes at her fiancé and continued to walk to a customer's table.

"Not me, I like being single. See you." Dylan stepped outside. Unexpectedly, several shrill laughs rent the air. A burn of jealousy scorched him. *Fortunate kayakers. I need to go soon. I'll see if Hope's up for it.*

Driving from the shop, he glanced over at the outfitters and saw his brother pull into the parking lot. Wishing he'd had time to talk to him and book a kayak trip, Dylan calculated with the clock on his dash that he would be late. He ran over questions he'd researched online in his head. Last night, he'd spent hours creating a list of necessary requirements for the firm's receptionist. Inwardly, he was thankful Hope would be there to be his second set of eyes. His were singed from the late night.

In a matter of minutes, he crested a hill which led to Briar Creek's Main Street. Surveying the parking spaces, he secured one near his usual spot. Parked beside his car was Minnie's turquoise two-seater convertible. Both she and Pedro were still inside.

Dylan moved the laptop bag from his seat to his shoulder and took the coffees after opening his door. He slammed it shut with a jut of a hip. "Good morning, Minnie. Pedro." That kind woman always wanted her pet to be acknowledged as well, it was as if he were a human instead of a parrot.

While Dylan waited for a response, Minnie did a delicate dance to get both her and the bird from the car. Pedro's marble black eyes fixed Dylan with an unblinking stare. He swallowed. The bird was interesting to observe, from far away.

"Morning, I see Hope's still here." Minnie pointed to the

coffee. "Smells like Hazelnut. I adore Briar Creek Bakery's coffee. I've got a bag of their River Run Decaf I keep in my store."

"That's a good one. Do you want me to get the door for you? You've got your hands full."

Minnie's shiny suitcase-sized orange purse dangled from her left hand and Pedro walked down to Minnie's free one. "Would you mind taking Pedro?"

Dylan's spine stood at attention, every particle in him wanted to make a quick exit. "I will."

"He doesn't bite all the time." She gave him a half-wink and put Pedro on Dylan's shoulder.

Pedro's big feet pressed heavily onto his right shoulder. Dylan prayed no "digestive elements" would appear on his shirt. Too late. Warmth coated his shoulder, he attempted to look at it. The perpetrator gave him a skeptical glance and squawked.

Minnie pulled her large key chain from her American Tourister doppelganger and unlocked the door. She eyed his stained shirt. "Oh, I'm so sorry. What size are you?"

"I'm a 15 X 34." Dylan croaked as he glanced in the shop window. Feathered things on non-seeing plaster people stared at him and one atrocious Hawaiian shirt. "I'm fine, it'll clean off."

"Let me turn off the alarm, come in. Pedro, you stinker come over to me." Minnie pointed a taffy orange fingernail at him as he walked onto her hand. "Say you're sorry."

"Squawk! Bad boy!"

Minnie marched him to his golden cage where he happily got onto his perch. "Let me see what I have." She threw several unusual shirts on top of the rounder, another Hawaiian shirt like the one in the window, this model in sherbet colors, a black short-sleeved shirt with the outline of North Carolina all over it. *Help me, Lord. Please.* The last one was beyond description.

Minnie laughed and hugged it to her body. "This is the shirt

Silas wore on his fiftieth birthday, we went to a car show in Asheville. Do you like it?"

Pedro let out a huge screech.

I agree with you Bad Boy. It's hideous. The shirt had six patterns of one-hundred percent pure ugliness sewn together. "It's special."

"You have good taste, young man." Minnie pushed it into his arms. "It's yours."

"It has memories for you and Silas, I can't wear it." Dylan tried to hang it back on the rounder. "Thanks though."

"I insist. He let me bring it to the shop. It's one of his favorites he'd said. Anyway, it's yours." She plucked it from the hanger and stuffed it in his laptop bag. "You'll look great."

"Thanks, again." Dylan lifted a hand in a parting greeting and exited. He slipped inside the firm's door before she could gift him with another object from the past. *Now to slip past Hope so I can clean my shirt.* The traitorous wooden floor creaked with each step. He heard footsteps down the hall. *Too late.* He turned on the hallway lights.

"Hey, I smell coffee. Are one of those mine?" Hope took it and gave it a quick sip. Her eyes grew large as she pulled the shirt from his bag. "Is that for a church rummage sale?"

"No, Minnie's bird." He pointed to the disgusting spot. "She wants me to wear it."

He noticed her lips quivering, and her eyes didn't meet his. It made the situation even more comical to him. Dylan burst out laughing. The front door groaned as someone opened it.

"Go wipe it off in the bathroom, they're early. I'll stall them." Hope threw the shirt back at him, and he caught it with a pinkie. "Hide that shirt."

Dylan walked with a purpose and spent several moments spot washing his shirt in the washroom. The shirt was wet on the shoulder, but clean. He blotted it with a paper towel wishing he'd had a hand dryer instead. The crazy pattern shirt might have been a contender had this not worked. He frankly wasn't in the mood to be a tacky tourist wannabe for the day. Opening the door, he heard Hope's very cheerful voice.

He walked toward the reception area, the wet shirt acting like a scuba suit with each motion. Dylan quickly peeled it from his shoulder before entering the room and pulled up the applicant's resume on his laptop.

"Dylan, this is Tessa. She's graduating this year from high school. And collects rocks." Hope's smile was strained. "We've talked about them for the last ten minutes."

"Oh. We've got plenty of them in our area to study." Dylan smoothed a hand over his thigh and eyed her resume. "Do you have plans to go to college?"

Tessa lifted her eyes from her phone screen. "In January, I'll be attending Duke University full-time and studying Geology."

That explains the rock fascination. He pondered how to say the next bit. "So, you'll be moving to Durham. I need someone who's going to live in this area."

"I get it." Tessa pushed from the seat and dramatically rolled her eyes. "My parents made me do this." She left with a slam of the door.

"That was really. Great." Hope managed to say.

"I'll mark her off the call-back list. Does my shirt look okay?" He swiveled in his seat so she could see.

"It's drying. What'd you do with the other one?"

"I left it in the washroom. I'll take it home later." Dylan opened his iPad. "Let's see who's next." He scanned the screen. "Cullen Leigh Thomas, she graduated from Asheville College and is a paralegal. A double plus." Dylan pointed to her resume as Hope looked on.

"We'll know if she's the one in about ten minutes."

The next candidate arrived on time, didn't collect rocks, nor plan to leave in seven months. In all, Cullen Leigh was a strong candidate, to Dylan's relief.

Three more quick interviews after Cullen's and they were finished. Dylan glanced at Hope as she made notes on her laptop. "What are you doing?"

"I've listed the top two persons, and why they'd be great for your practice."

"Efficient, you would make a great receptionist or administrative assistant." Dylan rose and stretched. "Treat you to lunch. It's already one o'clock."

"I've got my second interview with Briar Creek Elementary at three. If we hurry, it's a deal."

While Dylan hoped it would work out, a hollow feeling drummed inside. *I'd really miss her if she took the Tampa job. She's smart, fun to be around, incredibly positive too.* Dylan stole a peek at her long and shapely legs. *Get back on track, Gaines, she's not left, yet.* He couldn't let his feelings sway what was best for Hope.

CHAPTER TEN

After meeting the whole administrative team, Hope felt she had a place within Briar Creek Elementary. She wavered between going back home and interviewing for the job in Tampa or staying to see how things would turn out. Hope pulled Big Red from the space and drove toward Faith and Caleb's. As she passed downtown, Dylan's silver car was parked in the same spot when she'd left. Curious, she parked and went to the office and knocked.

"Sorry, we're closed." A male voice said from behind the door. "Please go to my website and fill out a request for an appointment or come back at 9 am. Thank you."

"It's me, Hope." She raised a fist in the air as the door opened, and he caught her hand mid-swing.

"You're pretty powerful."

"All those days of lugging my laptop around campus, and here."

"Come in, tell me about the interview."

They sat across from one another in Dylan's office, and she glanced out the window as the sky lit up with brilliant orange and pink colors. *That'd be a gorgeous photo.* "I couldn't tell if all the administrators liked what I said." She flicked a paperclip on his desk. It spun in a crazy spiral, which was a match to her unnamed emotions. "They didn't say I'd get another interview. . .or anything."

Dylan eased back into his leather office chair and rubbed his chin. "Did they ask a lot of questions?"

"Yes." Hope shifted in the seat.

"Check their phones?"

"No, that'd be rude."

"I've been in meetings where this has happened before." He shrugged. "It made me want to talk even longer."

Laughter sprang from her lips.

"Kidding. It sounds like everything went well."

"It did."

Dylan leaned forward, his chair squeaking, "Are you going home next week for the interview and to stay?"

"It's virtual, I'm here for another few weeks."

She couldn't decipher his expression after her admission. Hope blurted, "You'd like me to stay. You've said it several times recently."

"I would."

"Why?" Hope spun the paper clip faster and faster, her eyes fixed on the blur. "We hadn't talked in a long while, before I came."

"We've said it before, both of us have busy lives." Dylan leaned forward in the seat and ran his fingers through his hair as Hope kept flicking the paper clip. Dylan put a hand on top the crazy clip. "You've changed."

Her heart thudded in her chest as his critical words landed in the "don't-bring-that-up" tender spot in her heart. "Everyone does. You have."

"How?"

"You used to be less stressed, more casual." Hope turned her face back to the window seeking a focal point to calm her electric emotions.

"Having my own law firm takes a considerable amount of time, I'm the only one I can depend on. Soon I'll have a receptionist to pay. Adulting is stressful sometimes."

"I know." She weighed her words before speaking. "Going to Tweetsie Railroad with you and Jack was fun." Hope pushed her hair back from her face. The silver bracelet shone in the bright office light.

Dylan's asked. "You wore that today?"

"I like to wear it because it reminds me of the day we had." She twisted her mouth to the side in contemplation. "I'm not sure why I came by here. Maybe it was to get your level-headed assessment of my interview." She sighed. "Or maybe it was because for some reason I can't really say why, I wanted to see you again."

She noticed the smile increase on Dylan's face as he spoke. "To see, me?"

"Yes, Dylan. Don't get a big head over it, okay? I liked being in the office with you, the way you'd pop in and check on me, tell me something funny about your day. Ask me about mine." She checked the time on her phone. "Forget it, I'm late for dinner." She put the cellphone into her bag and hooked it over her shoulder and began to walk out of his office.

"Don't go."

She turned around. He'd moved beside her. Her arm hovered between the safety of her body, and the unknown of his outstretched hand. Their fingers clasped in the middle. She felt the warmth from his skin, and saw the dark stubble on his jawline, his pulse beating at his throat. Weightless strings drew her to him, and she moved closer. Silently, their foreheads touched. It was jarring to Hope. Fragments of memories burned in her mind as they danced within her thoughts. Swimming in the water in Florida, him holding her as the waves crashed around them, the feel of his arms around her and his kiss. Cricket music brought her to the present as she forced her eyes to investigate his as they darkened to a starless night sky. Her heartbeat pumped faster than normal, and she licked her lips. His eyes trailed to the motion, and he smiled. With their mouths so close together, she could see the bow of his upper lip, and Hope wanted to lean in farther.

"Squawk!" Pedro announced his visit, the bird's wings stirring the air between them.

They came apart, and Hope saw the bird's beady round eyes as he sat on Dylan's shoulder.

"Pedro, come back here. Dylan, are you here?" Shoes tapped the hall floor. "The wind blew your front door wide open, good thing I came back to the shop to get something." Minnie entered his office. One eyebrow quirked. "Evening you two. Did my boy interrupt anything?"

Hope sent a quick nod to Dylan, who spoke. "No, Hope was telling me about her interview."

"From that close? Come on, Pedro." Minnie held out her hand near Dylan's shoulder. "Let them finish what they were going to—discuss. Bye, y'all." She waved and left the office.

The security door chime sounded a short bit later.

"I think I'd better go." Hope slipped her bag higher on her arm. "Thanks for, um, listening."

"Yeah. I'll walk out with you."

Before Hope got into the car, Dylan asked. "Remember I asked you if you wanted to see one of America's castles?"

"I do. The Biltmore Estate."

"Would next weekend work for you? You could bring your camera and we'd spend the whole day seeing the sights. Am I tempting you?"

You are, but, the photos, no. "Maybe. What were you going to do back there?" She pointed in the direction of the law office and gave him a small smile. "Before Pedro flew in?"

"I think you know. And you would have liked it." He winked.

An unbidden thrill ran through her. She only hoped the next time that happened, Pedro was nowhere in sight.

CHAPTER ELEVEN

Biltmore Estate's immense limestone walls stretched toward the early summer sky. Hope's mouth flew open as wide as a baby bird's during feeding time, then she spoke. "As a kid, I recall this being big. Why. . .it's humongous. It looks like a storybook palace." She pointed to the entrance and continued to chatter. "Those gargoyles remind me of the ones in Windsor Castle." She panned the lush green landscape beyond with the Blue Ridge mountains shrouded in a mist. "This is gorgeous."

"I'm glad you like it. Want to see more?" Dylan pointed a thumb toward the entrance. "The wait's not too long."

"I wish I had my camera. The way the mountains surround the property, it's stunning." Hope put a hand over her mouth and turned away. "Scratch that."

Dylan put a hand on her shoulder. "I've noticed you aren't a fan of that camera. It used to be your sidekick. What happened?"

Can't we enjoy the day? He's going to keep asking, so I'd better tell him why. "I had an art showing for one of my classes, and some of my classmates excoriated my photographs. They said they were 'plebian art.' During the showing, my professor sided with them. It was my first, and only, 'C' in a class. I was humiliated." Wetness gathered in the corners of her eyes. She swiped it off and hoped he'd not notice. "I wanted to discount their critiques. Several of the critics became professional photographers, so they had credible talent." She fixed her gaze ahead, not wanting to see his expression. "I wanted to teach and do photography as well. It crushed me, and because of the low grade, it cost me the scholarship for an extra semester abroad in photography studies."

"I'm sorry that happened." Dylan ran a finger down her arm. "I've seen your photos, I think they're great. Don't let a few people keep you from doing what you love."

"You're sweet." She glanced at him and saw his compassionate glance and smile. "Thanks, I didn't mean to be a gloomy cloud."

"You're not. I'm here to listen to you. You'd do it for me. Not to dwell on the camera talk, but do you think you might do a headshot for my website?"

She knew after his kindness it'd be horrible of her to turn him down. "Okay. For you."

He gave her a one-armed hug, and they both walked through the grand entrance of the home. As she took in the grandeur of the large entrance hall, her leather soled flats slid on the marble floor. She hoped her bobble wasn't apparent.

"Everything okay?"

"I'm fine." She kicked up one leopard flat. "I wore the wrong shoes for marble."

"I'll make sure to catch you."

Hope smiled. "You were always good at watching me." She ran a hand through her curls and let out a long breath. "I meant out for me." *What a blunder.*

"I understood. The behind-the-scenes tour is over to our right, I see the sign." Dylan instructed. "We'll be going in about five minutes."

"I'm so excited, it takes me back to all the history, glamour, excessiveness of England's castles." Hope walked faster to match Dylan's strides and to expel the nervous energy from her gaff. "It's so romantic. I mean other people, not us." She caught her bottom lip on her top teeth. *Why couldn't she hush?*

"I agree. I'd love to stay in one of those drafty places someday. Live like a high-born gentleman for a few days."

"That'd be amazing. I'd like to do that too."

A dignified gentleman led their small group through the lower level at a clip. Hope paused in the library, the vibrant hues on the ceiling painting secured her attention. As she scanned the double level bookshelves it was hard not to reach out and touch the beautiful leather bindings and sink into one of the red damask chairs to partake of a story. She half expected the Earl and Countess of Grantham from Downton Abbey to appear if they lingered long enough.

"I thought this might be a favorite place of yours." Dylan chuckled. "The guide said there's secret stairs which are behind the mantle."

"Let's find them." Hope hurried to the dark carved mantle. Her eyes roved around the fireplace. "It's here somewhere."

"Sorry, Sherlock. We're two rooms behind the others. We need to catch up." Dylan held out his hand to her. "Take my hand, so you don't slip."

Their fingers laced together, they sped past another gorgeous room and into the majestic Grand Dining Hall, where ornately carved chairs were resplendent in bold red fabric, while taxidermy animal mounts stared loftily from their second story homes. Hope shivered against the cool winds from the air conditioner, and the glassy eyes of the animals.

"Cold?"

She nodded, Dylan wrapped an arm around Hope and rubbed her shoulder. As they climbed the stairs Hope had a protector in Dylan who stepped side-by-side with her. The serviceable carpet covering the floors was a humble sight compared to the marble on the family floors. "Thanks, I won't skid here."

"Too bad."

She nudged his shoulder with hers and rolled her eyes. Fireflies flitted inside at the words he'd said. "We're behind, again. Let's catch up. I think he mentioned something about a beautiful view."

"No need, there's one right here."

He lowered his head toward her. Hope's heartbeat quickened as his eyes sought hers. Dylan was so close that she could see each eyelash on his blue eyes and the way his one dimple grooved his left cheek.

"Next on the tour." Another guide stated loudly from the staircase. "The next group should be on the rooftop by now."

Disappointed at the botched romantic attempt, she mustered a smile. "We need to go, right now."

They hurried down the hallway past the single female servants' rooms as the open door near the end emitted a light to mark their path.

Once outside, the warmth made her chill bumps recede. In the distance, the Blue Ridge Mountains didn't hold their bridal veil of haze. Instead, they stood in soft purple blues, bold as the colors in the gardens of the estate.

Their group made the way downstairs, to Hope's great relief, and the couple thanked the tour guide and didn't mention them being tardy several times.

Under her feet the soft green spongy grass was a welcome change from the cold, unmoving, floors. They strolled through arbors of grapes, meandered through sun-seeking lacy flower gardens, and found themselves inside the Conservatory. Dynamic purples, and mystery forest greens predominated this beautiful space. The enclosed space held a humidity which matched Hope's home state of Florida, a small ache pierced her chest. She moved toward a palm tree and ran a finger over the prickly bark.

"They remind you of Florida, doesn't it?"

"Yes."

Dylan moved closer to her and took Hope's hand in his. "I'm sure you miss being there, it's gorgeous. We have beaches too. They're farther away in the Outer Banks. They have sand, water, and great seafood spots."

She gave his hand a confirming squeeze. "I'm sure they're absolutely wonderful."

"Stay here and find out." Dylan frowned. "Not meaning to be pushy."

"I might. I have to see if the Tampa school wants to interview me again. Everything was good with it."

"I won't try to sway you." He smiled and rubbed a finger on top of her hand. "Either place would be fortunate to have you as their art teacher."

"You're always patient, it's one of the qualities I like about you. This flower over here is to my liking too." Hope flitted to an orange bloom bending its head toward the planter. As she got on tip toes to sniff the flower, a syrupy-honey fragrance pleased her senses. "It's like the honey ice cream we had at UNC's ice cream shop several years ago."

Hope moved over a fraction to allow Dylan to experience the scent. She felt the heat coming off his skin, which made her aware how close they were.

He leaned in and smelled the aroma. "Nice, it reminds me of honey too. I recall reading that this plant, Orangeus Floralia, is like mistletoe in some tropical cultures."

"You don't say? Which ones?"

"Somewhere in the South Pacific." His voice lowered. "I don't know, really."

She glanced around at the empty building. They were alone, and shyness threatened to blanket her. "Prove it."

Both moved together as if magnetically attracted. Their lips were opposite poles. Her heart sang as they held one another in an embrace, and their kiss continued until Hope needed to get more oxygen in her lungs. Coming apart, she grinned, and gave him one last peck under the "mistletoe."

"I hadn't forgotten how great of a kisser you were." Dylan's fingers ran through her hair. "You're absolutely gorgeous, smart, fun. And I'm getting more than friendly feelings for you."

"Dylan, you'd better stop, I might get overheated." Hope fanned herself and moved away from the kissing flower. "Or I'd ask for more."

Dylan groaned. "I'd comply, whenever you want."

Hope's spirits flew like the beautiful yellow butterfly that had made its way into the building and alighted on a nearby tree. "I'll make sure to ask sometime."

He pulled on his shirt collar and grinned. "Don't you think we need some water? Lemonade? It's sweltering inside here."

"Now it is." Hope sauntered from the gorgeous building and planned when her "kiss request" would happen. If not in the next hour, then before the day was over.

On the drive home, the winding roads rocked Dylan's car. The combination of sun and the motion lulled her to sleep.

A gentle kiss awakened her. Hope jumped in the seat and moved closer to the door.

"You, okay? I didn't want to wake you, during the two-hour ride. We're at the house."

She ran her fingers through her hair and wiped her eyes. "Sorry I slept, we had a busy day."

"We did, fun one too."

"I agree. Wanna come in?"

"I'd better not. I'm volunteering with the youth at church tomorrow, during the early service."

"8 am." Hope stretched careful to miss hitting his shoulder. "That's early."

"My coffee pot will be going steadily until I leave for church." Dylan smirked.

"We'll all be there later, save some spots for us at the main service." Hope flicked the door lock. Dylan hovered a hand over the control, and she paused in the seat waiting to see where this might lead.

"Are you going to ask me?"

"I'm not sure what you're talking about?"

"It's what a couple does when they really like one another."

Sizzles ran through Hope. *He said couple.* "They go out on dates, do you want me to ask you out?" Her lips formed a grin.

"Ask away, I'd say yes. Right now, we need to have a proper goodbye."

"As in?" She raised an eyebrow.

"One moment." Dylan pulled a lip balm from his pocket and pretended to put it on his mouth. "Ready."

She read the bright yellow and red label. "Burt's Bees, nice. Next time, go for the vanilla. That's my favorite."

"I'll get some for our second date."

Hope brushed a quick kiss on his lips, which were so soft, no moisturizer was needed. "See you tomorrow."

"See you. I'll reserve the seats. We'll go again to Biltmore and investigate the elusive 'mistletoe' plant."

"We might have to try several times."

"I'm counting on it."

"Before you go, can we get the headshot photos done after church tomorrow? I forgot the website designer needs them by the end of next week. Is that enough time for editing?"

"Sure. I hope you like them."

"You'll do a great job. I appreciate it."

Hope waved and closed the door. *Tomorrow's going to be tough. Me and the camera.* She shoved the door open and stored the thoughts away for later. Wouldn't doing this for Dylan help her overcome the bad experiences? Hope was well and truly flummoxed. Was she ready to journey on this rocky trail?

CHAPTER TWELVE

Under the fluorescent lights of Dylan's office, the camera fought to adjust the lighting to a more natural state. Hope turned off the automatic focus and adjusted it herself. As Dylan's agreeable face, blue eyes, and generous lips came into view, she grinned.

"Laughing at me? I don't think I look too bad today." He pulled on the tips of his dress shirt collar. "I changed out of the church volunteer t-shirt."

"Never. You're handsome, all that dark hair, nice smile, even though it's a bit crooked."

He jumped up from the desk and took her in his arms. "Crooked? Look closely, this is the mug of a former Mr. UNC. I wasn't called a 'hot topic on campus' because of a wonky grin."

"You've never had a lack of confidence in what the Lord made you into."

Dylan's lips met hers. She clung onto her camera as they enjoyed a moment together a while longer. She moved away, rechecked her camera settings, and collected herself. His kisses lingered on her lips and in her thoughts. Drat. While they were otherwise involved, the aperture setting got moved. Any excess light in a photo, and the subject would be too pale and not stand out from the background. While he stood next to his desk waiting, Hope made a perfunctory appraisal of his current state. White dress shirt under navy suit, not rumpled. Good. Navy tie, off center. She walked over and straightened it.

"You wanted to touch me, didn't you?" His smile grew as her touch lingered.

"No. Yes. Maybe." She turned to face the opposite direction and kept her delighted grin to herself. "We need to take a few more shots. How about up front? The afternoon lighting might be better, and you've got that wooden wall as a backdrop." Before she could collect the camera equipment bag, he'd flung it over a shoulder.

"Are you getting tired of smiling, or can we shoot a few more? I'm liking the way you look against the color of the planks."

"I could smile at your beautiful face all day. Let's do more."

As the camera lens whirred, her excitement grew for the chance to show him what they'd created. "Last one." Hope pulled the camera to a better vantage point and flipped through the last set of photos. Dylan's professional demeanor showed in his upright posture, and the one dimpled smile represented his more playful side.

"These are great." He leaned over to view the series. "Don't ever doubt yourself. There's probably a good amount of folks around here who'd like you to photograph them for their business and their family portraits."

"I don't know. Thanks though." She cut off the camera and covered the lens with its cap. The cost of scratching a lens wasn't affordable to her now, or in the future.

"Before youth group, a realtor friend of mine asked me to check out a cabin in Beech Mountain. He's thinking of buying it to make it into a rental." Dylan opened the door, and Hope moved through onto the sidewalk. "Do you want to go up there with me?"

"I haven't seen that much of Beech Mountain. Sure, that'd be fun."

Along the way, Hope admired the quaint small towns spanning the short distance from Briar Creek to Beech Mountain. She took a stick of gum and began to chew it to make her stuffed ears pop.

Dylan motioned to his ear. "The change in elevation gets me sometimes, too. Can I have a piece?"

"I should've asked. Okay if I unwrap it for you?"

He nodded.

She held the tiniest corner of gum in the wrapper and offered it to him. It was difficult for her not to laugh as he opened his mouth wide enough for a visit to a dentist. "My Grandpa used to say you could catch flies with a trout mouth like that."

"I'll take it as a compliment, thanks, for that, and the gum." Dylan's jaw flexed as he chewed. A fresh licorice smell filled the car. "This has a unique taste. What is it?"

She dug the container out of her purse and quickly showed him. "From England, Airwaves, Black Mint."

"Never had it. It's kind of like if a jellybean had a baby with a plant." He scrunched up his mouth. "Not a fan." Dylan pointed in the direction of his glove compartment.

Hope pulled on the lever and found a stack of restaurant napkins. She shoved one into his flailing hand. Once he disposed of the gum, Hope passed his water bottle to him.

"I won't offer you another piece, if that's what you're thinking."

"Dang! That was so nasty." He took several more swigs of water before speaking. "Next time I drink a Cheerwine, I'll have to share it with you."

Hope slunk into the seat and pretended to shake. "That's the cherry cola, isn't it?"

"The one and only NC invention."

She folded one arm over the other and frowned. "You know I can't stand cherries."

Dylan's mouth turned upward. "I know. That's why I was teasing you."

"There is no other man on this earth exactly like you Dylan Walker Gaines."

"You remembered my full name." Dylan reached over and took her hand. "It means a lot to me."

"What's mine?" Hope rejoined their fingers and glanced away giving Dylan time to think of it.

"Hope Abigail Fuller."

Glitters of light filled the car from the large trees they passed by the side of the road. It was an identical twin to how she felt. Celebrated and cared for by this man. "You got it."

"I never forgot. We're here."

The car lurched into a pebbled driveway, and they hugged the steep incline. Her hand shot to the camera bag and held it secure as the vibrations threatened to topple it to the floorboard. "This drive would wake you up every morning. So bumpy."

"It's steep too. You might get trapped in a snowstorm, think of plowing it." He shook his head.

"You'd need a big truck to do it. Trapped in a snowstorm with a good book, that sounds pretty amazing."

Dylan parked the car. "As long as I could stream movies, I'd be happy. Though, being with someone you like would make it even more special." He brushed a kiss on her cheek. "Like you."

Like gunpowder igniting dry brittle branches, the barren edges of her heart simmered with his words. "Oh." She reached out and touched his face. "Like me?"

"No other person. But you."

They leaned into each another, and the seatbelts tightened. She fumbled with the seatbelt release as Dylan gently pressed it and Hope was freed. Together their arms encircled as their lips came closer.

Tap! Tap! Tap!

She opened her eyes to see a stranger next to Dylan's side of the car. "There's a guy out there."

Dylan sighed. "Probably the owner of the house." Once he turned around, he opened his door. "Great timing, guy. Did you see we were busy?"

"Sorry, I thought I'd come up here and let you both in so you could see the house." The smiling stranger held the keys on a finger. "You forgot these at church."

"It's my friend the realtor," Dylan said. "The one with really bad timing."

Both exited the car.

Smiling, the realtor held out his hand to Hope. "Hello, I'm Logan Whitlock."

Hope gave his hand a shake. "Hi, Logan. I'm Hope, so nice meeting you."

"Thanks, you as well." Logan gestured toward Dylan. "I've known this guy since high school. Seems you two have known each other a while too."

"For some years, his brother, Caleb, married my sister."

Logan's eyebrows rose. "You're Faith's sister? They're a great couple, I've enjoyed getting to know them since I moved back to town a couple of months ago."

"Where did you last live?" Hope inquired.

"Atlanta, the big city was fun for a while. I missed my family and friends here," Logan admitted.

"There's something really special about his area." Hope glanced around the front of the yard. A sweet scent perfumed the air. "It smells great here. Is it from those star-shaped flowers growing on the porch rails?"

"Yes, it's Confederate Jasmine. Grows like Kudzu around here." Logan plucked one off the vine and gave it to Hope. "Smells better than Honeysuckle."

She took a quick whiff, placed it on the porch bench and took out her camera. "Y'all go inside, I want to snap a photo of the front yard. Those trees and flowering shrubs are gorgeous."

Logan play jabbed Dylan's arm. "Dyl, you didn't tell me your girl was a photographer."

"An amazing one."

"I've been looking for the right person to photograph the homes I'm listing." Logan turned to Hope. "Can I see some of your pictures?"

"All I have on this card are personal shots."

Logan lifted his shoulders. "I need to see what kind of eye you have. If you don't mind, could you take some of this house?"

"I'd be happy to." She raised the camera and clicked several photos in a row.

"Do you live around here, Hope?"

"I might. I'll know soon if Briar Creek Elementary will hire me."

"I know Dyl wants you here. Can you send me some of those photos? If they're as good as Romeo says, I'd like to hire you part-time to work with me."

"I'll send some to you later on."

Logan handed her his business card. Hope tucked it into her front pocket and offered a small smile as she walked into the home. The two-story foyer demanded her attention, the stone stacked fireplace ran the length of both stories. Her camera told the story of the gorgeous home where the majestic mountains views didn't overshadow the interior of the house. From the screened in back deck, she spied a trickling brook below a stand of trees.

"Beautiful, isn't it?" Logan stated. "It's been on the market for two months already, no nibbles."

"I don't know why, it's a piece of Carolina heaven." She sighed and ran a hand over the live edge railing. "Someone would be fortunate to have this home."

Dylan smiled, "I'm right there with you. I would love to be stuck in a blizzard here."

Logan looked at Dylan and Hope. "Not me. There are too many things to do for my business. Speaking of it, could I see the photos you've taken."

A short time later, she'd backed up the camera's screen to the first home photo. "They aren't edited. I usually do that before anyone sees them." As he viewed the photos, she tried to ignore the growing lump in her throat.

"He'll like them." Dylan rubbed her back.

"I haven't let a stranger see my work since the art show."

"Let's go over there and pray."

"He'll see."

"Look at him, he's got a smile bigger than this home. He won't."

Dylan took her hands in his, and while they surveyed the towering mountains beyond the deck, he prayed.

A cool waved covered her, peace. Dylan's thoughtful prayer was exactly what she'd needed to deal with her preconceived ideas of what Logan would say.

"All the shots were clear, it was like you took the most important things in the room and gave them a place to shine. If you stay, Ms. Fuller, I'd like to hire you."

She threw her arms around the nice gentleman and gave him a lightning-swift hug. Once Hope realized her error, she backed away. "Sorry, I didn't mean to do that."

"As long as Dyl's not gonna punch me, it's fine." Logan gave her the camera back. "I've got a five o'clock meeting in Blowing Rock. Let me know if you're wanting to take me up on the job." He handed her a card with the imprint of LBW Realty on it.

Dylan chuckled. "I won't."

At their cars, the guys gave each other a back slap, and Logan smiled and waved at Hope. "Nice to meet you. I'll look forward to hearing from you."

"Thanks, you'll know soon." She and Dylan got into the car before she let loose an excited squeal. "He wants to hire me. As a photographer."

"Because you're good, shoot, great at photography. You could make this a whole side business if you'd like." Dylan revved the motor. "Logan's using your office now. I could kick him out, so you could come back."

"No. He's your friend." She laughed and fastened her seat belt. "We'd have a difficult time working, being so close together. It'd be hard to pay attention to business."

"That's a wise assumption. It'd be fun to see you though."

"Sweet talking man, like I've said, you have a way with words."

"As you have a knack for great photography. He doesn't do things like that, a job offer, without merit. Know you have substantial skills."

"It's hard to switch from one lane of thinking and veer onto another." She twisted a curl between two fingers. "I'm thrilled he likes my work. If I do stay, it'd be nice to have some extra funds coming in."

"As long as he doesn't try to make any moves on you. He was known by the girls in high school. Homecoming king, quarterback, might have well been Mr. January in the school calendar."

"I can see it."

Dylan cut his eyes toward Hope.

"Eyes on the road, please. All I meant was he was handsome in a perfect hairstyle, big smile kind of way. You're my Mr. January, tall, smart, hotter than this summer."

"Go on."

"You know you are, I'll hush."

"I don't think I'm that great, maybe a six out of ten. You're a ten out of ten. The gorgeous face and hair, sweet spirit, smart, kind, talented."

She slapped her knee and rocked back and forth with laughter. "Now who's making me more impressive than reality?"

"It's exactly as I see you. You are amazing."

"So are you."

All too soon the car ride ended. Dylan walked her to the door and gave her a quick kiss. "See you later, thanks for going with me."

"Welcome, maybe tomorrow I'll stop by Minnie's Treasured Things and then your office."

"I'll be waiting."

As he walked to his car, Hope paused and glanced back at him. She touched her tingly lips from the kiss. North Carolina looked better and better. Hope prayed there'd be a phone call soon from the school to keep her here. Without it, she'd be living in Florida.

CHAPTER THIRTEEN

"Congratulations, we'd love to have you be part of our Briar Creek Cougars team," Principal McTier all but shouted into the phone.

Hope rocketed off the guest bed and danced on the hardwood floor after she'd waited a long week and a half to hear the news. "Thank you. When do you need me to report to school?"

"In a month, we'll have new teacher orientation. The whole first week of August will be full of staff meetings and classroom readiness. I'll have Bea email the schedule and paperwork. Return it as soon as you can, please. See you in August."

She went down the hallway and into her niece's room. Faith rocked Isabella and sang softly. "I have a job."

"What?" Faith put a hand over her mouth, both stared at the sleeping angel who stirred. "You're serious?"

"I am, I've got a month to move here and find a place. I need to get busy." She smiled at her sister and niece. "I'll be able to spoil her and Jack all the time. The Lord is so good!"

"Congratulations." Faith whispered and gestured toward the door. "Go call Mom and Dad. They'll be thrilled. Dylan will be even more happy."

"We'll talk later." Hope went back to her room and called her parents with the great news. Both were jubilant to hear it. Next on her list to contact was Dylan. She put on her nicest outfit and an extra spritz of light-scented perfume. Hope met Faith in the hall, and they headed downstairs. "Can I borrow Big Red to go see Dylan?"

Faith pulled the keys from her bag in the hallway. "I guess, but I'll need you back before one because Isabella has a one-month checkup."

"It won't be long, thanks." Hope took the keys from Faith's hand. "Need anything at the Shop-N-Sack before I get back?"

"Milk, Jack drinks it like it's water."

"Got it. See you later."

Shifting the ruffled blue and white skirt underneath her legs, she fired up Big Red and made it to downtown Briar Creek by the time a second song played on the radio. Before Hope went into the office, she peeked her head inside Minnie's store. "Morning, Minnie. How're you this Wednesday?"

"Hi Hope. Can't complain. Silas and I are going on a rafting trip later with your brother-in-law. It's our date afternoon. I can't wait to ride the waves."

"You always amaze me, Minnie. Next thing you'll tell me you're going skydiving."

Minnie's lips split into a grin. "Already have for my sixtieth birthday. Silas won't go, though. He's too chicken. You look like something's going on? Something good?"

"Yes, I got that art teacher job at the elementary school."

"Congratulations, go tell that young man of yours. I'm happy you're going to be a Creekian."

"Creekian?"

"It's what I call new town people. I'm thinking of getting t-shirts made to sell here. Do you think it's social media worthy? I need more followers for the store's 'Gram account."

"Depends on the style, it might be. Maybe a v-neck short

sleeve for women, and a round neck for guys. A logo of Briar Creek on it would be cool."

"Thanks. I'll think about it." Minnie's plastic bangles clanked on her slim arm. "Don't mind me flapping and yapping like Pedro over there. We'll talk another time."

On impulse, Hope went into the store and hugged Minnie. "Have fun on your date with Silas, try not to fall in."

"And not have my hunky hubby rescue me." Minnie sputtered. "That's part of the fun."

Hope grinned and left the store. Her heartbeat ramped up as she walked through the office door.

Cullen, the receptionist, glanced over the top of her bronze horn rim glasses. "Good morning. Is Dylan expecting you?"

"Hi, Cullen. No, he didn't know I was coming."

"He's in with Logan right now. I'll page him." Cullen pressed the intercom and reported that Hope was there to visit. "He'll be here in a bit."

Hope nodded. "Thanks." She wandered to the other side of the room and stared out of the large window. Several people entered Briar Creek Bank across the street or strolled on the wide sidewalk enjoying the morning before the heat arrived.

"Hey. Come on back. Thanks, again, Cullen." Dylan held out a hand and Hope put hers in his. Once they were out of the receptionist area, he dropped a kiss on her cheek. "I like this surprise."

As they walked past Logan's office, Hope overheard his laugh and grinned. "He's having a good morning."

"The best. He sold that house we looked at the other week."

"Congrats to Logan." She eased into the low leather chair and put her thin-strap bag on the floor. Hope flicked an appreciative glance at Dylan. The color of his shirt made his eyes a brilliant blue. "You look-um, I mean." Once she regained her thoughts, she began again. "What I wanted to say was, I was offered the Briar Creek Elementary job."

Dylan jettisoned from the chair. "I'm the one having the best morning. Congratulations." He bent down and brushed a kiss across her lips. "Are you thrilled?"

"I am, but I'm worried. I've got to move up here and find a home to rent in a month."

Footsteps tapped down the wooden hallway beyond Dylan's office door. A knock sounded on it soon after. "Anyone, home?"

Dylan and Hope exchanged looks. Hope shrugged.

"Come on in."

Logan entered and began closing the door. "It looks like I'm interrupting something. I'll come back later."

"No, Logan." Hope waved a hand towards him. "Come on in, you're right on time."

"Did I miss something?" His eyebrows rose as he stood in the doorway. "What's happening."

Hope relayed her good news to Logan.

Logan entered the room. "Congratulations. Good thing you know a super skilled realtor." He shook her hand. "Tell me your list of must's in a home, and I'll start on it now. Does this mean you'll be my photographer too?"

"Once I get in the routine of classroom teaching, I'll be your part-time photographer."

"When do you think you'd be ready?"

Hope calculated how long it might take to have a strong command of her class. "By October, at the latest." She held out her hand and Logan shook it again.

"Deal. Congrats. I'm happy you're on board." He quoted her a per hour price that was more generous than expected. "Dyl, can you draw up a contract?"

"Let me know your particulars and I'll draft a contract."

"Thanks." Logan turned back to Hope. "Email me your list when you can."

"I'll do that as soon as I get back to the house."

"Good, we need to get a jump on this market. Rentals are going quickly too." Logan exited.

Dylan's phone rang and he frowned. "I was expecting this call. Can I pick you up later this evening. We can celebrate at my house. I'll cook."

"Make it around 6."

"6, then. See you."

Before she pulled onto Main Street, a turquoise sports car went past. Minnie had Pedro perched on a shoulder, his feathers blowing in the wind. She'd never seen the likes before. It caused her to laugh until she couldn't breathe. The 'Creekians' were a unique breed of people. Hope was tickled to become part of them.

"I'm home." Hope called from the foyer. A picture of a white jug flashed through her mind. "I forgot something. I'll be back, didn't get the milk."

"Don't worry, I already texted Caleb to bring some home tonight. I was pretty sure you'd forget." Faith patted Isabella's back as she went down the hallway. "How'd Dylan react?"

She followed her sister and niece toward the family room. "He's happier than me, it seems."

They sat near each other, and Hope looked away. "It's not like I'm unhappy, things happened suddenly. I love Florida, but to be near y'all, and him."

"I can relate. When I moved here, I was unsure of things. Small town, slow way of life. It's wonderful." Faith lowered Isabella into her arms. "Make sure it's what you want, not what everyone else wants more than you."

"I've already accepted the job, told Dylan, and have Logan ready to find a rental home." Hope pulled a throw pillow across her midsection and hugged it. "I'm being absolutely ridiculous, go ahead. Tell me."

"You are doing a great job of it already. You don't need my second opinion. I was scared, like I said a second ago. Relationships can fracture. Then you're stuck in a town where you weren't sure you wanted to live in the first place." Faith sighed. "Pray over it. Don't pop off on me about this next part. Do you care enough about Dylan to see this being more permanent?"

The question resonated inside Hope. Did she care enough to make this permanent in the future? "I want to live near y'all, see the kids grow up. Mom and Dad have mentioned getting a home here for vacations. They will probably retire here." She wrapped her arms around the soft pillow tighter. "Dylan and me permanent? We only dated about a month before. Who's to say this time we'll make things 'stick.'"

"Do you feel differently than last time?"

Air leaked through Hope's mouth as she took time to answer. "We've both matured, and it was over three years ago."

"Spend time alone together. Things like the Biltmore Estate are good."

"I'm going to his house later. Dylan's cooking."

Faith's eyebrows rose. "My brother-in-law cooking. He's been known to come over to the house since he moved in the area for dinners, lunches, whatever we'll feed him. Kind of like Kodiak the bear at Grandfather Mountain. He won't say much but will eat enough for three people before he leaves."

"He could be a competitive eater. Those arms and legs need lots of calories. Why he's as fit as..." She buried her head into the pillow.

"There's physical attraction, which you clearly have for him. How about emotional connectedness. Do you communicate well?"

"Don't get all analytical on me, big sis." She placed the pillow back against the seat and looked at Faith. "What do you suggest?"

"Twenty questions. I think I have a copy of a sheet. Caleb and I played it when we dated."

"And you still have that relic around?'

"Four years isn't ancient. Take Isabella." Faith put the sleeping baby in Hope's arms. "It's in my memory box. Hold on." Her sister moved with speed out of the room.

A bubbling noise sounded, and Hope encountered an obnoxious smell. She held a gag inside and carefully stood.

"Here's the paper. Isabella, daughter of mine, did you make some oopsies." Faith took her little one into her arms and cooed.

"Look it over. It's a nice way to learn each other's likes and dislikes."

Once Faith and her niece departed, she let herself breath. Glancing down at the paper, she scanned the twenty questions, some she already knew how he'd answer, but most she didn't. Tonight would prove to be interesting.

Dylan left work early and showered and changed. He rushed to the grocery store after and picked up chicken and steaks, safe choices for dinner. At exactly six, his car was parked in Caleb's and Faith's driveway. When she answered the door, his eyes roved her beautiful face, and cute pinkish dress. "You look beautiful."

"Thanks, I like that polo on you. The yellow looks great."

Both walked to the kitchen.

Caleb stood near the island, taking chicken off skewers. "Hey Dyl. Faith said you're cooking. Didn't know you could eat so much over here."

Dylan was used to his older brother's jabs. "It'll be better than that dried up chicken you cook."

"My chicken is legendary. Faith likes it, so does Jack."

Jack took the opportunity to grab a piece of chicken from the plate. Around his mouthful, he stated. "Delicious!"

"Told you, brother." Caleb smirked.

Dylan nodded and tried to get his sister-in-law's attention.

She shielded her face with Isabella's body as she burped her. His nephew's frown was in full view. "Sure, they do. Anyway, Hope and I need to get dinner started. See y'all later."

In the car, Hope said. "That was mean of you."

"Guys do that. It's the brother code."

"I know you're teasing him. His chicken is palatable." Hope wouldn't meet his eyes like her sister a while ago. "Men that cook are fantastic."

"Wait until you see my grill skills. Like a cross between Guy Fieri and Bobby Flay."

"I should've brought my camera."

Thank goodness you didn't. Dylan prayed he wouldn't set the meat on fire like he did a week ago. It took hours to scrub the grit off the grill. "Next time."

As the evening sky darkened, Dylan unlocked the door and left it open for Hope. "Go on in, I've got the groceries in the trunk." He ran back to the car and piled the three bags into his arms. Seeing Hope inside his house made his smile grow wider, it seemed like she'd been there many times instead of this initial visit.

"Your home is nice. I like the stone fireplace, it's really cabin-esque."

"Thanks." Dylan stowed the salad bags in the fridge. "Wanna follow me to the deck? I need to light the charcoal." Both went through the sliding doors to the wide deck. Dylan glanced down at the grill and snapped his fingers. "Forgot the lighter. Be back in a moment." His hand was on the doorknob. He turned and asked Hope. "Care for a drink? I've got water or sports drink."

"Water, please."

Dylan returned with a bottle of water and ignited the charcoal. He inhaled the primordial scent of new fire. As he slapped at a mosquito on his arm. "Let's go inside, I don't want you getting bitten."

She went ahead of him, and he tried not to notice how her fit legs moved below the length of dress. *Cook, guy. Ladies aren't meant to be ogled.*

"I saw you put a salad in the fridge. Do you want me to make it?"

Dylan opened several cabinets before he found a suitable container.

"A takeout container? Do you have something bigger?" Hope shook the large plastic bag of greens.

"No, this is it."

"We'll half it. You can eat the rest later."

"Great thinking. I could take it to work." *Or, spread it on my lawn for the animals out in the woods. Better them than me.* He shot a glance at the grill. Flames of orange red tentacles arced through the lid openings. Moisture trickled down his spine as he raced to save their dinner. With a cautious flick of the wrist, he lifted the lid and jumped away from the darting flaming arrows. He picked up a steak and inspected the top and bottom. White confetti stuck to the grill and steak. *I didn't remove the absorbent pads underneath the meat.* Dylan threw the steaks on the cold side of the grill and searched on his phone about what he'd done. The words *inedible, tainted, dangerous,* sneered at him. His shoulders fell, he couldn't look at Hope. *Way to botch it.*

"I like mine brown in the middle." Hope put a hand on his shoulder. "It's a more dramatic dining experience."

Dylan pointed to the remnants adhered to the grill. "I rushed and ruined the steaks. I left that on them. I apologize."

"It's okay. You were cooking for me. It's sweet."

"It is?"

"Yes."

They forgot about the scorched steaks for a while as they enjoyed a hug under the moonlight and fleeting kiss.

"I've got frozen pizza or we could do takeout."

"Umm, pizza goes with the salad better."

"I'll heat it up, but I won't forget to unwrap it."

Over dinner, they shared stories from their past. Dylan got to the fraternity singing, during a dance they attended. Hope covered her mouth with a hand. He pretended to be shocked.

"I know my friend Jake can't sing, that's what you're laughing about." He took a sip of water and continued. "At over six five with bright red hair he was hard to miss anyway. Good guy though."

"He was and I wasn't trying to make fun of him." She held up part of her hair, the red fire glints caught his eye. "Jake's practically my hair twin."

Dylan had trouble speaking around his warring thoughts. He pushed ahead. "His never looked as gorgeous as yours."

"I hope not."

He grimaced and hit the table lightly in jest. "I didn't mean he was a looker. But yours is stunning, like Merida's."

"The hair, yes. Do I have her stubborn nature though." She leaned closer toward him.

He was distracted by the cute freckles dotting her nose and the way her lips crumpled with laughter. "Stubborn." Dylan pulled at the collar of his polo shirt. "No, not as intractable as her. There's some give in your personality."

"Some give?"

"You need to have your own mind. Look at me, I'm the first to say my personality is type A. I thought I could cook tonight." Dylan motioned with a hand at the mess in the kitchen. "Look how it turned out."

"The night's turned out great." Hope took his hand. Fire shot through him at the contact of her soft skin to his. "You still cook better than me. I can't hardly make ramen noodles. The water evaporates before they are cooked."

"Stovetops can be tricky."

"I was referring to the microwave."

He hid a smile behind his pizza crust as it hovered between his mouth and the plate. "I've burned popcorn. If I hadn't mastered ramen, I wouldn't eat on the weekends in school. It's cheap and full of life-giving preservatives."

"It's the preservatives that are unsettling."

Dylan finished his pizza slice and began to take their plates.

She waved him away. "I'll help you clean up."

"You don't have to, I can do it later."

"No, you got dinner." Hope gathered things off the table with Dylan.

In the kitchen, he looked at Hope across from him, hands in soap suds and looking at home in his place. Dylan's thoughts veered to doing more things like this, spending time together without their family around. Maybe even having their own children someday. As Hope turned around to get the next plate, he looked away, feeling inexplicably like a teenager. The rush of attraction new and fresh, not sure where it was headed, but wanting to spend more time together.

"Your fish over there is cute. What's its name?"

"What?" Dylan had opened a window to let the cool mountain air hit his warm face. Crickets soothed his rumpled emotions as the sound of Hawk Creek burbled underneath the natural symphony. "You want to play a game?"

"No." She gestured with the spatula she held in her hand. "The name of your fish."

"Spartacus."

"Big name for a little fish."

"He's a Beta, a fighter fish." Dylan pulled a silver-colored scoop out of a drawer and held it to the fish's bowl. "Watch what he does, he is a fierce fish." Spartacus swam back and forth, bulging eyes staring at his reflection, in a quick moment, all his fins stood at attention and his gills puffed out.

"That's awesome, I see why he has his name. He's still cute though."

Dylan removed the shiny scoop from his fish's eyesight and began to dry the dishes. He glanced at Hope. His gaze lingered on her soft pink, pillowy, and irresistibly kissable lips. "I got some ice cream, your favorite."

"Blueberry Ripple?"

Dylan wanted to sink to the floor. "I thought you liked Blackberry. Man, I really botched tonight."

Hope handed him the last dish. "It's one of my favorites too. Yours is dark chocolate."

"Mmhmm. I bought that too." He put the last of the pizza in the fridge and pulled out the small pints of ice cream. "Share?"

"Of course, who doesn't like chocolate-covered berries."

"Meet you on the sofa, I'll bring the spoons."

Once he found two spoons that somewhat matched in his utensil drawer, he sat beside Hope and gave her the dessert. She licked her lips in anticipation, a wave of emotion shook him to the core. Dylan fought against giving her a kiss. Instead, he dipped his spoon into the decadent goodness and tasted it.

He noticed her big smile after the first spoonful, and relaxed. Tonight, wasn't about making mistakes but coming closer together, without the rest of the family around them. And it proved to be remarkably interesting. Hope more so than the chocolate dessert awaiting another sample. *I could do this every night. I wonder if she could too.* He was afraid to find out but thrilled she might be feeling the same way as him. Dylan dipped his spoon into the soft ice cream as a smile played about his lips.

With her sweet tooth satiated, Hope was blissful. When Dylan took the ice creams back to the kitchen, she checked her phone for the time. Although it was after midnight. It seemed they'd only been together an hour or two at most.

The sofa cushion sank as Dylan sat back down. His hand eased into hers as they watched a movie with the volume turned down. The tired, predictable, dialogue held no charm when compared alongside their conversation. As her eyelids threatened to close, she sat on the edge of the sofa and stretched her back. Warm hands surrounded her shoulders, and she fought against the urge to fall back into the cushions and stay longer. She rose to her feet. "I need to go."

"I don't want you to leave. But it's getting late."

The couple walked into the shadowed night. An alert sounded as Dylan hit the unlock button on his fob. The car's interior shined like a homing beacon. She blinked against the glare. "This was fun."

"We'll do it again, but with chicken." Dylan's fingers played with strands of Hope's hair, prickles rose on the back of her neck as the cool night air touched skin. She shivered. "You are cold."

"I am." Hope turned into him, and they stood inches away. She could hear him inhale and exhale in the silent surroundings. Their lips came together, and the pressure increased. Her heart skipped a beat, and she stepped back as swells of longing threatened to cause her to lose good sense. "We need to get going."

She noticed the labor in his chest as he breathed, the sigh that escaped his lips like a surrender to doing the right thing.

Hope entered his car and Dylan turned on the car and seat warmers and wound down the mountain road toward her temporary home. Hope realized something had turned in their relationship. She now had to make sure they'd continue down the peaceful path. Her heart would shatter if they didn't. Which frightened her more than she cared to admit.

CHAPTER FOURTEEN

"Here's the list of homes you wanted to see." Logan moved the papers over to the other side of the table. "Most are in your rental price range."

Hope took a sip of Briar Creek Bakery Coffee and combed the small stack, sorting them into a stack from "definitely see" to "maybe not." More papers lay in the reject pile than the other. "You've really done a great job." She held up the "hopefuls" in her hand. "What time are we going?"

"As soon as you're ready."

She drained the last of her coffee and pushed from the table. "I'm ready. I wanted to say hi quickly to Ryan and Willow."

"I'll meet you outside."

After she threw her cup in the receptacle, Hope looked around for her friends. Willow came from the back of the coffee shop holding a tray of cookies in her hand.

"Hope, I haven't seen you since you've been back in town." Willow put the tray down on the counter and gave her a quick hug. "Are you coming to the wedding? Will you be able to stay in Briar Creek?"

"I'm moving here, I have a job teaching art in Briar Creek Elementary."

"Wait until I tell Ryan. He'll be excited to hear it. We've missed you. It's been a while."

"Over a year. You're going to be the prettiest bride."

Willow ran a hand over her straight light blonde hair. "Thanks."

"I'll see you both at the wedding, Logan's waiting on me by the car."

"He helped me and Ryan get the apartment. We're going to rent over Minnie and Silas' garage. And, I haven't told Ryan yet, but we'll be bird sitting when we get back from our honeymoon. It's how we're getting the place for a discount."

"Congratulations. Pedro is a hoot. See you later." Hope exited and saw the realtor pacing back and forth near his car. She stopped to smell the rose bushes outside of the shop. The pink hues reminded her of Edgar Degas' ballerina series.

"I'm ready, so do you want to ride together, or meet me there." Logan inquired.

"I'll follow you, since I've got the addresses you sent me in my GPS in case I get lost."

"I was on the phone with the owners of 234 Aspen Lane, they've decided to stay in their house."

At the unexpected news about her top pick not being available, Hope gripped onto the strap of her purse tighter and consoled herself with the fact that the other choices were almost as great.

Down to house number four on the list, and doubts began to crowd into her mind that she'd not find the house she needed. Her heart skipped a beat as she followed Logan down a paved driveway. A charming wooden home with a front porch nestled between emerald green trees like a cottage in an enchanted forest. Hope entered the door Logan held open and noted the tall river rock fireplace in the family room. Beyond was an Lshape kitchen with concrete counters and neutral wood cabinets. "This is so pretty, Logan."

"I think so too. It's a two-bed, one and a half bath home." Logan scrolled on the tablet screen. "It's available in two weeks. There's a really cool feature in the backyard."

As she peeked into cabinets and closets, happiness ran through her. Hope glanced at the listing she held in her hand and winced. At the very top of her budget, she'd need to be miserly with her finances. The home seemed to well-constructed, and she saw a security system sign before she'd entered. "I've seen the whole house, what's the surprise?"

"Come on, you'll be really happy." Logan pushed open the back door for her. "It's really nice."

Once she stepped onto the deck, the woods behind the home sloped downward, and beyond the property, the gorgeous Blue Ridge mountains greeted her. "It's breathtaking."

"There's something down the hill. Be careful as you step." He held out a hand. "In case you need it."

Smiling, she made her way beside him, and he took her arm in his hand. "Thanks, this isn't too steep, but I appreciate the assist." Tumbling water sounds grew closer. A small trickle of water ran past her and opened to a small waterfall and river into which it spilled. "What river is this? It's gorgeous."

"We're not far from Hawk's Creek Outfitters and Briar Creek Bakery, three miles at most."

"That's amazing, I'd have Hawk's Creek running through my backyard, practically. Can I sign the papers on it?"

Logan's lips parted and a laugh forced out of his mouth. "I stored this home's documents in my iPad. I was pretty sure this'd be the favorite."

"I like confidence." Hope took a photo of the picturesque river and waterfall before they climbed the small hill. "I can see why you and Dylan are good friends. You are a lot like him."

"That's a compliment. He's a great friend. I'm happy you two are together."

"Me too."

Both pulled from the driveway after Hope e-signed the rental agreement, and she prayed the landlord would accept her as tenant. The other homes didn't please her as much as this one. It was a farther drive to school, but a closer trip to Dylan's.

Two weeks later, Hope spent the final morning in her Tampa apartment. She sealed the last of her moving boxes as the movers knocked on the door. The past few weeks flew quickly in comparison to the movers who emptied half her place by one o'clock. Hope and her parents found a bench outside her former apartment to rest on as the tall Florida palm trees gave shade to her warm face. She handed her parents the last of the water bottles from her cooler, and they both thanked her.

"Ready for the big change?" Her dad grinned. "Your mom and I might retire up there someday if most of our girls live there."

"I am. It's scary, but I'm ready." Hope looked around the apartment complex as part of her was already in North Carolina, and another still on the sunny beaches of her home state. It created a restlessness in her, one she'd not experienced since the first few weeks temporarily living in London. "I'd like y'all closer, and I know Faith and Caleb and the kids would too."

"You never know. We might move, someday." Her mom switched the topic. "Are you sure you don't need us to help you move in?"

"I'm good, thanks. You've been planning this 35th anniversary trip to Greece for a year. Grace is going to help me move. She should be home from University of Florida in a few hours." Hope took a short drink of water, and touched the dripping bottle to her face. The cold felt heavenly. "Dylan and Caleb are helping too."

"We're going to miss having you in the same town. It makes me want to retire even sooner." Her mom's smile faltered. "We'll be there at Thanksgiving."

"Cat, we can't go that long without seeing Jack and Isabella. They'll be bigger in five months."

"You're right honey. After the Greece trip in August, we'll visit."

Hope patted her mom's arm since she was too warm for a hug. "I can show you my place and then I'll need your advice for decorating."

Her mom thumbed through the phone's screen. "I've been thinking of a few cute things I saw at Haute Home the other day. This green vase would look darling in an entryway."

"It's pretty." Hope glanced at her dad who wiggled his eyebrows in fun. "Remember, Florida décor is different than North Carolina cabin chic."

"I'll have to rethink it. In fact, I think this vase would look stunning in our foyer. Honey, do you agree."

Her dad gave it a three-second glance. "Whatever you think, dear."

Cat grinned and pressed the phone screen. "Ordered. It'll arrive before our trip. I need to rearrange the hall table to the other side of the room. Can you move it for me?"

"Later on, darling. When my back's not hurting."

"Mom and Dad let's go home. Grace and I are leaving early tomorrow morning and the sun's already dipping on the horizon over Tampa Bay." Hope would miss the gorgeous views of the sparkling bay from her apartment and its manicured grounds.

Once in her old bedroom, Hope scrolled through her texts. Dylan had sent three. Two wishing her the best with the move-out, and another because he missed her. She called him after she freshened up and had dinner with her family. They conversed for several hours until sleep was too hard to hold away.

~

Three hours from Briar Creek, Hope was ready to stuff her ears with some of the cotton balls in the suitcase in the trunk.

"So, what do you think your class is going to be like?" Grace took a sip of her energy drink. "Are you excited to teach?"

"I don't know, and yes." Hope focused on the winding mountain roads happy she'd replaced her tires a few short months before. "I'm trying to concentrate. These are some challenging curves."

Grace opened the sunroof, and the wind began to blow the napkins from their fast-food lunch in a cyclonic pattern. When one clung to the window blocking most of her view, Hope reached a boiling point. "Close the sunroof." She balled the napkin and threw it in the middle console. "We don't want to get into an accident."

"Sorry, but this mountain air is different. It smells cleaner than Florida's." Grace turned away from Hope. "I wasn't trying to be a pest."

"I know, I barely slept last night. I'm sorry I snapped at you."

"I do talk a lot. Mom and Dad have always said I could be insistent. They thought I'd be a great lawyer."

"You would." Hope giggled. "All the questions you've asked were like one of them during a cross-examination in court."

"That bad?"

She didn't want to hurt her younger sister's feelings, so she kept silent.

"It's helped me in my writing, I always get the answers."

"Which is important." Hope kept her eyes on the narrow road. "Have you started writing your novel yet?"

Grace huffed. "My courses have kept me very busy, so I plan to begin when I graduate next year."

"Save me an autographed copy."

"I will."

Her words seemed to placate Grace as she quietly scrolled on her phone.

"Can you text Faith and let her know we'll be at their house by seven o'clock?"

"Okay. Are we stopping for dinner before then?"

"Graceful, you had a Moon Pie, Dr. Pepper, and a bag of chips at the last stop."

"I have a very high metabolism." Grace patted her trim midsection. "Will we?"

Patience. She's your sister. "Faith told me she made lasagna for you and homemade rolls."

"Forget what I said, and let's go straight to their house."

"No stops?"

"She cooks better than any restaurant, I'm so glad we have a professional chef in the family."

"Me too."

Hope's phone buzzed. Grace picked it up.

"There's a Florida number on the screen, want me to answer it?"

"I'll put it on speaker." Hope pressed a button on the dashboard. "Good afternoon, Hope Fuller speaking."

"Hi Hope, it's Melanie Ross from Tutoring Champs. Am I interrupting anything?"

"No, I'm in my car."

"You are the highest reviewed tutor we've had in our eight years of business. Congratulations."

Hope glanced at Grace who silently clapped. She held a giggle back. "Thank you."

"We at Tutoring Champs wanted to see if you'd be interested in being a trainer for our virtual teachers."

"I am very honored, and I loved working for the company this summer."

"You wouldn't have to travel, since it'd be via tele-conference. We'd need you at corporate headquarters in Tampa every other week."

"I see. What a great offer, thank you. I'm moving to North Carolina as we speak. I'll be teaching at an elementary school and doing photographs on the weekends."

"We'd love to offer you a competitive salary." Melanie quoted a figure which was substantially higher than the teaching position. "Think about it. Let me know by the end of next week." She ended the call.

"Sweet Florida oranges, what're you going to do?" Grace stared into Hope's face. "That's a lot of money."

"I already promised to work at the school in Briar Creek. She didn't give me a chance to respond. We were taught not to go back on our word, a responsibility is ours to keep. Maybe they'd want some part time virtual help? I've got praying to do."

Hope wondered what Dylan would think about it. He'd become a larger part of her life, and his opinion counted. She had decisions to make, and Hope longed for the simpler days of childhood, what games to play, which friends to spend time with. Adulting was difficult, and sometimes it came with sobering doses of reality.

CHAPTER FIFTEEN

The slate-colored sofa went past Hope as the movers carried it into the home. Dylan glanced inside the truck and shook his head. "Thinking it's too much stuff, Dylan?"

"When I moved, I had two rooms of furniture." Dylan wiped his forehead. "This is a house plus half another one."

"Every piece in that truck is something I love. It'll fit. I've measured. Thanks for helping, paying movers by the hour gets expensive."

A mover ran up the ramp. The clatter of his footsteps interrupted her thoughts. He came back down shouldering a tangerine orange chair.

"Glad to help. I'll skip my work out later." Dylan raised his hand and shook it at the chair. "You like that?"

"I adore it. The bright color adds personality to a room."

"It adds something, I'll agree." He brushed a kiss on her cheek as she attempted to move away.

"When it's all in there, you'll see. Like my décor versus yours, there's more in a crayon box than charcoal gray. My home's going to express my creativity."

"I guess. I'd better help these guys get the boxes in your

house, so you can decorate." Dylan moved toward the truck. "Caleb, come help me."

Caleb walked from his car to the truck and held out his hands. "Fill 'em up." Dylan deposited a big, square box into his arms.

As he moved past Hope, she patted his shoulder. "Thanks."

"Welcome. I thought your sister had a lot of things. It looks like you've got more."

"Funny, that's close to what Dylan told me."

"We're pretty similar. I'm the smarter one though."

"Hardly, guy." Dylan whizzed around Hope. "Who's the lawyer, and who has their MBA?" He darted into the door, as his short laugh made Hope's mouth twist into a grin.

"You chose Faith. I'd say Caleb, you're a smart man."

"I knew you were a clever person, thanks. We are really glad you'll be here."

"Me, too." Hope's phone buzzed. She looked at the screen. It was Tutoring Champs. She moved down the driveway, away from the noisy bustle. "Hello, it's Hope."

"Hi, it's Melanie. Any closer to a decision?"

She bit the inside of her cheek as her teeth clamped together in frustration. It was only mid-week, and Hope wasn't supposed to give an answer for two more days. Micro-management on any day wasn't welcome in her life. *Stay calm.* "Hi, Melanie. I'll let you know by Friday, I'm moving right now."

"Friday at noon. We'll talk then."

Glancing up at the sky, the calm blue quieted her roiling spirit.

Dylan walked closer to her. "What's wrong? You're pacing, and frowning. Something wrong with your things?"

"No." Hope sighed. "I wanted to talk to you later about it. Remember that company I worked for this summer?"

"Yes. That tutoring place. Was that who was on the phone?"

"It was. The other day, Melanie, the owner called me. She offered me a job training their virtual teachers."

"Back in Tampa?" Dylan crossed his arms, and she noticed his pulse beating in his neck. "You're moving here, today."

"No. It wouldn't be living there again. Let's go over this later. The truck's half full." She and Dylan headed toward the truck, carrying a burden of many unspoken questions. Hope was excited to get everything moved into her new place, but not as thrilled with the conversation later to come.

Throughout the day, Hope raced around the house, instructing the people where to place the furniture or boxes. After the last piece of furniture and heavily taped box was inside her home, Hope lowered onto the porch swing and Dylan joined her. Through the silence of nightfall, she heard Dylan's slow breathing and glanced over to see his blue NC State ball cap over his eyes.

"I'm awake, barely, but I can see you staring at me."

"I thought you were asleep."

"That comes later. Do you want to talk about the job offer?"

No. Yes. Possibly. What to answer? "Okay, with Grace conked out in bed already, we have the place practically all to ourselves." She pulled on his hand. "Let's go sit on the sofa, at least I'm pretty sure the boxes are off it." Hope led Dylan into the house, and it struck her how unfamiliar it felt to her, like being a foreign person in an unknown land. "I'm not going to accept the job, even though it'd give me a bigger cushion in my bank account."

"Turn it down? Are you sure?"

Hope blew air through her pursed lips. She stopped to gather her words. "I am. When I promise to do something, I do it. It's how my parents raised us. Commitments are important."

"Mine too. I get it about the finances. There's some weeks I barely squeak through with enough to buy groceries and gas." Dylan ran a finger over her hand. "Do what's right for you. It won't change how I feel about you. Man, I sound like a swelled-headed guy. Take me out of the equation. Forget what I said."

"You are part of this. Don't think you're not one of the reasons I moved here."

"I didn't want to assume, but I thought I might be." He held tighter onto her hand. "It makes me really happy to hear you say it. This is going to work."

"You're stuck with me for at least a year, since I signed the school and home contracts."

"I'd like to be together for longer than that." His voice softened. "I'm really, really, liking you Hope Fuller."

Blood pumped faster. She heard it in her ears. Fireworks popped inside. "More than your college football team?"

He came closer. She viewed the blond, long-past five o'clock shadow. He said, "College football, who?"

"How about extra strong espresso?"

"Most likely." He gave her hand another quick squeeze.

"Most? Likely?" Hope scooted farther away on the sofa from Dylan. He gently wrapped an arm around her. She bit her lip and looked into his sky-colored eyes. Their lips were a whisper apart. "Your fish?"

"Spartacus, non-starter."

When their lips met, Hope put her arms around his strong shoulders. It was as if the harried day was washed clean. Excitement trickled through her, for their future, together.

Wiping a hand across her face, Hope untangled the cord to her pod coffee maker and set it up. She surveyed the mountain of boxes in the kitchen and the family room. Over the coughing coffee maker, she heard the doorbell ring. "Coming." Hope peeped through the blinds and saw Logan's short brown hair and chocolate eyes looking back at her. Glancing down at the yoga pants and shirt she wore, she was thankful she'd changed out of her pj's. Smiling, she tugged open the door. "Morning."

"Hi, congratulations on your house." He handed her a basket filled with breakfast items, scones, English muffins, jams, and a large bag of Hazelnut coffee. "Sorry it's the day after your move-in and only 10. I'm showing a house near here. Wow, that's a lot of empty boxes. Looks like you've been busy."

"Thanks for the welcome gift. Busy, with still more to come." Hope held the door wider with her free hand. "Come on in. Want some coffee?"

"I'll pass thanks. I stopped at Briar Creek Bakery and had my triple-shot espresso in the car." Logan leaned against the counter. His quick smile reminded Hope of a younger Theo James.

"Hope, do you know where my. . ." Grace slid into the kitchen, in all her fashionable for sleep attire-neon pink cat socks and matching spaghetti strap pj's. Her mouth dropped in the direction of her knees. "I didn't realize someone was here." Grace wrapped her arms around her body.

Hope motioned to her sister's mouth. The silver from her mouth guard shined in the fluorescent light. Grace's hand flew to her lips. She stumbled from the kitchen.

When Hope looked at Logan, he had the good manners not to laugh at her younger sister. It was too early in the morning to correct someone's behavior. Even if he was a friend.

CHAPTER SIXTEEN

With more boxes now out of her home and in the carport, Hope began to become more relaxed, she looked at Grace fiddling with her phone, looking tired. "It's hard to think we've been at this for four days. Thanks again for your help. I know it was a lot."

"I'm happy to have helped." Grace yawned.

"Do you want to go shopping before I drop you off at the airport?"

"Give me a few minutes to put on a better outfit." Grace tossed her phone on the sofa and grinned. "We might run into someone. Maybe even what's his name."

"Who? Logan?" Hope questioned. "Only if we go into Dylan's office."

"I haven't seen Dylan hardly at all. And you probably miss him, we need to pay him a visit." Grace left the room.

A throb settled between her ribs at the thought of Dylan. She did miss him. Hope went to touch up her makeup in case they did see that handsome guy.

Once Grace's bag was inside the trunk, the two made the trip into town chatting all the way.

"This town in so cute. All these shops, hey, wait, what's Minnie's Treasured Things?" Grace nodded in the direction of the shop as they parked. "It looks very eclectic."

"Minnie is amazing."

The sisters only got as far as the first rack of clothes before both Minnie and Pedro came to greet them. "Look at you two." Minnie hugged Hope. "This must be your sister, she favors you."

"She is, this is my younger sister, Grace." She prayed Grace wouldn't look shocked at Minnie's purple streaks in her hair and the matching skirt she wore which sparkled like a disco ball.

"Nice to meet you sweetie." Minnie offered Grace a handshake after pointing to her shoulder. "This loud character is Pedro."

Grace grinned and shook her hand. "I love your hair, Mrs. Pickering. And Pedro's adorable."

"Thanks, call me Minnie. Pedro is pretty cute." The older lady patted her hair. "Silas, that's my husband, isn't too sure about my wild colors. He should know I always aim to surprise him. It keeps our marriage fresh." Minnie switched Pedro to her other shoulder. "Remember that tip girls, for future marriages."

Hope nodded as Grace blurted. "I will, it's a treasured thing like your sign says."

"Bring her by anytime, Hope, I like this young lady." Minnie swiveled her head around the store. "I've got a little something for you, Grace, the color would look so pretty with your black hair." She came back with a set of straw hats, a green one for Hope and a blue one for Grace. "Put these on, they'll look great on you."

Both sisters tucked their hair back and tried on the short-brimmed hats.

"You look adorable, Grace. Go, look in the mirror over there," Hope directed.

Grace wove through the racks to the mirror in the back.

"Do you have one with cats on it, Minnie? I think she likes neon cats." A man's voice stated.

Hope glanced in the direction of the voice and saw Logan walking closer. "Hi, Logan, thanks for the basket."

"You're welcome, so are there any neon cats Minnie?" A smile flickered on his face.

Minnie pulled on her chin in thought. "Logan, I can't recall ever seeing a hat with bright cats."

"He's kidding, Mrs. Picker, erm, Minnie." Grace swooped the hat off her head. "He thinks he's being funny."

"I didn't mean anything by it." Logan began to turn away, muttering, "No sense of humor."

"I'll show you what's funny." Grace pulled a Christmas hat with dangling ornaments and put it on his head. "This."

He moved the red and green elf ornaments out of the way as they jingled like a winter's sleigh. "I happen to love Christmas."

"So. Do. I." Grace found another hat and replaced the one of her head with it

"Did you read what it says?" Hope and Minnie giggled. She took a photo of Grace in the ridiculous hat.

"Tell me." Her sister's fisted hands sat on her hips. "Delete that photo, too."

He cleared his throat. "It says, I need a kiss. Did you miss the mistletoe on the brim? Can you send me a copy of that photo?"

"No, I thought it was a Christmas tree sprig." Grace threw the hat back on the rack and went to stand by Hope. "You won't get one finger on my photo."

Logan shrugged. "Are you visiting for Christmas?"

Grace shook her head and put the hat back on the shelf.

Hope blurted, "She is. I'll send a copy to you, Logan." She shoved her phone in a secure spot in the bag and smirked.

Logan took cash from his wallet and counted it. "Minnie, I'm feeling festive. I'll buy this hat." He pulled down the one Grace had just returned. "Grace needs it."

"Sure, I'll wrap it up. I don't have any Christmas paper. I do have some flamingo gift paper though."

"You're from Florida?"

"Yes." Hope answered.

"Flamingo paper is perfect." Minnie took the hats from him as Pedro flapped his wings apparently happy his owner had made a sale. "Follow me."

Logan moved his lips higher in a full grin and joined Minnie at the counter.

"Way to be nosey. He's a royal pain. Mom and Dad can come without me." Grace harrumphed.

"You're telling me you'll miss Isabella's first Christmas, and time with Jack? I'm not buying it." Hope began to walk toward the exit.

"No. I'll be here." Grace huffed. "Let's leave before he tries to put that hat on me again." She pushed Hope on the shoulder.

One could only pray he would. Grace had never been interested in such a lively man. Hope couldn't wait to see what could happen between them. Who said small towns weren't fun?

He followed them back to the office whistling a cheery Christmas carol, which made Grace groan and walked faster. His low laugh accompanied them down the hall.

"Hey, what're you two doing?" Dylan hung up the phone and went around his desk and gave Hope a kiss on the cheek. "What happened?"

"Nothing." Grace plopped in a chair and looked out the window.

"She didn't like her present I bought from Minnie."

"Who, Grace? Do you even know her?"

"Enough to affirm she has an affinity for cats and keeping her orthodontic work intact." Logan stated. "She's got a great hat for Christmas."

Dylan crossed his arms over his chest. "I'm perplexed. What happened?"

Hope caught Dylan up to speed.

Grace huffed. "Logan is ridiculous."

"He's always had a penchant for jokes. He'd be the one to set off poppers in our fraternity brother's rooms at 2 am." Dylan clapped Logan's shoulder. "Our house mom, Mrs. Mackie, didn't like it."

"I was the one who had to do dinner clean up on chili night. Still can't eat it. Disgusting." Logan shook his head.

"I'll make sure to get the biggest can of chili for your Christmas present. Extra beans."

Logan held his stomach and grimaced. "I'll return the hat."

"Don't." Grace shook her head. "It's pretty funny."

He wagged a finger at Grace. "I knew behind those bangs there was a personality somewhere inside."

"I've got plenty."

"I'd like to find out. You three have fun, I'm late for an appointment." Logan bobbed his head and left the office.

"I can't believe he's your friend, Dylan. What an absolute jerk."

"He can be, but he's also the one who will do anything he can for friends." Dylan folded his hands over his midsection. "He's a lot like your sister. But not as artistic."

"Hope is giving."

"Did you see the receptionist area?"

"It's beautiful."

"Everything in there's from her creative mind. Except there's a blank spot for a photo."

Doubts still tangled inside Hope. "I need to find the best location."

"I'll take you to this place, in the late afternoon light it's very nice."

"I'm flying out tonight." Her sister stood and declared. "Go Saturday."

"Saturday, eight o'clock, I'll pick you up."

"Okay." Hope brushed a kiss on his cheek. She didn't want her sister to gape at their affection. "I'll be ready. Come on Grace, we need to get you to the Asheville Airport."

In the car, Grace stated, "You've got me to thank."

"I don't know if I should thank or blame you." Hope turned the car over as her emotions revved along with the engine. Did she have it in her to create a gorgeous landscape. The soundtrack of the art show years ago replayed. Not quality. Not worthy of a show. Not enough. She prayed in a few days her camera would capture a photo as worthy as her blooming emotions for the man it was for. Hope prayed to be enough.

CHAPTER SEVENTEEN

As a yellow wash painted the sky, Hope braced the camera on her hand and breathed a prayer when she clicked the button. Sweeps of blue and grey vapor hugged the gentle mountain peaks. "Blowing Rock is beautiful. I'm glad you convinced me we needed to leave earlier today."

"Can't compete with you." Dylan's lips pressed onto her cheek. "In this light, I think even I could take a gorgeous photo with you as the subject."

"Flatterer." She kept her concentration on the scenery beyond the jagged rock where they stood. Comfortable silence kissed the air around them. "And I accept all forms of it." Hope checked the view screen to make sure the photo was to her liking. Waves of color blurred together to create a natural canvas more gorgeous than any museum display. "One more photo of the mountains and I'll take one of you. Go stand on that rock jut." Hope heard rocks sliding beside her as he stepped away. She swung her camera toward him and held a breath, his face was outlined in a radiant sheen. Her finger poised on the button, Hope continued to stare.

"Can I move?"

"I forgot to take the photo." She snapped it and released her hold on the heavy lens. "You look like a magazine cover. Come see."

Dylan peeked over her shoulder. "The ones of the mountains are fantastic. Me, I'm pretty good."

"Better than that, admit it." Hope softly touched his midsection with an elbow. "Brag about yourself."

"All I'll admit is you far surpass me, you, Hope Fuller, are gorgeous in all ways. I love you with all that's inside of me."

"You do?" Sparkles skyrocketed inside.

He nibbled on her neck and murmured. The vibration from his voice tickled. She laughed and moved to see his face.

"I love you too. Your sweetness. Your support for me. Your eyes when you look at me. I've never felt like this before." Hope lifted her camera before she put it in the bag quickly. "It's like I've grown, since we began to date again."

"We've never said we're exclusive." Dylan drew her into his arms. "We never needed a label. You've got all of my heart."

Hope stood on the tips of her tennis shoes to meet him eye-to-eye and reached her hands around his neck. "You've mine too." Heart beating faster with longing, she put her lips to his, and they shared a kiss full of promise and love.

With her camera safely stowed in Dylan's trunk, they put on their warmup jackets for a late morning adventure. She and Dylan walked into the mouth of Linville Caverns along with several others on the tour. The damp cold was a change from the warmer weather outside. On the narrow pathway, pools of water bisected each side, spotted fish swam in the clear pools. Their tour guide informed the group the fish were blind. A pang of sorrow overcame her. "They can't see how pretty the light is in here."

Dylan put an arm around her. "Maybe their senses can tell them."

"True." She was struck by his intuition to what was rumbling inside. "You're smart."

"I'm dating you, so I'd have to agree."

She gave his hand a squeeze. Before they went deeper into the cavern, Hope snuck a kiss on his cheek.

"We're going to cut off the light, folks, so you can see how dark this area is when no tours are going." The tour guide shone a flashlight on the ceiling. "This small bulb will remain on, for those scared of the dark." Titters of laughter sounded around the group. At once, the darkness enveloped them.

Hope's insides pitched at the void of light within the space. Trickling water was the singular sound in the room. She felt Dylan's arm tighten around her. Comfort eased her nerves. "Thanks."

"Welcome."

Through the tour, Hope marveled at the shiny formations clinging to the walls some resembled bacon, others, like an undone bed sheet. As the group progressed from the exit of the cave her eyes burned from the harsh transition of near darkness to the bright outdoors. Hope tucked her sunglasses behind her ears, joy-filled at the relief.

Dylan eased a grin across his face. "How'd you like it?"

"I loved it, I'm ready to do more caving."

"We will. There's some in Tennessee, and other states you need to see."

It permeated her with a fulfilled joy to hear he had future travel plans in store. "That'd be wonderful."

"I can't wait, let me know when you have spring break."

She was sure he knew her stance on being chaste until marriage. "Out of town. We'd have our own rooms?"

"I wouldn't ever ask that of you." Dylan took her hand as they walked. "We both agree on that matter. Faith first."

"Good. Do you want to come back to my house, and we can see how these photos can be edited?"

"I'd like to, but I have plans."

"Oh."

"It was supposed to be a surprise, I've booked a kayak trip for us."

She did a quick dance. "That's exciting, I've been wanting to go since I arrived here."

"You should have said something. I'll always go."

On the drive toward Hawk's Creek Outfitters, Hope answered Amelia's text and told her about what she and Dylan had said.

When's the wedding?

Hope let out a joyful laugh.

"Something funny?" Dylan glanced at her.

"Ame, my best friend being silly."

Gotta go, Dylan wondered what you said. Love you.

I'll start researching wedding venues and dresses, want me to email you some ideas?

Hope moved her phone closer to the door so Dylan couldn't see. She texted. *No, too soon.*

I think the timing's right. Love you too. Bye.

When she looked at his profile, everything about it delighted her. It was only matched by his wonderful heart. Hope's emotions flooded with warm light, and happiness filled all within her.

"We're here. Look who I see?"

Hope glanced past the parking lot, as a small blonde head peeked above the deck rails. "Let's go."

"Whatcha doing here?" Jack's big brown eyes were wide. "You surprised to see me?"

"I am. Happy too." Hope hugged her nephew and gave him a kiss on his head. He carried a scent of too-warm boy. "Are you here with your dad?"

"Mmhmm, he needed to get something, maybe it's books."

"Books? You've got a lot of them in your room." Dylan tousled Jack's hair. "I'll go in and say hi to the staff and check us in. Be back in a bit."

Jack dragged Hope by the hand. "Let's shoot pebbles into the water."

"We'll go by the trees over there." Hope pointed to their left. "This way Uncle Dylan can still see us."

Dirt clung to the "pebbles" Jack deposited into her open hands. When they began to rain from her hands, she asked him to please stop. Her adorable nephew tossed a stone into the water, it skipped once, then sank.

"I'll show you how, son." Caleb took a handful and showed Jack his technique. "It's a flip of the wrist." Her brother-in-law's skipped to the middle of the river.

"You've got it wrong, bro." Dylan picked one large size stone from Hope's hand. "Jack, you throw it like you're going in for a curveball." His pitch landed in the ripples of Caleb's throw.

Both stared at each other. Hope found a chair under a tree and pulled it over. A contest was about to begin. Each man had a small pile of rocks near their feet. Before they threw, Jack was taught the perfect way to get a good skip across the water or make the biggest splash. The sun rose higher in the sky and warmth touched Hope's arms and face.

Jack looked at Hope, his face was light pink. "I'm thirsty."

"Let's go get waters from the outfitters shop and get out of the sun for a while."

She and her nephew left the competitors to continue their "lesson." Neither one checked to see if Jack was watching. Inside the outfitter building, she veered to the cooler of water bottles while her nephew played with a sticky ball in the toy area next to it. After paying for the waters and toy, they went walked around the store before going back outside.

"Do you think your dad and uncle are finished?" She unscrewed the tight lid and handed a water to Jack.

He took a drink and wiped his wet mouth on his t-shirt sleeve. "No."

Hope glanced where they'd left the men, Jack was correct. The rock piles had grown, and she heard grunting from one or the other as they threw. "You need to get home. Your mom's probably wondering where you two are. I know how we'll stop them." Hope whispered into Jack's ear.

As quiet as the river, Jack snuck behind Caleb and Dylan. He glanced back at Hope who waved him forward. Water bottle in hand, he ran behind them and splashed as high as he could. It ended being waist level on the tall guys.

"Jack! Why'd you do that? I was beating your uncle." Caleb's eyebrows drew together.

"Not a chance I had you by two throws." Dylan swiped at the wet area. Hope giggled. "Your aunt asked you to do this didn't she?"

Jack began to shake his head back and forth, but mid movement, he nodded.

"Can I have the bottle, please?" Dylan held out his hand. Jack complied. "Payback!" Wearing a piratical grin, his long legs tore through the grass. Hope yelped and ran. "I was the baseball star, you can't beat me."

She stopped mid-stride, and he ran past her. "I can outthink you though."

Caleb walked by Hope with Jack on his shoulders. He bent down so Jack could give Hope a high-five. "You beat 'em!"

"I did, we won't' tell him though." Hope blew a long breath out and took a sip of water. Dylan came alongside her, panting. "Here's yours." She gave him the full bottle which he chugged in short measure. "Still wanna kayak?"

"A short trip? I really want to see the photos."

"I'll grab the gear, we'll be finished in two hours." Dylan

walked toward the kayak shed. Hope headed toward the dock and awaited a rafting party to clear it. Once they got into the boat, she stood on the floating dock and took two life jackets. Used to wearing one on her dad's boat throughout the years, she quickly fastened the neon orange jacket and tucked her phone in the inside pocket.

Dylan tied the kayak to a cleat on the dock, and she helped him get his life jacket on. "Thanks, I've done this before."

Hope fastened the buckle across his shoulders. "It gives me an excuse to get closer to you."

"You have a mischievous streak." He pulled her to him, the thick security devices impeding a hug. Dylan leaned over, and she met him in the middle for a quick kiss. "Go ahead and get in, I'll follow."

"All right. Don't you want to get in first?"

"And I like how you look when you get on the boat." Dylan's smile grew larger as he untied the kayak and pushed from the dock. "I've got one too. A fun side."

Her cheeks scorched from his audacious statement. She ran a hand through the chilled water and put it on her face before putting her oar into the water. Hope imagined what a life lived with Dylan would be like, all the fun and time learning new things about one another. Maybe she needed to text Amelia to start looking at wedding venues, in case.

CHAPTER EIGHTEEN

Carrying in her last heavy box of teaching materials, Hope slid into the office chair behind the desk. She glanced around the classroom, and her eyes landed on the teal and gray August calendar on the bulletin board and several half-completed decorating projects on other walls. *Five more days. I can do this.* With a push on the chair's arms, she unbent her kinked shoulders and stretched.

"Need help?" Taylor, Faith's best friend stood in the door-way. "It's looking great so far. I love the children's book cover poster. Where'd you find it?"

"It was a gift from Dylan." Hope ran a hand over the shiny poster and grinned. "It's my favorite."

"How's things going, with you and Dylan? We haven't seen each other except at church recently. And the kids are always keeping me busy with summer Pre-K activities."

"They are precious. Everything's going great, Dylan and I get to see each other almost every day." She moved a can of paint-brushes toward the stack of papers on the wide windowsill. "Not this week though. Readying my classroom makes me exhausted at the end of the day."

"Make sure to take vitamins, it'll keep your immune system strong." Taylor looked at the ceiling and a laugh sounded. "Sorry. I don't mean to 'mom' you."

"You're not, I appreciate it."

Taylor leaned on the whiteboard. "Are you excited?"

"About school?"

Taylor nodded.

She glanced to the empty desks and smiled. "I can't wait to see the students. It's going to be fun having Jack in a class."

"He'll be so happy to have his aunt at school. I'm looking forward to Olivia and Jacob coming with me to work in a couple of years."

"That'll be fun."

Taylor walked closer to Hope. "You sure you don't need anything?"

"I'm good thanks. I'll be getting out of here in another hour."

Her friend gave her a hug. "See you tomorrow."

Hope lifted a hand as Taylor left the room. She put on some soft music on her desktop, and it filtered through the speakers. Sifting through the box of things from her desk, she pulled out the Vincent Van Gogh doll she'd purchased in London's National Gallery. The bright yellow pants the crocheted doll wore made her smile. Another souvenir, a pop-up card of the London skyline, found a place beside her computer monitor. *Maybe Dylan and I can visit Great Britain together if we get married.* She imagined the rainy weather, West End shows, museums, and kisses they'd share. Many, many, embraces too. Hope smiled at the delightful thought.

The first day school bell and footsteps mixed with chatter filled the hallway. Hope stood outside of her classroom ready to greet the students. Several looked familiar from church. She grinned and waved at the kids. There was a tug on her midi-length skirt, and she checked to see who'd done it. A large set of blond eyelashes blinked back at her. She gave her nephew a hug and got down to his level. "Good morning. Are you excited about first grade?"

"Yes, and seeing you Aunt Hope." He gave her a squeeze around the neck, his breath warm on her neck. "I'm coming to your class soon."

"Tomorrow, we'll do some fun things then." She put a kiss on his cheek and stood. "Where's your parents?"

"They walked me to my class, it's down this hall, and met the teacher. They said I could go see you really quick." Jack grinned. "The nice lady who's the school mayor showed me your class."

A giggle bubbled in the back of her mouth. She pushed it away with a cough. "Mrs. McTier, the Principal."

"Yes, her."

"Why don't we walk back to your class. I'm sure your teacher's looking for you."

Both dodged the streams of young learners in the hallway. Soon Jack was in his class happily chattering away with the other kids. "He's my nephew." She explained to the teacher. "Jack wanted to see me."

"My kids are both here at school, they've come by two times already." The gentleman smiled. "They do this every year. Have a good first day, I remember Annie introducing you last week as a new teacher."

"Thanks, you too. I'm teaching your class tomorrow."

"See you then." He turned and announced to the class. "Please take your seats, class."

A bell sounded, and she picked up the pace toward her classroom. Even though first period was her planning time, she wanted to get ready for second period's class.

For the remainder of the day, she incorporated the classroom rules along with a coloring game. At the sound of the dismissal bell, Hope wanted to cheer. Her strained voice was dry and raspy. She took her things and closed the classroom door, excited for another day of learning tomorrow.

Driving home, she played the music louder than normal to keep herself focused on the snaking mountain road. Hope sighed when she opened the door, and dropped to the sofa, kicking off her shoes from her complaining feet. Daylight turned to dusk as she watched tv and vegged. Dinner sounded too complicated to think about that night. Her doorbell rang during the 6 o'clock news. Hope lowered the volume and hobbled to the door. As she opened it, a familiar hand stuck through the growing crack. It held a bouquet of blue and purple flowers. "Dylan, come in." She took the flowers as he entered the foyer.

He wore a pair of dress pants, an untucked polo, and one heart-ceasing smile. "How was your first day?"

"Sit down, and I'll tell you."

"In just a moment. I've got some things in the car." He gave her a quick kiss and went back through the door.

Sniffing the bouquet, the earthy-sweet smell of lavender introduced itself followed by the soft whisper of peony. Hope pulled an antique vase from her mantle and took it to the kitchen for water. While at the sink, she eyed the messy aftermath from breakfast. Once the dishes were put in the dishwasher, she trimmed the ends of the flowers and put them in the vase.

"I figured you probably didn't have any dinner." Dylan pulled out ready-made things from the bag and a box of tea. "This is for your throat. My mom recommended it."

"Thank you, how was your mom's first day back?" Hope pulled dishes from the cabinet.

"Busy, they've given her an extra class of Culinary Skills students and cut back the time on the others to accommodate it." Dylan scooped the food onto the plates. "She's not very happy about that."

"I'd imagine not. Do you want to sit at the table or in the family room?"

"On the sofa, we can sit closer together." Dylan put a hand on her shoulder. "Can I fix tea for you?"

"I'll do it later. Water's fine right now." She shook her glass for emphasis. "You are wonderful, this looks great."

"It should be, I didn't cook it."

"Same goes for me."

"One of us has to learn to cook, we can't eat out all the time." Dylan took her glass and put it on the side table as she sat down. "Too expensive and waistline expansive."

"I'll look for some easy recipes and give them a try soon."

Conversation came in waves, as both were weary from the workday. After dinner, Dylan scooped up Hope's legs and put them on top of his, which caught her unaware. With gentle rubbing motions, he eased her sore feet with tender care. "That feels amazing, thank you." Her limbs became loose as the relaxing ministrations continued. She captured a yawn with the back of a hand.

Dylan patted her legs and shifted on the seat. "I'd better go, even though I don't want to leave. We both have early mornings."

She scooted her legs to move off him and rose from the sofa. Hope took his hands and pretended to pull him up to standing. "That was incredible, thanks."

He pushed a lock of hair from her face. "Glad to help. Sleep well. See you soon. I have a client dinner tomorrow night, or you could come over."

Disappointment like a heavy winter coat wrapped her. "You too, have a good night's sleep."

At the door, Dylan crossed the threshold and turned around. "You know I'd rather be here tomorrow night with you."

"I know, me too."

One quick kiss led to four more before he waved and moved toward his car. She raised a hand as he backed from the driveway. Pain spread through her as his taillights disappeared. It was a totally unaccustomed feeling and as messy as an unfocused photo of fog. Hope closed the door and grimaced. She'd never had feelings so deep for a guy. It was both electrifying and amazing.

The following weekend, summer's heat made way for the cooler temperatures. Spots of tangerine, yellow, and mountain-brown colored the leaves. Hope spent the afternoon on her deck enjoying the change in air and editing the photos from the day in Blowing Rock. She maximized the photo of Dylan and ran a finger over the screen. It wasn't like touching the real man, but as close as she'd get for now. Flipping to the mountain shots, she was enthralled with the beauty shining through her screen. Hope had placed the order for a large print of her favorite one two weeks before. Daily she checked her email for the delivery date and was sad to see it was delayed. Once more she pulled up her inbox and noted today's delivery date. Hope hatched a plan to give Dylan his present on his birthday. She texted him to see if he was free Sunday afternoon. He immediately said yes. The plan was in action.

CHAPTER NINETEEN

All through church Hope noticed Dylan's furtive glances. While they walked to their cars, Dylan began his inquisition.

"Where and what are we doing?" He was not going to be thwarted from his fact-finding mission. "A man needs to know things."

Exasperated, her nerves were stretched to their breaking point. "You'll see, birthday man. See you at two."

"I need a hint on how to dress."

That remark made her tickled. "That's my usual question to you. Wear clothes." She gave him a chaste kiss in the parking lot and sped away before he wheedled the answer from her. Hope dressed in a pair of army green jeans, a brown lightweight heathered sweater, and matching low leather boots. She swept her long curls into a ponytail and glanced in the mirror. No accessories. Eyeing the small selection in her top drawer, she put the gold arrow loops through her ears and slid the bracelet Dylan had gotten her at Tweetsie Railroad a couple of months back. The doorbell pealed. Hope ran to the door and yanked it open. "Afternoon."

Dylan entered, the smell of sunshine and yummy man followed. "So, where are we going?"

"I won't tell you, I'll take us there." She was ecstatic she'd had the foresight to put the present in the trunk after church. "Ready to go?"

"A bit worried about what you've got planned."

"Something you'll like."

After turning on the alarm, she met up with Dylan at the car. On the drive, they talked about work, a big case pending for Dylan, and how the same student in Hope's class couldn't follow the directions. "She kept drawing squares instead of circles. Everyone's projects came out great in the end though." Hope tapped on the steering wheel with a finger to the soft music she was playing. "We ended up cutting hers into circles after she saw what the rest of the class had done."

Dylan's hand touched hers on the wheel and stayed for a quick second. "Did it work?"

"It was the cutest one of them all."

"That's like life, isn't it? Not getting things exactly right can turn into something really great."

"You're an intelligent man. That's very thought provoking." She clicked the turn signal and pulled the steering wheel to the right. "Close your eyes."

"A smart person would accept his girlfriend's suggestion." He covered his eyes with his hands. "I can't see a thing."

Once parked, Hope scooted to face him. "Uncover."

Dylan blinked several times before a large smile bisected his mouth. "Show Me an Axe. How'd you know I wanted to go here?" He bolted from the vehicle like a kid going to a birthday party.

"Hmm, was it the third, or fourth time, you mentioned it?" She alighted from the car and took his outstretched hand.

Once inside the building, the wooden walls reminded Hope of the cabin where she lived. Everything except for sporadic grunts, axes, loud thwacks. She jumped at the crack of an axe as a ladies throw met the target.

Caleb and Faith, Logan and some other friends from church came around the corner a moment later. They snuck up behind Dylan.

"Happy birthday, bro." Caleb clapped his brother's back. "Surprised?"

Dylan's eyes glowed. "Hey, everyone. I'm shocked not one person gave it away at church today. Especially Jack."

"We didn't tell him." Faith hugged Hope and Dylan. "He had no idea until Mrs. Settles came over to sit."

"This'll be fun." Another loud crack made her skin slither. Dylan put an arm around her. She appreciated the comforting gesture. Hope located the check-in area and began to lead everyone there. "We have to do the lesson first, all."

With the safety spiel completed, the boisterous group took their lanes. Dylan and Hope shared a lane with Logan. The others took the one beside them. Dylan grabbed the axe from the holding box. Hope and Logan stood back the prerequisite six feet and cheered him on. His first throw landed on the outer edge of the bullseye. Her hands came together to celebrate his score. "Nice work."

"Thanks." He sauntered over to the table after putting the axe into the box on the wall in their lane.

"Hope, do you want to go next?" Logan inquired.

"Go ahead, I want to see how everyone's doing." She glanced at her sister and brother-in-law and another couple. They were all cheering each other on. Logan planted his axe near the bullseye.

"Nice work, guy." Dylan clapped his back. "Your turn, Hope."

Pulling on her sleeves, she eyed the circular painted rings. As she hefted the axe, the weight of it felt as familiar as a quadratic equation in her artistic-minded brain. Hope adopted a wide legged stance as the instructor had said, and locked her wrist tight, releasing the axe. It arced two times and landed near the bullseye. She raised her hands in happiness and ran back to the table.

"Awesome." Dylan's lips joined hers in a fast kiss. "Prepare to be astounded."

"I'm watching."

His throw landed an inch or so closer to the center. He whooped and hurried back to the table. "Nice, huh?"

"It was breathtaking. The way you threw that axe. Wait until I get this bullseye." She tweaked his chin for fun before scoring her next almost bullseye.

When Dylan was throwing, Logan asked Hope. "How's Grace doing?"

Interesting. "I spoke with her the other day. Three more semesters until she graduates."

"That's going to be finished soon. Happy she's doing okay." He twisted the straw in his tea. "Do you think I could text her?"

"I think she'd like that." Hope sent Logan Grace's number. "I'll let Grace know."

"Let it be a surprise. Thanks." He tapped the table and went to take his turn. He scored a bullseye. As he walked back to the group, he received a flurry of congratulatory wishes.

Hope got closer to Faith and whispered, "Logan asked for Grace's phone number."

"He did?" She quirked a brow. "Our little sister will be excited to hear from him. I think she found him as interesting as her literary hero, Mr. Darcy."

"At least he isn't brooding. My husband got his second bullseye a while ago." Faith pointed to the electronic scoreboard. "All the guys are comparing scores while we women couldn't care less. It's fun though. Good idea to do this."

"I'm happy he likes it so much. I pray he loves his present." Hope chewed on a hangnail. "I'm really nervous."

"Hush, it's gorgeous. Text me what he does when he sees it."

Faith hugged her sister. "Mrs. Settles is probably going nuts right now. We've been gone a few hours. I'm going to grab my man and head home."

The partygoers departed. Hope and Dylan took his birthday cards and checked out with the host. Dylan held a copy of the scoreboard and the two compared scores. Both declared themselves victors which led to a flurry of comparisons about who came closer to getting a bullseye. Outside, Dylan stood by the passenger side door. Hope waved him to her trunk.

"What's going on?"

"There's a second part to your surprise."

"In your trunk?"

She popped it open and picked up a blanket-covered object that spanned half the size of her trunk. "Unwrap it." Hope held it in between them. An expectant frizzle of energy charged inside.

As the blanket fell into his hands, Dylan glanced at her and softly said, "Wow. It's so much more than I could imagine."

In Hope's hands was the first work she'd created for her love. The portrait of soft skies against the metamorphic ancient mountains were postcard perfection. "You like it?"

"The fact you made it for me, yes. How you put yourself into it for me, yes. Even though you were scared." He kissed her lips. "This is a present from your heart. I can't think of a more meaningful gift. Thank you."

"I thought I was hiding my nerves." She carefully placed the framed photograph in the blanket and covered it. Her focus was on making sure it was secure.

As she stood, Dylan's finger whispered across her cheek. Hope ventured a look at him. All she could see were big, kind eyes which made her extremely comfortable.

"You don't have to pretend around me. I love you no matter what."

Hummingbird flutters winged in her chest. "I won't."

"Good." He brushed a fast kiss on her lips and the two separated. "Now for an unromantic question."

"Fire away." Hope grinned.

"Can we go to the hardware store?"

She squinted against the sunlight and looked at his face. "Are you going to take up axe throwing?"

"No. I'll come here again, this was great. We need a picture hanging kit to display this artwork properly in my office."

"Would Pickerings have it? Didn't we pass it on the way here?"

"We did."

Down the mountain road they went, she was careful to pump the brakes to not speed. The white clapboard of the store came upon them fast, she swerved into the lot, parked, and cut the engine.

"You might need a few driving lessons about how to navigate these steep roads."

"It was fun, like an amusement park ride. Where's the joy in poking like a turtle?"

"My stomach left my body about a block back."

"Come on. The ginger ale's waiting inside." Hope rubbed his back. "You'll be good as new."

Dylan groaned, and the pair walked slowly to the store.

Silas Pickering gave them a wave as they entered. "Afternoon. Looking for something in particular?"

"Picture hangers."

"Check the back of the store. Say, Dylan, you're looking the color of the grits I sell. You, okay?"

"Fine. My girlfriend needs—"

Hope thrust her words in front of Dylan's. "He needs a ginger ale. Do y'all sell it?"

"We do, it's called Blenheim, it's in the cooler over yonder."

"Thank you, Mr. Pickering."

"Call me, Pick."

"Thanks, Pick." She looked up and down, side to side, in search of a sign, and whispered to Dylan. "Where's yonder?"

He let loose a robust laugh. "We North Carolinians use it to describe a direction. It's the left of the jars of Mount Olive Pickles."

"That explains it." Hope frowned. "Show me yonder."

"You don't show." He wiped a hand across his forehead. "Never mind. Here's yonder."

Hope stood in front of the old-fashioned soda cooler and assessed the selection. She reached a hand inside the frigid, red-painted aluminum box and pulled out two soft drinks. When they went to pay for their drinks and the picture hanging supplies, she spied a red handled axe behind the counter. "Here's your chance to get one for yourself."

"Sorry." Pick shook his head. "That's my personal axe. Minnie got it for me the last time we went to throw."

"How'd you do?" Dylan leaned on the counter. "Did you win."

"Have you seen all the jewelry and kerfuffle Minnie wears? Her arms are strong. Almost as big as mine." He held up a stick-like arm and flexed. A hill raised under his plaid shirt. "I won. Didn't beat her by much."

"Same. Hope almost had it."

"Don't listen to him Pick." Hope put her hands on the counter and leaned in. "It was a draw."

"I'm not getting between you two young folk." He handed the bag to Hope and eyed Dylan. "She's a lot like my Minnie. Feisty."

"That she is." Dylan held the door open for Hope, and she ducked under his arm to exit, snugging the cold bottles closer in the damp paper bag. "See you later Pick."

The older gentleman waved in response.

In the car, she pulled the bottles from their sack. "How're we opening them?"

"Be back." Dylan took the bottles and went back into the store. By the time she started the car, he'd returned. "Pick had an opener in the cash register."

She took a long pull of the spicy-sweet drink and held back a carbonated bubble. Women didn't emit bubbles. Her mom had taught her and her sisters that fact. Not that she didn't. 'Biological bubbles' happened. They didn't happen in front of Dylan. Hope started the car and pulled out from the lot and headed turned toward Briar Creek.

"Do you have time to go to the office? We can hang the picture together."

"Of course."

Hope was soon parking in front of the building. Once inside, the two began exchanging their opinions on the best height to hang the picture. Hope won the discussion. They sat on the sofa looking at the photo as the sun slipped into the room and shone on the dazzling mountains.

"It's gorgeous, this has to be one of the best birthdays in a long time." Dylan eased back into the seat. "I've got a beautiful, smart girlfriend and an amazing present. Thanks again. It was fun."

"You're welcome." She rubbed her hand over his strong, light-haired arm.

"Know what be better?"

"Cake. Ice cream?"

"No. Something more grown up." Dylan brought his lips to hers, the sunlight touching her face. Hope ignored the beams as they moved closer together and broke the connection between them.

A blue glow in his eyes and Dylan's shallow breath let her know he did indeed enjoy their kisses. She kissed his cheek as his stubble tickled her lips, Hope giggled.

"What was funny?"

"Nothing. I liked kissing you."

"Me too." He sunk his mouth on hers, and she ran her fingers through his hair. This way to celebrate was much more special than flour and sugar. She wished it could continue but knew it wouldn't be wise. Someday, if they were married, they could kiss and cuddle whenever they wanted. That idea made her smile. She hoped it would come true.

CHAPTER TWENTY

Getting into her car, she shielded the screen with a hand. Her second job was beginning with Logan's realty company. Hope combed over the photography list and times for each he'd texted. The bright October afternoon sun made it difficult to read the directions. Once she moved the phone below the sunlight, she put the address into her phone and pulled from the driveway.

Through the curved mountain roads, she glanced to the side to see piles of rocks on the ground from the side of a mountain. Down the road, slight trickles of water cascaded to small ponds. The ever-changing beauty was as unique as fingerprints. Jesus was a gifted artist. A quick peek at the house number again and she realized it was coming up ahead. The narrow gravel driveway caused her car to shimmy and shake like Minnie Pickering's bangle bracelets. Hope darted a hand as her camera case almost toppled off the passenger seat. She inhaled and relaxed slightly.

Her eyes focused on the gorgeous home and how to best capture it for Logan. Four stone pillars held the front porch's expansive overhang. A large set of glass doors revealed a wooden floored entryway larger than her old apartment. She grabbed her black jacket from the passenger seat and glanced in the rearview mirror. With a quick tug to straighten her mustard-colored blouse, Hope gathered all the things she'd need for the photo shoot. As she approached the door, a little girl darted across the foyer inside. The blonde hair and sweet face resembled a student of hers. Hope was unsure whether to knock or ring the doorbell. Once again, the child hurried across the foyer. She waved at the girl whose mouth rounded. "Hey Sydney, how are you?"

"Ms. Fuller, you're here at my house. Let me tell my mom." Sydney sped toward the heart of the house. Her shrill voice sounded through the glass. "Mom, my teacher is here."

Sydney came back tugging her mom's hand and smiled.

The woman opened the door and glanced at Hope. "You're Syd's teacher?"

Hope smiled and spoke. "I am. I'm the art teacher. I'm here today to take photos of your house. Logan Whitlock said he'd told you."

"He did, come on in. I'm Vanessa Ridgeway, thank you for coming out here."

Hope shook Vanessa's hand.

"Hope Fuller, you're welcome, your home is absolutely spectacular."

"Thank you. Thomas, my husband, is an architect. Our family really loves it here." Vanessa led Hope to the family room. "Syd and I can leave for a while so you can take the photos. How long will you be?"

She took in the mountain mansion and stated. "An hour or an hour and a half."

"We'll be back in a while. Come on, Syd. Let's go get an ice cream at Fred's Backyard."

"Yes!" Sydney shot a fist in the air and did a wiggle dance. "Can we bring one back for Ms. Fuller?"

Vanessa looked at her and smiled. "Would you like one?"

"No, thank you." She began to take her camera equipment out of the bag. "Have fun, Sydney."

The seven-year-old grinned and waved, the door closing softly behind them. Hope stored her bag out of site on the porch and came back into the home snapping photos of all the extraordinary rooms. When she went to the upper back deck, the clouds were beginning to gather over the mountains some miles away. Shapes danced across the tops, enthralled, Hope snapped photos of the scenery.

"Did you get what you need?"

Hope jumped at the unexpected voice piercing the quiet. "Thanks, I did."

Vanessa and Sydney came out onto the deck.

"How was the ice cream?"

"Good, I got chocolate sprinkles on my chocolate ice cream."

"Yum."

Vanessa pointed to her camera. "Can I see some of the photos?"

"Sure, they'll be edited before Logan posts them online." Hope scrolled to the beginning of the photo series and gave Vanessa the camera. "I started at the foyer."

Sydney and Hope talked about school, while Sydney's mom viewed the photos.

Vanessa handed the camera to Hope. "These are superb, do you ever do magazine work?"

Hope maintained a calm façade, breathing in slowly through her nose. "I've not done any yet. I'd like to, though."

"I work for an online magazine, *Mountain Living*, we're always looking for people with talent like yours." Vanessa handed the camera back to Hope. "It's freelance. The pay isn't going to make you leave your teaching job."

"Is it steady? Or more sporadic?"

"Every few weeks or so."

Hope's excitement built, getting magazine credit for her work would give her a boost in becoming known in the industry. "Do you have to travel?"

"No, it's all local. The farthest we reach is Asheville." Vanessa lifted a shoulder. "It's not an overly large magazine and readership."

"Could you send me more of a description about what it entails. I'm interested." She gave Vanessa her business card.

"I'll contact the Managing Editor, and he'll be in touch."

"Thank you." She held out her hand to the nice woman. "Nice to meet you, Vanessa. See you Monday, Sydney."

"You as well."

Vanessa held the back door open for Hope, and they walked to the front of the home. Hope turned and waved before stepping off the front porch. She wanted to skip like a girl to her car, but reined the impulse in. *I can't wait to tell Dylan*. Hope headed North on the country road toward his home. Close to his house, her pulse rammed in her throat. She pulled into his driveway and observed him raking leaves in the front yard. The car door swung open, and Hope bounced from the seat and over to Dylan. "Hey, hottie."

"I'm that." He smirked and wiped his forehead. "Been raking leaves for an hour. What's going on?"

"Logan sent me to take photos of a home." She flicked a leaf off his shoulder.

"What was that about?" Dylan grinned. "Couldn't resist touching me."

How very true. "A leaf decided to hitch a ride."

Dylan brushed a hand over his shirt. "All gone?" He rotated in front of her.

Hope inspected his black shirt. "You're good, no more tag alongs."

"Back to the home. How'd it go?"

Hope shifted her stance in the soft grass. "Turns out it

belonged to one of my students. The mom works for an online magazine. She's offered me a freelance photographer job." Hope wrapped her arms around Dylan's midsection. "I'll accept if the job description fits my skills. Isn't that great?"

"Congrats." He kissed the top of her head as they stood side by side. "You'll be working for them instead of Logan some weekends?"

She kicked the leaves in front of her, and they scattered in the light breeze. "I can do both."

Dylan crossed his arms over his chest and rocked back on his heels. "You'll teach full-time, do photography for both a magazine and Logan. When will we see each other?"

"There's time."

He went back to raking the leaves, the dust from his motion made Hope sneeze. "I don't want to squeeze our relationship into an hour here or there." Dylan gathered a pile of leaves into his arms and stuffed them into an oversized brown paper lawn bag. "Are we part-time?"

"No. We can make this work." Hope collected some leaves and carried them to the bag. "I love you. We'll be okay."

"My business is picking up." Dylan grabbed the rake and dragged it through the small pile. "Weekends might get crazy for me too. Where does that leave us?"

"As long as we both agree to see each other every weekend. It'll be fine." Her mood switched to become less happy. "We can do this."

Dylan dragged the bag to the edge of the road. "I love you too. I don't want anything to jeopardize what we're building here."

"And I don't either." Hope put a hand on his arm. "We'll both pray on it."

"We will. We can't mess this up. . . again."

Again. The weight of the singular word hit her like an axe slamming into its target. Burning tears blurred her vision. Hope glanced away and swiped at them. "We won't mess anything up. Look, maybe two part-time jobs are too much."

He rubbed her arm and his voice softened. "See how it goes. Maybe there's enough time between the jobs for us." Dylan pressed a kiss to her hair. "I don't want to lose you."

"You're not." Hope ran a hand down his arm and laced her fingers with his. "You, Dylan Gaines, have me for as long as we want this to go on."

"For life?"

Rolling warmth covered her back and arms. Hope's smile increased. "Like, maybe getting married?"

"Would you consider it?"

"I dunno." She turned away. Dylan put an arm around her and gently directed Hope to him. Pain pierced Hope to think about not being with Dylan. She forced the emotional words to blossom from her lips. "I would."

He let out a lengthy breath. "Thank the Lord. I thought I was the only one feeling it."

She motioned with a finger for him to come closer. Hope kissed his left cheek, and Dylan's lips arced. Her lips moved to his chin. He laughed. The right cheek seemed lonely, so it too received a quick lip smack. Like in the axe throwing, she wanted a bullseye. Lips meeting, an explosion of tingles ran from the soles of her feet to the top of Hope's head. A bullseye was scored.

CHAPTER TWENTY-ONE

After being convinced by her new friend Vanessa and some cajoling from Dylan, Hope packed the last of the framed photos into her trunk. She ran over the checklist for all the necessary things for that day's Land of Oz craft fair. Even though the hour was early, the sun was barely awake over the mountains. Hope was running on adrenaline. She was honored to be part of the artists featured in the fall festival.

A motor thrummed nearby. Hope peered around her car to see Dylan's vehicle swing into the driveway.

"Morning." He brushed a kiss on her cheek. "Need anything else put in here?"

"Hi. I thought we were going to meet there."

"Change of plans, I was told by Minnie yesterday that parking is hard to come by on property." Dylan grinned. "I thought I'd tag along."

"I'm glad you are here. You'll keep me calm." She slammed the door to her trunk. "I've only had one cup of coffee, yet my jittery nerves are acting like it's been three cups instead."

Dylan took her in his arms—she loved the warmth from his navy pullover and strong arms. "You're going to be amazing."

"I'm really hoping."

"Remember the great reviews you got on your photos for Mountain Living? Your boss loved them."

The old insecurities threatened to lash at her newly gained confidence. "I was grateful. He was more than kind."

His eyes narrowed. "No. He knows talent when he sees it."

"You're one fantastic ego builder. I love you for that and so much more."

"I love you too." Dylan opened her passenger side door. "How long's the drive to Land of Oz? I haven't been there since I was a kid, and it was an amusement park."

She moved to the driver's side of the car. "GPS says twenty-five minutes."

"Good, thanks. I forgot, I need to get something." He dashed back to his car and soon held several shopping bags in each hand. "Can I put this in your fridge?"

"Of course, what is it?" Hope threw him the keys, which he caught with a single hand.

"You'll find out later. Not right now." Dylan disappeared into the house and returned folding his tall body into the car. "You know what I'd love to do right now?"

They said simultaneously. "Get some coffee."

Barely turning the odometer to the next number, Hope pulled into Briar Creek Bakery. "Let's hurry, I need to set up my tent for the show."

"Taskmaster." Dylan alighted from the car in an exaggerated stretch.

"Let's go."

They greeted the newlyweds, Ryan and Willow, who were wreathed in huge grins. Both chattered to them about the honeymoon to New York City and the Broadway plays they saw. Hope felt small at being a green-eyed monster in the face of their wedded bliss. She prayed this would happen soon for them as well. Coffees in hand a quick few moments later, and they pulled from the parking lot.

With each twist and turn of the serpentine mountain road, Hope gripped the wheel more tightly.

Dylan's fingers rubbed over hers. "Relax. This is probably the steepest road you've driven on. Don't think of it as scary. Be challenged. You can do this."

"It does remind me of the driving game we played at your house a while back." She eased the pressure on the leather wheel and her bone-pale fingers began to return to normal. "I'll beat this road."

"You will."

They turned onto the wooded parking lot and parked. After all was unpacked, mostly on Dylan's back and arms, they headed to the entrance tent.

A woman who sat at an emerald-colored table greeted them. "Welcome to the fall fest. Vendors will set up beyond the yellow brick road."

Hope's little girl dreams were coming true, the Wizard of Oz was her favorite childhood movie. Her heart skipped when she spied the first golden bricks footsteps from where they stood.

Gathering her manners, she thanked the person and headed toward the designated spot. "I'll take some more things." Hope took several more framed photographs from his arms. "You're carrying too much."

"Thanks." Dylan shook his hands. "I had a cement grip on 'em. I didn't want them to break."

Both travelled through the curving brick road. Hope stopped in front of a metal-framed gondola and a circular structure of wires. "Dylan, my mom has some photos of me riding this as a teen. It had a colorful topper over this wire. This is so neat."

"It looks like a chicken coop with a basket." Dylan snapped a quick photo of Hope near the shell of a balloon. "Do you know what it was?"

"A skyride. Mom said it was scary. The wind made it swing side-to-side." She chuckled. "Most of my family doesn't like heights."

"So we won't be skydiving together?"

"Um, no." Hope glanced at the vendor map again. "It's to the left of this tree." She placed the artwork against the trunk of a stately oak and took the wooden scaffolding from her arm.

Dylan maneuvered around the site and assembled the bright blue tent. He grabbed the display holder and put it on the left side of the tent bracing it against the tarp cover Hope fastened to the interior.

"This looks good, thank you." Hope paced around the area, rearranging things from one side to the other before planting her booth sign into the ground. "Briar Creek Photography. Sounds nice, doesn't it?" She ran a hand over the carved wooden sign, the wood smooth beneath her palm. "I like how the river is running through it, don't you?"

"It looks very professional. I could see this hanging in a shop window."

Hope took his hand and looked up at him. "That'd be nice. I want to teach though. The kids when they get sparkles in their eyes from learning. It's amazing."

"You're going to make a great mom, someday." Dylan kissed her cheek. "You're wonderful with our niece and nephew."

"Thanks. You are too." She focused on the words as her mind reviewed what needed to still be finished before the show's opening. She paused, "I have to go back to something you mentioned me being—a mom?"

"Mmhmm."

Hope's heart unfolded like the photo of the blossoming soft pink Rhododendron she'd brought to sell. Hope stood in silence, unsure of how to share her thoughts. "You'd be an excellent dad."

"So, you'd consider having my seven children someday?"

Ready to answer, Hope opened her mouth to speak.

A man and woman came into her booth and pointed to one of her favorite photos, an early morning mountainscape. "Excuse me, is this photograph for sale?"

Hope's neck torched, and she hoped the couple hadn't heard the exchange. She smiled at the lady who was close to her age. "It is, let me check the price on the list." Quick dancing fingers over the iPad screen resulted in the answer. She showed the couple the price tag and beamed a prayer that it wasn't too high."

"We'll take it."

After the sale was made, the couple strolled past the tent promising to pick up the piece on the way out. She located a "sold" sign in her bag and hung it on the frame. "I can't believe it, my first piece sold."

"Congratulations, from the looks of the crowd coming in this direction. They'll be some more soon." Dylan gave her a quick kiss.

With nary a break until her feet complained, all but three of the twelve photographs had been purchased. Hope eased into the nylon seat next to Dylan and rested her head on his shoulder. "I'm so glad you're with me. You have a flair for sales."

"Appreciate it." Dylan's head softly laid on hers. "This is fun, I'll be your assistant for more of these. Where are we going next?"

"I haven't checked what coming up. I'll need to take more photos to sell." She disguised a yawn in the palm of a hand and rose from the seat. "Only three left. Think we'll get them sold?"

Dylan's eyes widened. "There's two more hours until it ends. I'd say it's going to happen."

Packing up at the close of the fall fair, Dylan had predicted close to correctly. They carried one solitary photograph to the car. As she closed the trunk with a thud, a weight settled within Hope. Her eyes were weary, and she resisted the impulse to rub them. Now to face the car ride back down the mountain.

Dylan asked. "Mind if I drive? You need a rest, and the road's pretty crazy, especially with the sun in your eyes."

Almost shouting with glee, Hope slid the keys into his outstretched hand. "You don't know how much I was dreading that. I might need the driving lesson you mentioned sometime back. Offer still stands?"

"Anytime."

They fell gratefully into the car's interior.

With soft music playing, Hope's heavy eyes began to close.

"Wake up."

She stretched like a day-old piece of Hubba Bubba Bubble Gum. "How long was I out?"

"About twenty minutes."

"I didn't mean to be. Thanks for driving." She pushed the door open as the cool air teased the curls around her face. Dylan began to pull things from her car. "I'll get all this tomorrow."

"I'll do it." Dylan pointed to her home. "Go have a seat."

"I should help."

"Nope. This way you can relax after church tomorrow.

"You're amazing." Hope squeezed his shoulder. "I'll get the door and when you're finished, you can show me what's in the bags."

"I think you'll like it."

Once everything was stored, they found their way to the kitchen. She pulled open the fridge. "Want some lemonade or tea?"

"You made the lemonade?"

Her hair flew into her face as she shook her head. Hope pushed it away. "No, it's that strawberry one in a container."

"Sure."

She poured two glasses. "I can't cook, but I can pour a glass of lemonade. What are you hungry for?" Hope glanced down at her phone. "We could do that pizza place we had some time back." The slam of the fridge drew her attention. Dylan held the mystery bags in his hands. "Or, I guess we could have what's in those."

He pulled fresh chicken, some asparagus, and bread from the bags.

She clapped her hands on his shoulders and leaned in for a kiss. "We're cooking?"

"Sit back, relax. I'm cooking." He winked and put his phone on the counter. "It worked when I made it at home. We won't have anything burned tonight."

"I can help."

"Keep me company."

As he cooked, Hope's eyes slid to Dylan's forearms now bare from his folded shirtsleeves. She sipped the drink and cooled the internal temperature threatening to rise. "I can't believe you are doing this."

"Anything I can do to make you happy. I love you and want to feed you." He hung his head down. "Sounds so pathetic, doesn't it?"

"No, you're a caring man. I'd love to have two point five kids with you in the future." Hope glanced away embarrassed at the sudden admission. "As long as one looks like you."

"Both like you, little redheads full of mischief and love." Dylan brought the skillet over to the table and plated the food some minutes later. "Don't think I have a whole repertoire of recipes. This is it. By the time they'd come along, we better know how to fix more things."

"Let's not rush or anything. We need to grow as a couple." She held the plate closer and took a sniff. "Heavenly. Thanks."

"You're welcome. I'm right there with you. Traveling, becoming more familiar with each other in likes and dislikes." Dylan took her hands. "Let's pray." He led them in a prayer which included their lives coming together in the future as man and wife.

During dinner, both shared stories about their childhood, future aspirations, couple goals. It was both exciting and uncharted waters for Hope, she feared it'd be hard to wait to get married. Elopement sounded like a great solution. Could she convince Dylan of the same?

CHAPTER TWENTY-TWO

A splash from Spartacus' bowl got his attention. Dylan rose from the sofa and pinched a few pieces of blood worms into the bowl. The greedy fish came to the top and gulped them down. "No more tonight. It's my turn to eat." Dylan figured he sounded a little wacky talking to a fish. Spartacus was the only one keeping him company tonight. With his cellphone in reach, he opened to his photo gallery and reviewed the photos he'd taken at the art festival a week ago. Hope's bright smile made his heart skip. The candid photo of her on Dorothy's front porch caused a grin to tease his lips. Glancing around his home, the number of shades of browns and man decorations shouted, "Here's a single guy." Dylan needed color and whimsy in his life and home. Hope.

He texted Caleb to get Mr. Fuller's phone number. It was time to ask for his blessing to propose to Hope. Energy like after a ten-mile run rushed through Dylan as he texted the gentleman. A rumble filled his family room as the phone buzzed in his hand. He read Mr. Fuller's response.

"We need another lawyer in the family. Her mom and I can't be the only ones. When's the big day?"

Dylan froze. He wanted to give her a memorable proposal, it'd take some planning. Thumbs running on the keyboard, he responded. *"Not sure. It's in the planning stages."*

"Let us know."

"Thank you, sir. It's an honor to become part of your family. Will do. Text you soon."

"Have a good night, son."

"Yes, sir. Thanks." The thought of calling Mr. Fuller "Dad" felt awkward. Maybe someday though. Dylan put the phone on the side table and went to his basement to his home gym. A little sweat and a lot of prayers, and he'd figure something worthy of Hope to do for a proposal. Dylan wanted something sooner than later. Loneliness covered him at times when he came home from work, and all he had to share the days happenings with was a sullen fish.

Sweat dripped from his face and down his back. It was great to get in a hard, heart-pumping weight workout. He unhooked his towel from the bar above him and wiped his face. His phone flashed. Who's at the door? A picture showed his answer, Hope. Dylan pressed his cell speaker, "Be there in a bit. Warning though, I finished a workout."

"That's okay. I've got school-kid cooties. We're even."

He laughed and ran up the stairs stopping only to apply some stick deodorant and wash his face. As he pulled the door open, Hope's eyes held his. All he wanted was to touch her and show his love in a kiss. "Come in. I'm happy you came over."

She entered. "Me too. I missed you today."

"So, did I. We saw each other yesterday and it wasn't enough."

He held out a hand, and she grasped it. "Come inside. I'll go shower quickly. I'm sure I ripe."

Hope went to see his fish. "Spartacus and I will chat."

Dylan carefully put his lips on hers in a quick smooch. "I couldn't help myself."

"Good. I wanted to do that since this morning."

"That long?"

"Didn't you?"

He nodded. "I wanted to stay and kiss you longer last night. Imagine when we're married. We can kiss as much as we'd like. I'll hurry." Dylan walked to his bathroom and made himself presentable after his shower. He ran a comb over his damp hair and put on pants and a shirt. "Fast enough?" He slid onto the sofa next to her.

"It was. What you mentioned before. Kissing and marriage. I'd like that." Hope kissed his cheek, and he yearned for more of them. "You know, I had an idea. We aren't engaged yet. So, it's premature."

"Tell me, I'm curious." Dylan played with her soft fingers on the counter. "What're you thinking?"

"Do you want a wedding, or to elope?"

Dylan looked in her face for any sign of hilarity. "Elope? Don't you want a huge wedding, like Faith and Caleb's?"

Hope's fingers stopped moving in his. "No, not me. Family and friends, a pastor. That's blissful to me. What do you feel about it?"

His mouth was dry like a loofah sponge. "I've never given my wedding a lot of thought. Always figured it would happen in my mid-thirties."

"Oh." Hope hung her head down, blocking his view of her face.

Dylan gently lifted her chin with a finger. "Until we began to date again. Now, I can't see myself going one more second without you with me. I love you."

"Dylan, you're my one person I must have in my life. I love

you so much. It hurts." Hope put a hand on her upper chest. "Goofy, I know."

"No, I feel it too." He leaned over and kissed her. "We can do whatever you want wedding-wise, as long as we're married. What do you think our families would do if we did elope?"

"They'd not forgive us, you know they want to be there too. What can we do to hurry this along?"

He chuckled. "I'd propose to you now if I had a ring. Hold on a moment." *There's gotta be some ring around here.* Dylan ran around his kitchen, opening drawers and combing through them. Finding a small ring binder in a drawer, giving it a test run on his larger fingers, he slid it into place. It was a tad bit too small. With a dash of dish soap, he rubbed it around the stuck clip.

"What are you doing?"

Dylan kept quiet.

"Let me help." Hope took the bottle and squeezed more onto the finger. "Got bar soap?"

He moved away from the sink. "Under my bathroom counter. Third door on the left."

She ran down the hall. He heard the frantic pace of her steps and his heart felt light. Some tugs later, he pulled the ring from his finger before she returned.

"Got it." Hope began to unwrap the soap.

"Don't." He held it in his hand the water cascaded down his arm, a beaming grin on his face. "Let's go out onto the deck." Dylan ran a towel over his wet hands. He noticed they were shaking. The pair went into the cold dark air. He flipped on the floodlights and stood on the opposite side of Hope. Dylan prayed that eloquent words would touch his tongue. His heart-beat and mind were twined in Hope's luminous eyes and that caused him to not think straight.

CHAPTER TWENTY-THREE

She fought against clutching her hands together in rapt ecstasy. Hope's emotions were dancing as joyfully as the lightning bugs swirling in the edge of the forest. She saw Dylan's hand shaking with the office supply ring, glistening in the bright wash of light.

Dylan bent down on the deck, his eyes shining in the spotlights. "We've been friends for a while. Then much more. Hope Abigail Fuller, you've made me, a tongue-tied lawyer, happier than ever before. You are my camera lens, bringing my life into brilliant focus. There's not one single person walking this earth who is more wonderful than you. I love you. Will you do me the honor of being my wife?"

With shaking legs, she bent down to kiss him. Her heart floated above them and joined his in that moment. As he slid the temporary ring on her finger, the weight felt permanent and wholly right.

"Is that a, yes?"

"Yes. Yes. Yes. I love you too, Dylan Walker Gaines."

They rose together and folded one another in their arms and their lips joined. Quiet night sounds played a melody. Hope heard his heartbeat as she laid her head on his chest. She was happier than happy. Like she'd created the most gorgeous photo, or seen a student come to love art. This man. He was her fiancé. Hope flicked her hand around the "ring," and it made her laugh. "We don't do anything normal?"

"No. That's what I love about you. We can go kayaking, axe throwing. Hiking. Anything's amazing together."

"It is." She reached up and pulled lightly on the back of his head. As his head bowed, she sealed her lips over his and sighed in happiness. Their arms surrounded one another and peace washed over her.

Soon they separated, Dylan picked up her left hand and kissed the ring finger. "This is temporary. You'll be getting an upgrade soon."

"It's perfect for a teacher, I use these all the times in class. Are we going to tell our families about this?"

"We will, or do we want to surprise them with something a little more formal?"

"I'd like that. Why do the usual thing? Surprises are much more fun." She ran her hands over her arms, the hard ring a reminder of what had transpired. Hope smiled and ran a hand over her fiancé's handsome face. "Let's go back inside and talk about the wedding. It's starting to get cold."

Dylan opened the door and Hope moved over the threshold. "As long as it's soon, I can't wait to have breakfast with you, in our home."

Delicious chills dotted her body. "Neither can I. Where will we live?"

"My place. I have a mortgage, and we can expand on the back of it." Dylan gave her a quick kiss, "for our growing family. About the wedding, when and where?"

They worked on their plan until Hope's mind couldn't function properly. "Ugh, I'm exhausted and need to leave. School's early tomorrow." She pulled him from the sofa cushion and ran a hand through his wavy hair. "I love you, you are my heart."

He pecked her lips with his. "I love you so much, I don't want to let you go. But I must. We'll get together tomorrow night and finish planning."

"I'm ecstatic."

"Me too." He gave her a kiss and closed her car door.

When her hands touched the steering wheel, the unfamiliar feel of a ring on the hand gave her a jolt. She smiled at the dull glow of the band in the streetlights. Happy things were forming for one big celebratory party. Together with their families.

CHAPTER TWENTY-FOUR

Leaves danced and swirled in the September breeze, Dylan paced in front of the Vanderbilt Estate. He glanced at his watch. 3 pm, Hope was thirty minutes late. He tugged on his suit jacket as it flapped in the wind.

When she grew nearer, his heart lurched. *She was worth the wait.* Her long ivory dress matched the lushness of the green lawn and brought out the fire in her gorgeous curls. She was more stunning than the mansion behind him. Dylan plucked words from his mind to say to her. "You look amazing." *Original, verbiage, guy.*

"Thank you, you're gorgeous yourself. That dark gray suit fits you well." She pulled on his lapel. "Did everyone get here?"

"Logan texted a bit ago to tell me all of them had arrived." He cleared his throat "Are we ready?"

"They'll be shocked." Hope's arm slid around his waist. "They think it's a proposal. I can't imagine how my folks didn't know, nor my sisters."

"My parents neither. It'll be a surprise. Like we wanted." A rise swelled in his chest. He glanced at her as she surveyed the bright orange mums in the plantings. "These remind me of the candy corn you liked to eat."

"You're right, I wish we had some now."

"Maybe later." Dylan slid a kiss on her cheek.

"Promises."

The photographer stood in front of them and snapped a photo.

When they walked by the greenhouse, he pretended to head toward it. "We can do a repeat of our first kiss."

"We're already late. I couldn't get my eyeliner to go on correctly."

"You look gorgeous, whatever you did, worked." Dylan was elated. They went further into the gardens and marveled at the fall topiaries dotting the landscape. "We can come back tonight.

"I'll be back in a bit, I need to tell the photographer something." Dylan whispered instructions to the younger man who nodded and walked away. He prayed it wasn't too obvious, the surprise planned for her couldn't be ruined.

Hope lifted her head and glanced around. "He's meeting us, isn't he?"

"We'll see him later." Dylan pointed to her camera bag on the opposite side of Hope.

"It's a gorgeous day, with an equally gorgeous woman. And we're going to become an official couple. Life couldn't be better." He took her hand and kissed it leaving the tingles behind on the place where he kissed.

She paused on the walkway.

"Everything okay, pebble in your shoe?"

"No, I've been thinking about the kiss you promised me in the greenhouse." She grabbed his hand and tugged him toward the tree. "Pay up."

Laughing, Dylan bolted ahead of her. "Not yet."

Under the rustling branches, the leaves fell off their homes and floated to the ground. Hope turned to Dylan, her heartbeat pulsing in her ears. She took several steps closer to him and pushed to her full height to meet his gaze. Click!

Stepping back from Dylan she swung her glance to the photographer.

"Great photo," The man said. "I think you'll like it."

They neared an evergreen tree that had one of its fingers hooked over the pathway. She raised a hand and brushed the prickly branch, releasing the scent of fresh, woodsy evergreen, like Christmas in the fall. "It's gorgeous, all the varying shapes these trees make."

"The same man who created New York's Central Park designed the grounds," Dylan informed. "We'll have to go there and take a walk."

"And a carriage ride. And a show."

He nodded.

Walking along the curved path, Hope cut a glance at a sinuous tree. "I wish I had my camera. I like how the shaggy branches almost touch the ground." Hope led them under the bower and slid a kiss on his lips.

"We were going to wait." He kissed Hope in return and took her hand.

"I couldn't."

When Hope could see a slate peaked roof and stone pillars of a gazebo, she saw the photographer in position beside the structure. She picked up the pace and stopped in front of a large statue of an elegant lady from ancient times and a dog.

"Logan's waving to us. He's bringing our families."

"Let's go." Hope took his hand as they strolled toward the crowd. "They're going to be shocked and amazed." She squeezed his hand and looked beyond the stone walls at the gorgeous view. Gray veiled mountains held pumpkin, sunlight, and deep forest green colors. It made her hitch a breath. "We're pretty crazy, aren't we?"

"They are. And, we might be, look what all we planned in less than three months."

Hope touched her midsection. "I've got butterflies."

"I'm nervous too." Dylan squeezed her hand. "It's going to be great. I can't wait to call you wife."

"And I'll call you husband." Hope breathed slowly and willed her heartbeat to slow. She noticed her mom's cap of dark hair in the distance. The navy dress she wore was far more formal than the cryptic invitation had asked. Her handsome dad's suit complimented his wife's dress.

As they neared, her mom's eyebrows winged upward. "Sweetie, what's happening?" Her mom swept a kiss on her cheek. "You look gorgeous, that dress looks like you're ready for a wedding. I thought this was an engagement. You're getting. . .married?"

"Mom and Dad, we've been engaged for a couple of months. Yes, you know me, I'm not one for a big event. Dylan and I wanted something simple and small. Shocked?"

"It's exactly what your dad and I would have done. I wanted to elope, but my parents wouldn't hear of it." Her mom swiped a finger under an eye. "We're happy to call you son, Dylan." She hugged her soon to be son-in-law.

By the time her mom and Dylan had finished hugging, the rest of her family circled around as well as Dylan's.

"Congratulations are in order." Dylan's dad clapped his son's back and hugged Hope. "Welcome to the family."

"Thank you." She reached over to Dylan's mom and gave her a hug as well. "I hope you're not too upset."

"I'm bowled over the two of you were able to keep it from all of us. I'm elated." Dylan's mom, Georgia, ran a hand over her green midi-dress. "May you both continually surprise one another like you did us." She swiped at tear.

Grace moved beside Hope. “That’s a gorgeous dress, I love the ivory lace capelet over it. Am I your maid of honor?”

“Glad you like it. You look beautiful in your long dark orange dress.” She hugged her younger sister. “I’d be honored if you’d be. Faith, will you be the matron of honor?”

“I’d love to be in the wedding. How funny that Grace and I are wearing similar colors.” Faith pointed to her pumpkin-colored long dress and put her arm around her sister. “I’m so happy, Dylan’s a great guy.”

“Thanks, he is.” A tear threatened to topple from her lashes. She swiped it away with her lace handkerchief she’d been carrying. “Jack, will you be the ring bearer?”

Jack dug his hands into his pants’ pockets and shook his head. “I don’t have a ring.”

Dylan rubbed a hand over his nephew’s head. “I’ve got them.” He opened his coat pocket and Jack looked inside.

“I get to wear both of those?”

Caleb opened his dark suit coat and pointed to the inner pocket. “Son, I’ll hold onto them. You get to walk down the aisle.”

“Okay. What about Isabellie?”

Hope kissed her niece’s head. She’d grown so much in the last four months. “She’s sleeping in her stroller.”

“Sorry, sister.” Jack patted his sister’s arm and skipped away.

An elegant woman walked over to the group and introduced herself as the estate wedding coordinator. She carried a box of breathtaking flowers. Grace and Faith were given bouquets of flame orange, yellow, and greens. Dylan and his groomsmen, Caleb and Logan were given orange boutonnieres. Both mothers were gifted wrist corsages while the fathers were bestowed yellow boutonnieres. Lastly, she opened a box another estate employee had put next to her. Green foliage haloed the same riotous colors of flowers in her wedding parties bouquets but with an addition of parchment-colored fragrant Carolina

Jasmine. She brought the spectacular flowers closer, and the light kiss of floral scent made her smile.

"Everything's set up." The coordinator took the wedding party aside and gave them quick instructions.

Pastor Tim from Briar Creek Community Church and his wife Jeana had arrived.

"Hello y'all. Can we pray?"

The couple nodded as the four of them circled and Pastor Tim led the prayer.

A stringed quartet began to play the first strains of "Jesu Joy of Man's Desiring."

"This is it. I can't wait to call you, my wife." Dylan took her hand and kissed it before walking into the gazebo.

Her father, looking dapper in a navy suit and green tie walked beside her. "Ready to do this?"

She kissed his cheek, holding back a small sob.

"You're marrying a good man."

"I am, thanks, Dad."

Arm in arm they walked the path lit by flameless candles and into the large gazebo. Candles from the chandelier flickered in the wind as well as those placed along each pillar.

Throughout the ceremony, Pastor Tim used some of their favorite scriptures from first Corinthians, and all recited the Lord's Prayer as the quartet played quiet hymns below the voices.

During the exchanging of the rings as Dylan put Hope's on her finger, she had to look twice. The replacement for the short-lived office supply ring was a square cut diamond which fit elegantly on her slim hand. She was still awe-struck by its beauty. As she repeated the vows, Hope put the black enamel band on Dylan's finger. The warmth from his hands gave her comfort. She smiled at him and her heart ka-thumped at the love he demonstrated for her in his blue eyes.

"You may kiss the bride."

As their lips met, she rejoiced internally for the bond of matrimony they'd created.

The small group of attendees milled about ready to congratulate the couple. Her parents were followed by Dylan's parents. Next were Faith and Caleb. Trailing behind was Grace with Jack.

The youngster had his eyes covered. "Is the kissing over, Aunt Grace?"

"It is for now champ." Grace gave each a congratulatory embrace.

Jack lowered his hands and grinned. "Good. Mom and Dad do that enough at home. Yuck!"

The families laughed at that oh-so-very all-boy remark.

"Jack." Hope hugged her nephew. "You did great."

"Sure." He ran back to his parents. "Mom, Dad, I did great."

"We heard." Faith kissed her son's cheek. "Nice job son."

Life couldn't be any sweeter than in that moment, with family encircling them under the lowering sun as the lights from the estate shined almost as brightly as Hope's smile.

A whirring camera shutter sounded as Hope and Dylan entered the conservatory. The fragrance of sweetness perfumed the air. Hope breathed in the beautiful aroma. She squeezed Dylan's hand as Hope spied the kissing plant from a while ago and pointed it out to her husband. "Our spot, later on."

"My wife, you have a date."

She stopped and nuzzled his neck, happy the three-inch heels made her within range of his face. "I love when you say that husband."

Dylan uttered a low laugh and led them into the room. Applause rang in the gorgeous space.

"Your table is over here." The wedding coordinator pointed to a two-seater linen topped table.

"Thank you." Hope eyed the orange-red flowers in her

Grandmother Inez's cut crystal vase. "How did that get here? It was at my house."

"I brought it with me. That's one of the reasons I left earlier."

"Thank you, it's part of her here with us."

Dylan kissed her cheek.

"It's time for your dance." The wedding planner smiled.

The first notes of "I Will Always Love You" were played by the quartet as Hope and Dylan danced in the middle of the room. Once the song was over, they made their way to the seats.

Dylan began to sit down when he bounced back up. He held a baseball card in his hand "What's this?"

"Turn it over."

His eyes grew larger. "It's a Babe Ruth Rookie card. How'd you know?"

"I had some help from your parents. I said it was for a Christmas present. Think they'll forgive me?" She glanced to their table where they sat with Caleb and Faith and the kids. Big smiles were present as they enjoyed the chicken dinner.

"I think so. They've gotten another daughter, my mom's dream." He fed her a piece of his chicken. She accepted it and smiled.

"That's good. I should've gotten that instead of the fish." Hope put a piece in her mouth and chewed. The lemon zing danced on her tongue. "Try it?"

"No, thanks, I'm happy with this."

Dinner was completed, and it was time for them to cut the cake. Hope was absolutely thrilled with the two-tiered ivory cake with orange and rust sugar flowers and green petals. She put her hand on the large silver knife, and Dylan placed his atop. The knife slid through the cake like silk. Rich chocolate wafted from the piece placed on their plate.

Small bites were exchanged, and the milk chocolate pleased her along with the coffee-flavored ganache filling. "Do you like it?"

"We'll be taking the rest of this home."

She laughed, as the quartet played some more classical tunes. Several people took to the small wooden square to dance. "I can't believe it."

"What?"

"Grace and Logan are dancing."

Dylan held his fork near his lips. "They're having fun."

"Look how close he's holding her. It's like he's familiar with my sister."

"When we get back from our trip. You can question her."

"I will." Hope satisfied herself with another bite of the amazing cake.

As the reception ended, their family came by for more well-wishes and hugs.

"I am so thrilled, honey. For the both of you." Her parents hugged her and Dylan. "Text us before you fly to Paris."

"We will."

Grace and Logan came up last after Dylan's parents and their siblings had left.

"Can I stay in your house while you're gone?" Grace looked at the newlyweds.

"You have school."

"Fall break. I'll clean and everything."

Hope wasn't sure of what everything meant, but she could tell how much Grace wanted to stay by her expression. "Is it okay? She can stay in your, um, our guest room."

"That's fine by me. Logan, are you going to keep her company?"

"Now and then."

Grace's mouth set in a firm line.

"I'm kidding. I'll feed Spartacus."

"Who's that?"

Logan smiled at Grace. "You'll meet him soon."

"Come over here." Dylan took her hand and they walked to

the orange flower where their love bloomed. "Don't worry about them. We have our life to live, Mrs. Gaines. We can be nosy later."

Under the bower of the arced flower, the new Mr. and Mrs. shared a kiss in the place where their love bloomed. Hope's journey to find both a life to treasure and her one love had been fulfilled.

The End

ABOUT THE AUTHOR

Stacy T. Simmons writes uplifting fiction that delights the reader's romantic sensibilities. Thirty-four years of marital bliss is a great contributor. She is a mom of two grown children, and she and her family have a menagerie of pets she likes to call "Noah's Ark." You can find her working on her next manuscript with a piece of dark chocolate and a cup of coffee nearby. She loves to connect with her readers via her website at www.stacytsimmonsauthor.com

facebook.com/Author-Stacy-T-Simmons-103608105545337
twitter.com/stacytsimmons
instagram.com/stacy.t.simmons
amazon.com/author/stacytsimmons

ALSO BY STACY T. SIMMONS

Briar Creek Love Series

A Promise for Faith (Book One)

A Journey for Hope (Book Two)

Collections

Keeping Christmas Volume Two

LOVE IS ABLOOM: MATCHMAKER IN 3B PART TWO

A JOURNEY FOR HOPE BONUS SHORT STORY!

STACY T. SIMMONS

"Flowers appear on the earth; the season of singing has come, the cooing of doves is heard in our land." -Song of Solomon 2:12 NIV

"If you look the right way, you can see that the whole world is a garden."
-Frances Hodgson Burnett

CHAPTER ONE

"He loves me, he loves me not." Shelby Thomas sighed and followed the vocal trail of sadness to the rear of the floral shop. Her best friend, and assistant manager Phoebe plucked the drooping petals of a tired daisy into the trash.

"Phoebes." Shelby laid a hand on her friend's back. "What's wrong?"

"Tristan texted." Her friend plucked the last petal and tossed the stem in the trashcan. "According to him, we're no longer dating ."

"I'm sorry." Like a prick from a rose thorn, Shelby felt her friend's pain. "He's missing out. You're a super person." It didn't seem right to remind her bestie that he was her second boyfriend in less than three months. "You'll find the right one, in time."

Phoebe swept an electric red curl from an eye and declared, "I thought he was it."

Shelby hugged her friend, "Will you help with the last of the Mother's Day arrangements? We have several orders we need to finish." Shelby gently reminded her. "Customers will pick them up tomorrow."

"Sure. I'll take the next order."

"I've got it ready on the screen." Shelby pointed to the Park Avenue order blinking on the workspace counter. "Mr. Smithson's getting his usual for his wife."

"He gets the same one every year. Can we mix it up a little?" Phoebe questioned.

"No. There are probably a hundred other florists here in New York City. He's an important customer. Although he's a man of little change from what we've seen over the last three years." Shelby giggled. "He probably schedules their dinnertime and breakfasts."

"Bor-ing." Phoebe declared. "Give me a man who's adventurous, handsome, and unpredictable."

Shelby retrieved a bundle of soft pink Ranunculus from the refrigerator and ran a gentle finger over the petals before giving them to her friend. "Not me. I like order, predictability."

Phoebe pointed the bundle toward Shelby. "We're best friends because you and I are opposites. What I wouldn't do to see you with a male form of me. Fun. Slightly messy."

The bell buzzed up front. "I see where this is going. I have enough to do running my floral shop." Shelby turned to leave the workroom. She looked over a shoulder and declared, "There's no need for any man. At least anytime soon."

She heard her friend's laugh as she made her way to the front. Shelby tucked a piece of hair behind her ear and eyed the shop. A tall man stood facing the refrigerated case at the far end of the store. "Can I help you?"

He didn't answer. She raised her voice. "How can I help you?"

The man jabbed a finger toward an ear. When he came closer, then she could see he was the new visitor to her church group, and that his Bluetooth glowed in his left ear. What was his name? She tried to remember. Nothing. Unnamed man kept talking to the caller. Shelby tapped a foot, and slowly exhaled.

A bit later, the man spoke. "Sorry, new client. I need some flowers for Mother's Day. Am I too late?"

She calculated the late hours they'd need to undertake to finish the current orders and coerced a smile to her lips. "No. What does she like?"

"Mom things. Pinks, roses, things like that." He exhaled. "Can I get it in the morning? I'm picking her up from the airport at noon."

"Sure." She extended the iPad to him. "Would you please fill out the order form?"

He returned the unfilled form blinking on the iPad and waved a hand in front of him as his phone screen glowed. "I need to take this, I'll be by around nine thirty to pick it up. He rattled off his last name and phone number." The man clicked on his Bluetooth and spoke to the caller as he walked to the exit.

"Don't you want to tell me about—" Shelby yelled as the door closed in answer, with rapid typing, the last name and phone number were entered on the screen. She marched to the back of the store and stood near Phoebe.

Phoebe's eyes widened. "You have that I'm-going-to-yell look. What happened? It didn't take long."

"His Highness ordered flowers for his mom." Shelby took the scissors from the worktable and picked up a rose to put in the bouquet Phoebe worked on. "He barely had time to say three words."

"Give me those." Phoebe took the shears from her hand. "You're bleeding. You'll get it on my flowers. He sounds like a Grade-A louse."

"I'm pleading the fifth. He was in our group last week, can't remember his name." She glanced at her hand as red appeared on a finger, Shelby put the flower down and grabbed a paper towel from the sink area. "I never do this. How clumsy."

"What did he order?" Phoebe stopped snipping. "I want to see."

"He left before we chose any flowers, because he had a phone call." She lifted the paper towel to see if her wound had stopped bleeding. A throb followed as the air hit it and Phoebe wrapped a bandage around her finger. "Thanks."

"Welcome. Going back to the customer, he might not like the order."

"I don't think he'll notice. He's coming by before ten to pick it up. He said his mom likes pink and roses." She eyed the array of flowers in the refrigerators. "We've got enough of a variety to suit his royalty."

Phoebe lightly pushed her back. "Go take a coffee break. Come back when you're more. . human."

She whipped her head around and eyed her friend. "I'm fine."

"You're not. Can you fix me a coffee too? Espresso, no milk."

"I'll go. Be back in a bit."

"Nope. At least fifteen minutes. That gives me enough time to finish this order and then take my coffee break."

Shelby frowned and went to the tiny breakroom. As soon as the coffee reached her mouth, her mood lifted. *I can get through this day. Lord, please help me not to be ill tempered tomorrow when that man shows up. Forgive me for my crabbiness.* She hoped tonight would move quickly and tomorrow would be a better day. After she'd seen "His Highness" again and he was gone, it would be.

As the taxi driver coasted to a stop, Blake Knowles grabbed his things and put the Bluetooth in his leather work bag. Enough chatter for one day. He alighted from the car and waved to the doorman for his apartment high-rise.

"Hello, Mr. Knowles. Good night, isn't it?" The navy suited doorman asked.

"It is, George." Blake's grin crossed his face. "Have a good one."

George opened the door and smiled. "Thank you. You as well."

Blake entered the building and headed to the elevator, where the lit elevator panel alerted him that someone was descending. He shifted his bag to the other hand and waited. Soon the elevator dinged and the doors opened. A trim woman stepped onto the lobby floor. Blake's smile was immediate. "Good evening, Mrs. Carlucci. How are you doing?"

She tapped a pink fingernail on his arm. "I'm doing well, how're you?"

"Great, thanks. My mother's coming from Austin to visit tomorrow."

"That's wonderful. I hate to chat and leave, but I need to get to Blooms before they close. It's my cousin Gina's birthday party tonight. They do the most beautiful flower arrangements in the city."

"Blooms is a very nice place."

"Especially the owner, Shelby. She's such a great young lady." Rose smiled. "Remember, Wednesday is our small group dinner at mine and Harry's place. I'm cooking manicotti. Will you and your mom come?"

"She's having dinner Wednesday with a college friend."

"Then I'll see you at 6:30pm." Rose stepped away from Blake. "Have a good night."

"You as well. Happy Mother's Day tomorrow." Blake got into the elevator and pushed the button for the fourth floor, happy the crotchety elevator worked. It had a mind of its own most days. With a small lurch, the elevator carried him homeward. He was soon in his one-bedroom place and seated near the television, a store-bought dinner reheated and ready to enjoy. His mind went back to the florists visit, and he felt a ping of remorse at how short he was with her. Flipping through the streaming channels, he found a spy movie to watch, happy the focus wouldn't be on the sad dinner he consumed. Why didn't he learn to cook when he lived at home some years earlier? Maybe his mother could teach him a few things while she was here. He was looking forward to Mrs. Carlucci's cooking next week—she cooked at an expert level. He glanced down at his pitiful dinner and sighed, putting it on the side table. Blake smiled at the thought of meeting his mother tomorrow and presenting her with the flowers.

~

Early the next morning, Shelby unlocked the door to Blooms, and pushed it open wide with a hip. Her travel mug jostled and matcha tea spilled on the floor. She stepped over the mess and put her things on the shelf in the back. Retrieving a towel from the breakroom, Shelby wiped the floor and stood to face his highness. "I'll be with you in a bit, come in." By the time he'd reached the counter, she'd put the dirty towel away and found his order in the back cooler. Smiling, she put it on the counter. "We used roses and a lot of pink like you said."

His wide smile caused a trip in her breath. She glanced away before looking back toward him.

"This is pretty, it looks like my mother." He ran a hand over his chin. "Mrs. Carlucci is right, you do create the best arrangements in the city."

"Thanks." She rang up the order. "Rose is so sweet, so is Harry."

"Agreed. They were the first neighbors I met when I moved from Austin." Blake handed a credit card to her. "Great people."

"They are," Shelby told him the total before taking his card. "Her cooking is as wonderful as she is."

"She's making manicotti for small group next week." Blake grinned. "Are you going?"

"Planning on it." Shelby smiled wistfully and slipped a glance at his name. Blake Knowles. Nice to meet you. "I wish I could cook like that."

"Me too." Blake held the flower vase in his hands. "Thanks for this, Shelby. See you next week."

"Have a good visit with your mom. Bye." Shelby waved, surprise shot through her at the niceness of the man and how he recalled her name. Maybe he wasn't uppity like she'd thought, but more down to earth.

Phoebe entered the store and proclaimed in a voice loud enough to be heard over the Hudson River into New Jersey, "Was that 'His Highness?'"

Shelby nodded. "Don't call him that. I know, I did. I feel guilty, he's from my small group at church. Barely said anything a few weeks ago."

"With ice blue eyes, and dark hair." Phoebe winked. "Who cares? Besides, he's more like 'His Hotness' did he like the flowers?"

"He did."

"Good." Phoebe pivoted toward the back room. "I wouldn't mind him being a repeat customer. In fact, is there room in your small group for one more?"

Her friend's boldness never failed to surprise Shelby. "It'd be good for business, and I'm not sure. Harry and Rose Carlucci are leaders. "Let's get all the orders to the front refrigerators. The Mother's Day rush is about to begin, and we need to get prepped."

"I'm ready. I've already had two cold brew coffees. There's enough caffeine in me for a few hours work."

Shelby laughed. "Come on."

The friends hurried to prepare as the next few customers came into the store. Shelby assisted all the customers as Phoebe ferried the orders to them. She took a quick sip of her now cold matcha before the next swarm came buzzing in. A springtime scent akin to new mown grass tickled her nose as she swallowed and frowned. *I thought lemon would make it taste better, but I was mistaken.* Shelby went to put the nasty concoction on the shelf in the workroom.

"Don't like it?" Phoebe breezed past her and grabbed the mug and took a long sip. "This stuff reminds me of the contents of bags from summer yardwork while growing up. Disgusting!" Her friend gave it back to her. "I'll stick with raspberry herbal tea or coffee."

"Me too, sad thing is I bought it thinking it'd be healthy and taste good." Shelby lifted one shoulder as she pointed to the tin behind her. "I can't imagine anyone actually likes it." She stepped back into the front of the shop.

"Hello you two," a woman voiced from a nearby refrigerator. "I overheard your conversation. What doesn't anyone like?" Rose patted her bright blonde hair and grinned. "I wasn't trying to be nosey."

"What a treat to see you two days in a row." Shelby walked over and hugged the sweet mature woman. "We're talking about matcha."

"Watcha? Is it that Wizard of Oz colored tea?" Rose's mouth puckered for a moment before she continued. "Harry got some for me at the corner mart, we both tried it and gave it away to a neighbor. He likes it."

Shelby hid her smile behind an arrangement she moved to another spot, Rose Carlucci's mispronunciations were endearing. "He can have mine."

"I'll let Blake know, he said he ordered flowers from you yesterday." Rose's eyebrows drew toward her brow. "You know he's single. Good job. Are you looking for anyone?"

"Me?" Shelby moved to the refrigerator and opened the door, the cool air restored her over-warm cheeks. "Not really, I don't have time for that, this business is only a year old. Did you need flowers today too, Rose?"

"I did, gotta have a nice table for family dinner. Are you coming to small group dinner next week? It'll be manicotti. Blake said he's going."

Phoebe came and stood beside Shelby. "She's coming, thank you."

"You can come too, Phoebe." Rose held out a hand in front of her. "I'll see you two, Wednesday. Happy I can put a bit of meat on your bones," Rose chortled.

Her best friend shook her head. "Shoot. I start night classes on Wednesday. Can't come, thank you though."

Shelby looked at her friend and saw a sparkle in Phoebe's eyes as she raised her eyebrows. She'd deal with her friend later as more customers were arriving for pickups.

The early May night was crisp and cool, Shelby gathered her jacket around her as she walked the three blocks to the Carlucci's apartment building. She'd not found a polite way to turn down the small group dinner invitation, as she didn't want to hurt her friend's feelings. Shelby glanced at the bright yellow tulips wrapped in bloom paper that she held in her hand. By accident, she'd coordinated with the flowers as her top peeking from the navy jacket was also a sunshine yellow. A smiling gentleman greeted her at the building door and let her in. "Thank you."

She passed the larger part of the lobby and pressed the elevator call button. It creaked and groaned like a granny's rocker as the doors opened. Shelby glanced around to see if anyone rode with her in case it broke down. No one else entered the elevator. With a quick prayer, she pressed the button to the fourth floor as the arthritic doors shut. Once she reached the floor, she looked heavenward and thanked the Lord for his deliverance. A few steps away was their apartment—3B.

When she knocked, the door swung open. A tall smiling man greeted her. "Shelby, welcome, come in."

"Hello, Harry, it's great to see you. Thank you for having me over." She pressed a quick kiss to his round cheek and entered. The scents of garlic and spices made her stomach rumble.

"Rose is in the kitchen, I'm supposed to do door duty." He grinned.

"I'll help." She walked down the hallway and followed the bright lights to the galley kitchen. "Hi, these are for you." Shelby offered the large bouquet to her friend.

"Thank you." Rose wiped her hands on her black and red checked apron. "They are gorgeous. Have a seat, I'll pour a tea for you." She gestured to the nook in the corner of the kitchen.

She slid into the wooden bench and smiled. A peace blanketed her. Food was her love language. "It smells divine."

"I hope so, Harry started the sauce yesterday. My US History students didn't do so well on their tests, I had a lot of emails to send," Rose sighed.

"Your kids are so fortunate to have you."

"Thanks, it's me who is the lucky one." Rose handed her a glass of tea with a lemon wedge on the side. "In a few more years, I'll retire. I'm gonna miss teaching."

The doorbell sounded. Shelby's middle began to tighten, unsure if Blake was coming to dinner.

By the time Rose had checked on the manicotti in the oven, two male voices drew closer to the kitchen. Harry entered and was followed by a person a half head taller behind the kind older gentleman. Shelby raised the glass to her lips and took a quick sip.

"Blake, glad you're here." Rose patted the man's shoulder. "You know Shelby."

Blake smiled before speaking. "Hello, Shelby."

"Hi." Her pulse ricocheted in her veins, she tightened her

grip on the glass, the cold sweat on the glass calmed her. "Where are the Collins and Moores?"

Silence hovered in the breadbox sized kitchen. She noticed Rose's rapt attention to her already baked bread.

Harry blurted. "Couldn't come, it's a surprise that both couples couldn't make it."

Rose kept fiddling with the bread. "Mmhmm."

"Next time. Blake, did your mom like the flowers?" Shelby offered.

He nodded. "Loved them, she wanted to be here tonight, but she's having dinner with her old college roommate and her husband."

Rose waved a hand in the air. "Since we don't have any other people here tonight, there will be plenty for you to take home, and you too, Shelby. Such a sad thing that they couldn't join us."

Harry snorted. "Isn't it surprising?"

"Help me with the manicotti, Harry." Rose handed the fire engine red potholders to her husband. "They might burn. We'll bring the food out. Go and have a seat at the table."

Shelby led the way to the dining table in the adjacent room and sat, and Blake followed suit. She asked Blake, who sat across from her, "Are you having a good time with your mom?"

"I am, it's a real thrill for her to be in New York City. Austin is a big city too, but not nearly as large as this," Blake laughed. "She couldn't understand all the food vendors along the streets. Back in Texas, there are food truck parks to grab snacks or lunch."

"I've not been to Texas. Does everyone have there have horses?"

Blake shook his head. "No, the only horsepower me or my family own are cars."

"I'm confused. Why do TV shows make it out to be the norm?"

He shrugged. "Stereotypes."

Shelby questioned again, "But you do have a cowboy hat and boots?"

"In the past I've worn them, I gave mine to a younger cousin," Blake's lips moved upward for a second before he continued, "I figured if I wore them here, I'd be a source of laughter."

"Good call. Do you even like country music?"

"It's okay, I prefer jazz."

Thrills ribboned inside her. "Me too."

Before either could speak, Rose and Harry arrived at the table with their arms full of manicotti, salad, and breadsticks. Shelby sniffed the garlic-infused air and sighed. "I can't wait to try it."

"It's worth all the effort my Rosie puts into it." Harry beamed.

The older couple made eye contact with one another and smiled.

Rose ran a hand along her husband's jaw. "Har, thanks."

Shelby found it endearing to see the tall gentleman's cheeks pink slightly.

Once Harry had said a prayer over dinner, she eyed the large, tossed salad near Blake. "Would you please pass the salad?" Shelby took the bowl from Blake. "Thanks." After heaping it on her salad plate, the other dinner components followed. "Rose, this smells so good. I wish I could cook like you."

Rose smiled. "Need a cooking lesson? I'm teaching some at the church the next few Saturdays. You and Blake should come."

"I need some, thanks Rose." Blake smiled and Shelby noticed his plate was half full already. "This is the best cooking I've had since last time you brought the cheesecake by when I moved in."

"Glad you like it. I'll look forward to seeing you two at church. Sign up on the website. Last time I checked the Rose's Kitchen and Fellowships were filling up fast."

"I might need to book one to eat lunch that day." Harry chuckled. "My Rosie's a blessing to my heart and waist." His hand went to his contented husband-sized midsection.

After the last of the meal was enjoyed, Shelby and Blake offered to help put the dishes in the washer and put up the food.

Rose ferried the manicotti to the kitchen as Shelby followed. "Don't worry about it, thank you though. Harry and I will get them. After this many years of marriage we work well together in the kitchen." She spooned the leftovers into several containers. "You can get the bread from the table, and I'll get the wrap ready. Seems the men are in there talking. That Blake is a great young man."

"Sure," she retrieved the basket from the table, the two men were deep in conversation and returned to the kitchen. "Still talking. I thought it would be us."

"Harry loves to chat. He keeps us at church longer after the service than I do, and that's something." Rose's ebullient laugh made Shelby smile.

"You two are a match."

"Thank you, we are. My aunt fixed us up when we were in our early twenties. Matchmaking runs in my family." Rose snapped the cover over the salad and put it in the fridge. "A few years ago, I introduced the cutest couple, Faith and my stock-broker Caleb. They now live in North Carolina with his son, and they have their own little one together on the way."

Rose's words warmed her heart. It felt like she'd heard one of her romance storylines in a novel. "What a story. You need to write it down."

"I'm a history teacher. The Lord gave me a love of our world through events, not words." Rose packed the leftovers into two bags. "Maybe I'll tell it to someone who likes it enough to write it down. Who knows?"

"That would be wonderful, I'd read it." Shelby eyed the clock on the oven, an hour before her usual bedtime. "Rose, this has been a fantastic night, thank you so much." She kissed her friend's cheek. It smelled of flowers and powder. "I'm going to enjoy this." The bag was heavy as she picked it up.

Blake and Harry entered the kitchen.

"We were in there talking, let me do the rest Rosie." Harry moved next to his wife and took the sponge from her hands. "So glad you both were here. What a good night."

"It was. Thank you, Rose and Harry." Blake smiled.

"Don't forget your leftovers, and the both of you, sign up for Saturday's class. It's pasta making," Rose reminded them.

"I will." Shelby held the heavy bag tighter. "Are you going Blake?"

"Who could turn down the invitation? This was delicious. I'll be there."

"Good. We're so happy you two came over. Next time everyone will be together." Rose hugged Shelby. "See you soon, honey. Have a good week."

She returned the hug. "Thank you, I hope you and Harry do too. And Blake." Silly, you sound like a sappy greeting card commercial. Her ear tips burned. "Bye." Shelby exited through the door Harry held open.

"Wait for me, Shelby." Blake asked. "I'll walk you home."

"You don't have to," She pressed the elevator button. "It's pretty safe in our neighborhood."

Blake walked behind her into the elevator. "I wanted to walk you home so we can talk more. I enjoyed our talk about Central Park at dinner. How do you know so much about it?"

"I like to walk through it when I get a break. What Jesus has created is gorgeous." She held back a sigh and walked from the elevator. "The flowers, green leaves, remind me of spring back home in Pittsford."

"Where's that?"

"About eight hours east of here. There are farms, friendly

people, and the Erie Canal even runs through the town. It's beautiful." She smiled as the doorperson held it open for them.

"It sounds like a great place."

"I'd like to move back there someday. Not anytime soon because of the shop, but all my family is there." She pulled a strand of hair that crossed her face.

"Mine's all in Austin. It's kind of strange living in a city by myself. I like living here, but I've heard the snow is brutal."

The pair dodged a quick-walking pedestrian laden down with grocery bags.

"Get heavy duty boots, they come in handy and a big winter coat." She reached out a hand to pat his arm but pulled it back slingshot fast. "Does Austin get in the negative degrees?"

"In the teens occasionally, I'd better look into those things before winter comes."

She shook her head. "Before fall, we get a taste of winter sometimes earlier than expected," Shelby instructed and pointed to a door to their left. "It's my building. The walk was so sweet, thanks. Will I see you Saturday?"

"I'm going. My sad dinners are enough to make me want to learn to cook. That and good company."

Silence hovered between them.

"I'd better get in and put this in the fridge."

Blake waved. "Night, see you in a few."

As the doorman pulled the door open, she whisked through it. The cold air conditioning iced her face, Shelby picked up her steps. Once inside her apartment, she stored the food in the refrigerator and folded the bag to save to give back to Rose. A crinkling noise sounded, she opened the bag and ran a hand along the bottom. The soft feel of paper met her fingers, Shelby and *pulled out a folded note.*

Shelby, make sure Blake gets to the cooking class. He looks like he needs a friend, you are a sweet young woman, and could help him get used to the city. I'll save two spots near me at the table. Hugs, your meddlesome friend, Rose.

She took a magnet from the side of her fridge and put the note front and center on the stainless-steel door. Rose is a treasure. Shelby grinned and went to ready for bed. Her Bible and then, a romance novel needed her attention. She was excited for Saturday and to learn how to cook something real, not fake tasting. And, to develop a friendship with the handsome, nice Texan.

Saturday morning, Blake went to his fridge to fix breakfast. He groaned. There was exactly one egg and half a plain bagel. With some effort, he had created a misshapen egg and bagel sandwich and brewed a strong cup of coffee. He sat at his two-seat table and opened his Bible app to read his morning scripture. "Behold, how good and pleasant it is when brothers dwell in unity!" Hmm, Psalm 133:1 seems to be applicable to today. Except today is with kind Rose and a beautiful woman, another rose named Shelby. He wiped his hand over his face and pushed from the table. The last thing his busy schedule could handle were dates. He'd not had one for over six months before he moved to NYC. A long, dry, dating desert. Soon, Blake had showered and dressed. He eyed himself in the mirror and ran a comb through his hair, then flexed his muscles. Small humps formed beneath the cotton. He needed to work out more. He headed to the elevator a short time after flexing and walked out into the bright May morning. Four Knish stands and two "designer" bag stalls into his walk, he had a hand on the church fellowship hall door.

"Good morning, Blake." A feminine voice greeted.

Shelby wore a bright green dress which hit above her knees. Her legs looked great. The bright smile she wore made his mouth tilt upward. "You look amazing, I mean, good morning." Not cool. She's a friend. Shelby can be a smart, beautiful, acquaintance. Blake opened the door. "After you."

She walked beside him and smiled. His middle tightened. A scent of berries and a feminine spice followed her. He wanted to sniff the air but didn't relish the thought of getting caught. He hurried to catch up to her. "Ready to cook?"

"I'm so excited. If I can do this, I'll be able to make dinner for friends and family. Someone else always makes it."

Both entered the large church kitchen.

Rose was standing at the head of the long island and six people were seated around it. "Welcome, come on in. You two will be over here." She pointed to two places to her right. "There's one more person we're expecting." Their instructor friend went over to the refrigerator and brought several cartons of eggs to the island.

Harry walked over to his wife and brushed her cheek with a kiss.

"We're ready." Rose clapped her hands and grinned. "Harry's here. Let's all introduce ourselves."

The group exchanged names and what they hoped to gain from the lesson.

"I don't want to eat takeout every night or a microwave dinner. One's too expensive and the other is awful." Blake's comment earned a few nods and chuckles from some people.

"I want to be able to have people over and not be embarrassed by my lack of skills." Shelby stated.

Blake noticed her pink cheeks as she spoke, he felt a sharp poke in his heart at her admission. She's so genuine and open. He whispered to her, "Me too. I'm glad you said that."

Shelby's smile was adorable, Blake focused his attention on Rose who instructed them to measure the flour.

"Now put it in front of you after you have it all measured out. Then put a well in the middle, like a bird nest."

The group followed her instructions. Blake slipped a glance at the couple next to him, their "nest" looked perfectly shaped. He began to readjust his flour, and Rose marched ahead with the instructions.

"Add your eggs, oil and salt," Shelby instructed. "Don't worry, look at mine, it's horrible."

When he glanced at her mixture, it reminded him of a piece of modern art he'd seen at the Guggenheim Museum. "Not bad." Blake put the ingredients inside and mimicked Rose's gentle hand motions regarding the mixing.

While waiting for the dough to rest, the group chatted. He was happy to hear some of the others hadn't been born in the city either. An older married couple finished each other's sentences. Does everyone do this? He listened to Rose and Harry who were standing beside him.

"Harry, what's that little city outside Morristown in New Jersey? You know the one we went to and they had the great fish place?"

"You mean Flanders. It was good. Nice little town."

"It was. Have you two ever been to New Jersey?"

"Not me." Blake shook his head.

"I haven't either." Shelby seconded.

"You ought to visit sometime. There are some charming small towns closer to us," Rose stated. "Morristown has George Washington's winter home, it's fascinating."

"Rosie, honey, not everyone breathes history like you. Isn't it time to do the rest of the dough?"

Rose's shoulders fell. "I get lost in history." She ran a hand over her husband's cheek. "Thanks, sweetie. He always keeps me stay down to earth, he's, my gyro."

"Welcome."

Shelby didn't meet Blake's glance at their friends 'Roseism.' Rose Carlucci was precious, and a great matchmaker as well.

With more careful direction, the pasta was ready to be rolled out. Blake held the long rolling pin in his hands and began to press the dough down.

"I can't get it." Shelby muttered beside him.

He covered her hands with his. "Let me help. Once you press into it, it softens." Blake resisted the urge to hold his hands over her soft ones longer. "You've got it."

"Thanks so much."

"Welcome."

When it came down to putting the pasta into the roller, Rose told them to work together. As the thick pasta pressed through the roller, it became thinner.

"I'll catch your pasta sheet." Shelby laid out her hands beside his. "I had no clue this would be so fun."

"Me neither, I was worried about how bad I'd be at it. This looks like pasta."

"Because it is. Good work." Rose tapped his shoulders and went to the next couple, giving praise to everyone around the island.

Soon, both dough balls were transformed to thin noodles, cooked in boiling water, and enjoyed with some green spices and oil.

At the close of the lesson, Rose issued a challenge. "You need to make the pasta yourself or with a friend sometime in the next week and send me a photo." She held up a finger. "The best-looking pasta wins. It's dinner for two at my nephew's restaurant, Antonio's."

"I love that place." Shelby nudged Blake's arm. "Want to join together to win?"

Surprise warmed Blake. "Sure. We made a pretty good team today." He walked his trash to the can along with Shelby's.

"I think so too." She carried the dirty rolling pins to the sink.

Everyone made the church kitchen clean as they worked together. Several people exclaimed they'd take all of Rose's cooking classes. Blake didn't miss his friend's broad smile.

Before leaving, Rose hugged everyone and the duo continued their cooking plans as they walked back to their homes.

Shelby asked. "Does Friday or Saturday work for you?"

He contemplated his schedule, the workload was intense right now with a new client needing more time than he'd originally thought. "Saturday. Friday's a late night of work."

"I understand, sometimes Phoebe and I work late nights too. Come over to my place after lunch, say two? We'll have time to make several batches and see which one looks the best."

"I thought I was an uber-planner. You might be more of one than me." He looked at Shelby's profile, it was dainty without being model perfect. "Don't tell me you have a schedule for your schedule?"

"No. I'm not that bad. My calendar is synced to my home and work schedules. Gosh, that sounds bad."

"Do you ever think of pitching the thing, throwing it in the proverbial trash. Having freedom?"

Shelby sighed. "Not now. I've not had a vacation in um. . .three years. Can't find time for it."

"You need a day off. No schedule. Do what you want." Blake resisted the urge to check his phone as it vibrated in his pocket. "I'd like one."

"Sometime. I've never been to the shore in New Jersey or to the beaches on Long Island. It'd be so great."

He slowed down, the surprise arrowed through him. He found his lips saying, "I'll take you to the beach soon, for the day. No schedule, just down time."

"I'd like that. Can I put it on my planner?"

"Funny. We'll both leave ours at home."

"Good, mine's more expensive than my shoes. Crazy, huh?" Shelby laughed.

"No. A coworker convinced me to get a leather-bound one. By the time I walked out of the store, my charge card had no more spending power." He joined her in laughter and they stopped in front of her apartment.

"See you Saturday." Blake wanted to hug her but kept his arms to his sides.

"Until then. Apartment 5A. I'll have all the things we need for the pasta."

Saturday would be fun. A pretty lady and some hopefully good food. Blake shot a prayer to Heaven and thanked the Lord for a new friend.

Flicking through her closet, Shelby pulled out two different outfits. What do you wear when cooking with a friend? She snapped photos and sent them to Phoebe for her review. Soon, her phone buzzed. She read the text.

"Shel, why do you care what you look like with Blake? Besides, it's Saturday and I'm at brunch with my new guy friend."

"We have to send in a photo to Rose." Weak excuse, be real. Shelby added to the message. "I want to look cute, is there anything wrong with that?"

"No, I thought you were friends. Do you like him?"

Her heart tripped several beats. She exhaled, then typed, "I wouldn't mind dating him. Let me know how your date goes later." Shelby closed her eyes not wanting to see the results of her admission. Finding the resolve to see, she opened her eyes and read the response.

"He's a good guy from what you said about dinner and the cooking lesson. I approve."

She leaned against the dresser and smiled. "I was hoping you would. Your advice means a lot to me." They'd been through a great deal together in the years since the shop had opened. Phoebe had become like a second sister to her.

"Go get changed. Tell me about all the details when you can and I'll tell you mine. Love you."

"Deal. Love you too." Shelby sent a hug emoji after the words. She walked back to the bed and plucked the blue embroidered dress off the bed. It reminded her of the trip to Mexico she'd taken with her family after her floral design graduation. She slid her feet into low silver sandals and put silver hoops in her ears. On her dresser, the silver bangles she often wore cried out to take residence on her arm, but they'd get dirty. Shelby fluffed her hair and slid on a light pink gloss to match some of the colors in the dress. She awaited his arrival as butterflies glided in her midsection. The seconds passed in slow motion.

Cutting the quiet, the doorbell rang and she sprinted from the bedroom to answer it her lips raised in happiness. Once the door swung open, Shelby's smile widened. "Hi, come on in."

"Hello, how are you?" Blake crossed the threshold, a shower-fresh scent tickled her nose. "You look great."

"Doing well, thanks, ready to win the contest?" She closed the door behind her. "Can I fix anything for you while we cook?"

"Water, please. It's warmer than I thought out there."

"One water." Getting the glass from the cabinet, she quickly got his drink and handed it to him.

He smiled in thanks and began to drink.

Her eyes skimmed his jawline. To her delight, it was smooth shaven. The last guy she'd dated let his winter wool grow in, and he'd looked practically paleolithic by Christmastime. "Need any more?"

Blake set the glass on the counter. "No, thanks. Maybe later. Ready to start the dough?"

"Of course. The winning dough, right?"

"We'll see."

Shelby was thankful she'd taken the extra time to clean the

countertops after work. A busy life creates a chaotic kitchen, even if it rarely includes cooking. She read the directions aloud from last Saturday's class, and Blake followed them step-by-step. Soon the mixture was incorporated and the dough needed to rest. "I'll put the timer on, we can go in the family room and talk, if you'd like."

They both found spots on the small sofa and side chair. Shelby brushed a sprinkling of flour off her dress with the back of a hand.

"That color looks great. Blue's my favorite."

"Oh, you're sweet, thanks. So, how was your week?" She ran a finger along the arm of the seat while awaiting his reply.

"Challenging, the new client is demanding. I've been glad to have some downtime today because of it. And, to see you."

Warmth flooded inside her. "I'm happy to see you too." She fought the urge to lean closer to him. "Last Saturday was fun. I need that in my life."

"Me too." Blake leaned forward putting his hands on his knees. "You make things more special. Wait, that sounded so ridiculous."

As she shook her head her hair spilled over a shoulder. Blake brushed it back with his fingers, and her lungs froze. Every heartbeat was like a call to him to come closer. With mere inches between them, she could see the tiny lines fanning from his eyes. They deepened she noted, and it caused her joy. She inched her face closer to his, not daring to make the first move. As their lips joined, he put an arm around her shoulders.

The blaring buzzer fizzled any further romantic gestures. They sat back in their seats. She rose and Blake followed her to the kitchen.

"Now I'm not so interested in winning." Blake shrugged. "I'd rather invest more time in conversation and kisses."

"Me too." She ran a finger over her lips. "If we win the contest, we can do one of them over dinner."

Blake leaned into the counter. "Maybe both when I take you home after."

Shelby unwrapped the dough, her hands shook from the unexpected excitement. "That sounds like the perfect date."

His warm hand covered hers. "I rushed things, we haven't even dated."

"I wanted that kiss. Can we consider last week our first date, that way we're already onto our second?"

"Happy second date." Blake brushed a quick kiss across her lips and took his hand away from hers.

"Glad you agree. We'd better get to rolling this out." Finding the rolling pin in a nearby cabinet, she floured the roller. "Since you're better at this than me, can you, do it?"

"I'm game." He took the rolling pin and began to roll the dough. She enjoyed the muscles flexing at the end of his polo shirt sleeve. "It's ready to be divided."

"Hmm? I must've zoned for a bit. Not enough coffee today." No more glances. Pay attention. The next steps were finished in the prep quickly. "Who will feed the dough through and who will catch it?"

"I'll feed." Blake moved behind the stand mixer.

"Then, I'll catch it." Cranking her trusty stand mixer on, they began the numerous parts to working the dough. She caught the long stream with both hands, which earned a large smile from Blake. After a few more steps, the bands of pasta were cut into long, slender strands. She took some photos of the pasta they'd made. "We did a pretty good job."

Blake nodded. "We might have a chance to win."

Shelby turned up the heat on the stove as they waited for the water to boil. "Rose really likes us. She might choose our pasta."

"I believe she'll be impartial." He crossed his arms over his chest. "It looks better than some I've had at restaurants."

"Me too." Her hair dangled over a warm cheek as she checked the pot, small bubbles danced at the bottom. Warm lips brushed over her cheek. Shelby's attention veered from the water. Her heart picked up speed she looked into his smoky green eyes.

"I had to give you a little motivation." Blake's voice was low as he spoke. "And you looked beautiful standing there." He ran a finger over her hair and pushed it back from her face. The cool air prickled the nape of her neck. "I'm sorry. Too soon." He frowned.

"No."

She noticed Blake's frown.

Emotions rose within her, she attempted to say intelligent words. "I mean no, you're not rushing. When we're together it's like I've had you in my life for a while. I do want to continue seeing you."

"I'm relieved, so we'll see where this goes." He ran a finger over Shelby's cheek. "You're beautiful. All that blonde hair, a business brain, a person of faith, and kind. Whether we win or not, I'd say what we have decided is more than a victory to me." Blake's face drew closer to hers. Hot water bubbled from the pot, the eye of the burner sizzled.

"Pasta time." Shelby moved around Blake and picked up the pasta, dropping it into the pot. She stirred it, the swirls in the water were a twin to her emotions. What to say to him? "You are so much more than a great looking guy, the more I get to know you. . .I really enjoy being around you. The first time I met you during small group, I thought you were shy. And, at Blooms you were. . .abrupt."

"Me, shy? Never. I was exhausted that night during small group and in a hurry at your store before Mother's Day."

"And you apologized the next day, which was thoughtful."

"Thanks." He lightly wrapped his arms around her as she continued to man the pot and put his hands atop hers.

Shelby wanted to laugh at how this totally unromantic cooking session could make her knees weak with the addition of Blake. She felt a kiss on the top of her head, so she gave his arm a squeeze, finding it firm and warm. "The pasta should be ready soon."

Blake released his hug, to her disappointment, and stood beside to her.

After lunch, the cleaned up the mess in the kitchen, and sat down on the family room sofa, tired from a busy afternoon.

"Where do you want to go next weekend, if you're free?"

"I am," Shelby agreed. "What'd you have in mind?"

"When we win, dinner at Antonio's." His fingers closed over hers.

She gave them a slight squeeze, and smirked before saying, "I love how confident you are in our cooking ability."

Blake nodded. "I am, the pasta looked better than before. After dinner we could go to a jazz club if you like that kind of music."

"I'd love it. I've not been to one in a long time." She swiveled in the seat to see him better. "Who are some of your favorite artists?"

When Blake began to name some of her beloved artists, she cheered. "Some of mine too. My parents would play jazz music daily, usually during dinner. They loved Charlie Parker and Kenny G. So, it was a big part of my childhood."

"I think that sounds amazing." He twirled a lock of her hair around a finger. Blake turned on a soft jazz song on his phone.

"Good song." Shelby snuggled into his outstretched arm, enjoying the warmth of his side and being near him.

They sat together for a while, several songs played as she ran a finger down his arm. His skin was lightly tan and smooth. When the next one ended, Blake pushed from the sofa. "I don't want to go, but I still need workout, will you walk me to the door?"

She raised her hand and Blake gently pulled her from the seat.

He gathered her in his arms and murmured. "I'll see you at group Wednesday?"

"You will, unless we win the prize. Rose came into the shop the other day and mentioned the dinner reservation was for 7 pm on Wednesday."

Shelby gave his back a quick rub and glanced up at him. "If we don't win, I'll be walking in the direction of your place to get there. Wanna go together?"

He gave her a light squeeze of a hug, and the two headed toward the door.

"I'll be outside the building by 6:30, ready for dinner." Blake's lips found her cheek. "Have a good one, see you in a few days."

"See you." The spot on her cheek felt warm. It'd been nice to sneak another kiss. He's a great kisser.

Blake waved and began to descend downstairs.

Her gaze lingered on his retreating form before she closed the door. The quiet sat uncomfortably within. Shelby picked up her phone from the kitchen table and flicked through her photos. A large grin spread across her face as a photo of Blake sprinkled with flour was on the screen. *We're so compatible. He's a great man.* She locked her phone and plugged it into the charger, like technology, relationships too take some time to come about. Shelby hoped she could be patient.

Sweeping some of the cast off stems and leaves off her shop's floor, Shelby walked faster than normal to the supply closet. "I'm nervous, do you think we'll get chosen to do the Vincent wedding?"

"I'm hoping and praying, it'd be a huge help for us. The wedding party alone will cover the rent for a month or so." Phoebe smiled.

After putting the broom away, she cleaned the countertops. "I'm praying too."

"It's going to work." Her friend took the cloth beside Shelby and helped clean. "We'll get it. Why the rush?" Phoebe questioned, "Wednesday night plans?"

"Mmhmm." She finished the last counter and put the cloth into the laundry bag. "Our consolation prize for the pasta contest. Rose gave us tickets to the new Hugh Jackman Broadway musical."

"I'm jealous." Her friend's gaze roved head-to-toe. "I'll close the shop. You'll want to dress up before you see that handsome man. And I'm not just talking about the hot actor."

"You think he's good looking?"

"Any man who could make Wolverine be second best is truly hot." Phoebe winked. "Go, wear something really cute."

"Blake's nice too." One glance down at her shirt, and Shelby frowned. "Thanks a bunch. Busy days mean messy shirts." She slung her bag over a shoulder and blew her best friend a kiss. "See you tomorrow."

"Have a good time." Phoebe smirked.

"Guaranteed." She waved to her bestie, exited the shop, and arrived at the front doors of her building faster than the subway rapid commuter line. Shelby showered and changed into a blue sleeveless, mid-length dress and ebony flats. After she braided the sides of her hair, she clipped them together on the back of her head. Her phone chimed, and she ran to cut off the alarm's cacophonous melody. With a quick application of makeup, she retrieved her bag and departed. The tepid May evening winds brushed her arms as harried pedestrians flashed past like a New York Jets linebacker. She sighed and kept pace with the flow of traffic. Shelby searched for a thatch of dark hair in the crowd in front of his building.

A deep masculine voice rose above the usual loud noises of the city. "Shelby, I'm over here!"

She switched her focus from a group beside her and glanced in the direction of the voice. Shelby threw a hand in the air and waved. "Coming!" Sidestepping some speed walkers, she played a game of pedestrian Frogger to reach him. "Hi."

"Hello. You look so pretty."

"So do you." *Goodness, what an absolute goof I am.* "I meant handsome. It was a long day."

"Mine too."

They continued to walk and chat. It was as if they were the only two people on the sidewalk, everyone else fell away from Shelby's attention, except Blake. Three blocks later they'd arrived at the Lyric Theatre, the bright marquee lights heralded the title of the show.

As they wound through the milling crowds, Blake kept a hand on the small of her back. She felt safe and secure next to him as the glass-like marble floor was slick underneath her feet. Shelby panned the gorgeous two-story rotunda. "I've not been here before, it's stunning."

"Me neither, it's very nice." Blake grinned and took her hand. "Our seats are on the second floor, and the stairs look slippery. I don't want to see you get hurt."

His words danced inside her. She'd not been on a date with such a kind and protective guy. "Thanks." She squeezed his hand and walked with him upstairs.

Settled into the crimson seats, the chatter surrounding them grew as more attendees filed into the grand theater. They conversed about work and plans for the jazz lounge after the show. "I can't stay out late, even though I'd like to." She shook her head.

"We'll stay long enough to hear a few songs—"

A loud voice intruded over the discretely placed speakers. "Ladies and gentlemen, please silence all electronics. Enjoy the show."

Two hours later, and after many curtain calls, they rose to exit the theater.

"Hugh Jackman was wonderful. This was an absolute dream to me." Shelby grinned and looked up at Blake.

"Me as well, I've not been to a Broadway play before. And, to attend with such a gorgeous woman. It made my night." He brushed a kiss along her cheek before they descended to the main floor via a crowded staircase.

Chill bumps raised on Shelby's arms. She was glad he couldn't see the reaction his kiss gave her. Delicious warmth spread throughout as he kept close contact with her while the crowds surrounding them tried to hurry past.

Beeps and scattered engine noises made Shelby wince as they stepped onto the sidewalk. "You think I'd be used to all the loudness at night. Somehow it still gets me now and then."

"I couldn't sleep well the first few months. Nights in Texas are full of crickets chirping and some emergency sirens once in a while." Blake held out a hand. "This takes noise to a whole other level."

The pair headed north up Broadway to the jazz club and waited in line.

"Did you check to see if there was an entry fee?" Shelby pulled her phone from her bag and opened a search engine.

He shook his head. "No, I didn't know there could be."

Typing the club name into the screen, she soon had an answer. "It's fifty dollars a person to enter if there's a special performer." Shelby pointed to the sign next to them encased in glass along the front wall. "Tonight's a band from New Orleans, there's going to be a charge."

"I should've checked. Can we come back another time?"

She covered her disappointment with a smile. "It's a date. I think Antonio's is around here, we can split an appetizer, or something else."

"I'm up for Italian, thanks for being flexible."

"We'll come here soon." She tugged on his arm. "I'm starving, let's go."

A short walk east of where they had been led them to Antonio's. Blake held the smoky glass door open and Shelby headed inside. Delicious herbaceous scents made her mouth water. A black-suited woman escorted them to a table. A flickering candle and flowers in a crystal vase decorated the white-linen square.

Shelby looked at the menu and pointed to a particular favorite. "They have gnocchi. Do you like it?"

Blake laughed. "I have never had it before, but if you like it, I'll try it."

"You choose the appetizer please."

"I always have caprese salad."

She smiled. "Me too." Shelby reached across the table and took his hand, it was warm and soft. "You have great hands, strong and smooth."

"Thanks, I think."

"I work in water all day, so it makes me self-conscious about whether they are rough, or not." She rolled her eyes. "So, when I feel some that are really nice, I say something."

"Yours are wonderful." His lips briefly touched the back of her hand. "I could hold them every day, all day."

I wish you would. She took a sip of her water instead of answering.

The server arrived and took their order.

A handsome dark-haired man walked to their table. "Good evening, I'm Antonio Bintelli. My Aunt Rose said to give you the VIP treatment. Whatever you'd like is on me tonight."

"Thank you, how did Rose know?"

Antonio laughed. "Uncle Harry came in right after you two arrived for their usual mid-week takeout dinner. Aunt Rose knows everything thanks to my uncle."

"Thank you, she is definitely a wonderful woman."

"And a really good person, she and uncle both." Antonio smiled and spoke to one of his waitstaff. "Excuse me, I'm needed in the kitchen. Nice to meet you two." He walked away with the person, speaking Italian back and forth with them.

"That's amazing." Blake raised an eyebrow. "Rose is one remarkable woman."

"She is." Shelby raised her water glass in the air. "To Rose."

Their glasses met in the middle of the table and clinked.

Once dinner was completed, the couple took their leftovers in a large brown handled bag and again, thanked Antonio before leaving.

Putting her purse closer to her side as they made their way outside, she felt a buzz from her bag. "I need to get this, it might be a client." She scanned the message and cheered.

"What happened?"

"Phoebe and I got an immense floral order for a wedding. This should help put my name out there." She swiped happy drops of water from her eyes. "We both prayed and it happened. Thank you, Lord."

Blake kissed the top of her head. "Congratulations."

"Thanks. I feel as if I could run all the way home, I'm so excited."

"Don't, I've eaten too much." Blake put a hand on his midsection.

"Me too."

As they neared her apartment building front door, disappointment hovered amidst the joy. *I'm going to miss him.* Like tight piano strings, Blake's kindness had found a place in her heart, this was more than a friendship. Did he feel the same way?

~

"I can't believe it's already the end of June." Phoebe plucked thorns off a rose stem. "The Vincent wedding is in three days. We've still got a lot of arrangements to make. Plus, this mess of a shop to clean."

Carrying a bucket of baby's breath in her arms, Shelby breezed past her bestie. "Blake's coming by after work tonight. He said he'd do anything he could to help us."

"If he can push a broom and ferry the buckets to us, I might be less stressed." Phoebe frowned.

"Phebe's, he will. I've never seen a time where he wasn't pitching in to help during small groups or when we cook together some nights."

"You're fortunate, because I'm still on the lookout for a good guy." Phoebe hugged her. "I'm happy that you two have something really good together."

"We do. This arrangement needs more greenery."

A male voice answered, "I'll get it."

She turned and walked toward Blake. He wore a faded University of Texas shirt and jeans. Shelby bit back a sigh. Instead of a lingering kiss, she settled for a quick one on the cheek. "Thank you. They're in the back room in the right-side fridge."

"Got it." He moved with a purpose to the back room.

"Like I said, you are fortunate. Doesn't he have a brother?" Phoebe raised an eyebrow.

"Nope, an older sister."

"Just my luck." Phoebe shrugged.

The friends assembled several more arrangements which Blake put in the empty coolers at the front of the store. She was delighted at how efficient he was during the busy process. They'd had him in the shop for a few hours now.

"I'll be back. We need some waters." Shelby's feet throbbed, she went to the break room to get them.

She heard Blake speaking to someone. *There's no one else here, maybe he's on the phone?* Shelby walked into the back room and noticed the floor had been swept clean. He's amazing.

He held a wilted yellow rose was in his hand, a castoff from an arrangement. Shelby drew closer for a better look.

"She loves me, she loves me not." The petals fell into the wastebasket.

Her heart sang as he plucked another petal from its home. Risking it all, she blurted, "She loves you."

Heartbeat thundering in her chest as he turned to stare at her.

"Shelby." Blake took her in his arms. "I've loved you since we stood over that boiling pot together. I wouldn't want to spend any time in this city without you. You are my love."

His lips sealed over hers, and they wrapped their arms around one another. She made low noises of happiness in her throat as the kiss deepened.

"It looks like we'll prep for someone's wedding in the future," Phoebe giggled.

Shelby broke away from Blake and surveyed his face. He nodded.

"Sooner." Blake rejoined. "I can't wait long to marry you. Do you agree? We should get married?" He dropped to one knee and took her hand in his. "Will you ma—"

Shelby interjected. "Yes!"

Blake rose from the floor, beaming. "You do?"

With a firm nod, water traced down her cheeks.

Blake scooped up Shelby and swung her around.

"I love you. Do we want to get married in June or July next year?"

"I love you too, Blake." She kissed his lips. "Winter wedding. December."

"Put it on the schedule, Phoebe. Someone else can do the flowers though." Blake's grin widened. "My bride-to-be will be too busy. First, we need to pick out your ring. Then thank Rose for her matchmaking."

All three of them laughed.

Shelby held her fiancé's hand and added, "Love is indeed abloom, thanks to Rose Carlucci."

The End

Made in United States
Orlando, FL
21 April 2023

32286845R00150